THIS TOWN
IS NOT
ALL RIGHT

M. K. KRYS

THIS TOWN IS NOT ALL RIGHT

Penguin Workshop

PENGUIN WORKSHOP
An Imprint of Penguin Random House LLC, New York

Text copyright © 2020 by M. K. Krys. Cover illustration copyright © 2020 by Shane Rebenschied.
All rights reserved. Published by Penguin Workshop, an imprint of
Penguin Random House LLC, New York. PENGUIN and PENGUIN WORKSHOP
are trademarks of Penguin Books Ltd, and the W colophon is a registered
trademark of Penguin Random House LLC. Printed in the USA.

Visit us online at www.penguinrandomhouse.com.

Library of Congress Control Number: 2019057445

ISBN 9780593097144   10 9 8 7 6 5 4 3 2 1

For Ben and Sophie—

to the moon

I

It had been ten minutes since they'd passed the "Driftwood Harbor, Population 203" sign, and ten minutes since anyone had said a word.

Out one window, the Atlantic Ocean stretched out like a big gray void as far as the eye could see. Out the other, a fog so thick, you could choke on it hung over a dense forest of scrabbly pine trees. A few miles back they'd passed a tumbledown house with an old truck in the driveway, but they hadn't spotted any actual life since they left the interstate more than an hour ago. (Unless you counted the seagulls that circled overhead, and even they looked like the type that would purposely poop on your head.)

It was desolate and depressing, and Beacon could tell from the way his twin sister, Everleigh, glared out the window that she was regretting not flinging herself out of the car when she'd had the chance.

"I hear they have fantastic lobster," the twins' dad said.

The tires' whirring underneath the Ford Taurus came into focus. A breeze whistled through a cracked-open window, ruffling the fine brown hairs clinging to the top of their dad's head and sending his tie over his shoulder.

"I love lobster," Beacon said, just to break the tense silence.

From the front seat, Everleigh snorted.

She was part of the reason they were moving from Los Angeles all the way to the tiny fishing village of Driftwood Harbor on the Eastern Seaboard. Their dad was hoping that the fresh air and change of scenery would help her. Nothing else had.

That's why Beacon tried to be optimistic about the move, even if he wasn't actually happy about it. He'd had friends in LA. He had the skate park downtown, where he practiced his jumps until it got dark. He had his bedroom full of Tony Hawk posters and a spot under the floorboards where he hid private stuff from his nosy twin sister. But he just wanted his family to go back to normal. Or as close to normal as they would ever get, now. After. If this place helped, then none of that other stuff mattered.

"Where is the actual town?" Everleigh grumbled. "If there even is one."

"Should be coming up to it soon," Beacon said brightly. "Right, Dad?"

He'd been doing that lately. Saying everything as if it had an exclamation point at the end, as if his enthusiasm might be contagious. So far, it only seemed to make Everleigh more annoyed.

Beacon looked out the window at the forest blurring past.

Suddenly a flash of movement caught his eye. A figure darted out of the trees. It was white and hunched, with a pair of huge round eyes.

And it was looking right at him.

Beacon gasped.

"What?" Everleigh said.

He was about to explain, but his words were cut short by a loud clunk from under the car's floor. Before he knew it, the car was fishtailing wildly across the road. The kids screamed as their dad fought to get control, the forest and road spinning around them in a streak of gray and green. The car careened toward a thick pine. Closer, closer, closer—they were going to hit it!

At the last moment, their dad braked hard. The car jerked to an abrupt stop. Beacon's head slammed against the window. Stars exploded across his eyes.

And then everything was still. The engine knocked over the ringing in Beacon's ears. Beacon blinked away the spots in his vision, searching through the cloud of dust outside the window for the creature in the woods. But if it was there, he couldn't see it.

"What. Was. *That*," Everleigh finally said.

"I don't know." Their dad gripped the steering wheel with white-knuckled fingers. "I was driving along normally and then all of a sudden something just *gave* and I lost control."

Beacon blew out a relieved breath.

"You okay, Beaks?" their dad asked, twisting around to check him over for injury. "Is everyone okay?"

Once he confirmed that no one was missing an arm or needed CPR, he climbed out of the car, briskly wiping the wrinkles out of his suit. The twins weren't far behind. Smoke billowed from underneath the hood of the car like a huffing dragon. Their dad coughed and blew away the fumes as he tried unsuccessfully to open the hood. Everleigh released an annoyed sigh and nudged him aside with her hip, then she unlatched the hood with a practiced flick of her wrist and peered underneath at the tangle of metal and wires.

"What is it?" their dad asked eagerly.

"Radiator's blown," Everleigh said, hands balled on her hips.

Everleigh was practically a pro mechanic. She'd been fixing cars with their older brother, Jasper, ever since she was in diapers.

Now she fixed them alone.

"Can you fix it?" their dad asked.

"Not without some leak sealant, and we don't have any on hand. If we were back at *home* . . . ," she said meaningfully, "now that would be a different story."

Their dad ignored the barb.

"We'll need to call a tow truck, then." He ducked away to the driver's seat, and Beacon got out his cell phone. He tapped the screen, but the browser wouldn't load.

"The Internet isn't working," Beacon said.

Everleigh snatched the phone from his hand.

"Hey, give that back!" Beacon said, but his sister twisted out of his reach to type.

Even though they were twins, Everleigh had at least two inches on her brother, a fact she used to her advantage at every opportunity.

"No reception," Everleigh said. "That's just great." She shoved the phone back at Beacon's chest.

Beacon grumbled and stowed the cell in his pocket. Then the twins looked down either side of the isolated road. That's when Beacon realized just how late it was. It hadn't exactly been bright and sunny before, but now the trees looked black against the bruised-fruit sky. It was so quiet, he could actually hear insects chirping and trilling in the long grass on the side of the road, instead of just cars and people like back in LA.

A fine mist sprayed off the ocean, and the air bit through Beacon's thin sweatshirt with razor-sharp teeth. Everleigh rubbed warmth back into her arms, which were prickled with goose bumps. Their dad had warned them that it would be chilly by the water, but it seemed to be getting cooler with every passing second.

Beacon thought of the movement he'd seen in the woods before the car broke down, and a shiver scuttled down his spine. Those eyes had been *huge*. He didn't even want to think about what kind of animal they belonged to.

"Well, I guess we'll have to walk," their dad said, jolting Beacon from his thoughts.

"I am *not* walking." His dad and sister stared at him, and Beacon crossed his arms stiffly. "I saw something in the woods before the car broke down."

"Don't tell me you're worried about aliens," Everleigh said.

"Don't be stupid," Beacon retorted.

They'd googled Driftwood Harbor before the move. The only things they could find about the place were some old newspaper articles about a large object that had crashed in the water back in 1960-something-or-other. Of course, a bunch of weirdos on the Internet had insisted it was a UFO.

"It was probably just a deer," their dad said.

"Or a bear," Everleigh said casually. "I hear they have tons of them around here. Huge ones, too, with paws the size of dinner plates and claws like Wolverine."

Beacon's eyes widened.

"Leave your brother alone," their dad said.

Just then, a white light beamed across the road. Beacon shielded his eyes as a pair of headlights rumbled toward them, the vehicle kicking up dust.

"Someone's coming!" Beacon said.

"Boy, nothing gets past you," Everleigh replied dryly.

Beacon didn't even care about coming up with a good comeback—he was just happy help was on the way.

As the vehicle got closer, a crane and rigging equipment took shape in the moonlight. A tow truck. What were the odds of that?

The truck pulled to a stop next to their car. There were at least two inches of dust and grease on the windows, and the wheel wells were so rusted, it looked as if the car was disintegrating. *Murray's Auto Body* was written on the side of the sun-faded, burnt-orange body. The driver leaned across the empty seats to look through the window. His cheeks were ruddy and deeply wrinkled, and a cigarette dangled from his lips, sending smoke curling into the air.

"Need a hitch?" he asked. Or at least that's what Beacon thought he'd said. His accent reminded him of some of the Irish action movies his uncle Stanley liked to watch, where Beacon could only make out about one of every dozen words, and it was usually a cuss.

"Wow, perfect timing!" their dad said. He tripped over himself to thank the man, and ten minutes later, they were all crammed into the box of the tow truck as they rumbled toward the town—term used loosely. Beacon was grateful when they finally saw some signs of civilization. They rolled slowly past a harbor. The weathered pier didn't look trustworthy enough to hold the weight of a toddler, let alone the dozens of boats anchored to it. If you could even call them boats. He saw tattered sails and broken masts and barnacles clinging to thick rope nets. Fishermen in chest waders and rubber boots stood in waist-deep, murky water, yelling at one another around a partially submerged tugboat with a big hole in its side.

A short while later, the tow truck lurched to a stop in front of a service shop. The domed, corrugated roof was sloping in the center and looked as if a strong breeze might knock it down.

They climbed out of the truck and followed the adults inside through the metal delivery bay doors. A van hovered on a platform in the middle of the room, and there was a giant puddle of oil underneath it. There were tools and gas cans and tins of nails everywhere. The smell of gasoline hung in the air.

Their dad and the mechanic fell into a discussion about the radiator, and the twins began wandering through the shop. Beacon was looking at some old pictures tacked to a corkboard when he heard Everleigh gasp. She had her hands cupped around her face and was peering out of a dirty window at the back of the shop. Beacon joined her and saw dozens and dozens of cars stretched out across a dusty lot, the metal shining dully under the orange light of a single lamppost. Before he could say anything, she was tumbling through the back door. He followed her out into the junkyard.

"I don't think we should be out here," Beacon said.

"Then go back," Everleigh said.

She weaved through the makeshift aisles, peering into the cars with a grin tugging at her lips. She looked like she was in heaven. Beacon was pretty sure it was the first time he'd seen his sister smile since . . . he couldn't even remember.

Maybe that's why he couldn't quite convince himself to tell her not to climb into the cars like she owned the place, as she was doing right now.

Beacon followed his sister's path through the junkyard. Before he realized it, they were near the back of the lot, where the light of the lamppost struggled to reach. The aisles melted into darkness. The bodies of the cars were swallowed by jagged shadows. The light flickered, and Beacon once again thought of that movement in the woods. A crawly feeling roiled inside his gut.

"We should go back," he said.

"Quit being such a wimp," Everleigh said.

"I am *not* a wimp," Beacon said defensively.

Everleigh gasped, and Beacon yelped.

"What, what is it?" he asked, whipping around.

"A 1968 Mercury Cougar," Everleigh said, pointing at an old car. Beacon's face melted into a scowl, and Everleigh laughed riotously, clutching her stomach. "Oh my God, you should have seen your face!"

"You're a real jer . . ." Beacon's words trailed off, his eyes widening at something behind his sister. Three sets of gleaming eyes stared out of the darkness.

2

"Nice try," Everleigh said. She turned around on a laugh, but her face froze as a body materialized from the darkness. She screamed, scrabbling back into Beacon.

Three kids stepped out of the shadows, wearing matching puffy gold-and-blue varsity jackets and strangely blank expressions.

"Sorry, we didn't mean to scare you," the girl said. Her hair was the kind of bright blond that almost looked white; the glossy curls bounced around her shoulders as she moved. "I'm Jane Middleton. And this is Perry Thompson and Nixon Sims." She nodded at the two boys standing on either side of her. One was short with shoulders so wide Beacon couldn't be sure he wasn't wearing football pads under his jacket; his light hair stuck up in spikes all over his head. The other was tall and thin, with tight, wiry black curls that matched his dark skin.

"I'm Beacon McCullough," Beacon said, then nudged his sister when she didn't offer her name. "And this is my rude sister, Everleigh."

Everleigh narrowed her eyes at the kids. "What were you doing out here in the dark?"

Before they could answer, the twins' dad ran out into the yard. The mechanic stumbled behind him.

"What's going on out here?" their dad asked breathlessly. "Is everyone okay? I heard a scream."

Jane stepped forward stiffly, her hands clasped in front of her like a mannequin.

"I'm afraid we scared them. We cut through the junkyard to get to the church on the hill, where we hold our meetings." She pointed up at a big stone church that loomed ominously out of the fog on a hilltop overlooking the ocean. "We don't usually come across anyone."

"Hey there, Jane. Nice to see ya. Nixon, Perry." The mechanic nodded at the kids.

"Hi, Mr. Murray," they all responded together.

"Meetings?" the twins' dad asked.

"We volunteer for the Gold Stars," Jane explained. "We're a youth group that aims to promote social responsibility in kids."

"Isn't that something!" their dad said.

"We're always looking for new members." Jane looked at the twins. "If you two want to join, we'd be happy to take you to a meeting."

Everleigh snorted, and their dad cut her a look that could slice through a ten-ton truck.

"That's a very nice offer," their dad said, a warning note in his voice. "I'm sure they'd love that."

Jane smiled, though it didn't reach her eyes. "We should get going so we're not late to our meeting."

"Oh, by all means!" He stepped aside to let them pass. "It was great to meet you."

"You too," Jane said.

The Gold Stars gave them another one of their blank-stared smiles before they disappeared through a hole in the fence.

"They seemed nice," their dad said.

"They seemed *weird*," Everleigh replied. "I've seen livelier personalities on some two-by-fours."

"Everleigh!" Their dad darted an embarrassed look at the mechanic.

"Oh, it's all right," Mr. Murray said, waving away his concern. "Probably just tired from the long drive. Why don't we go inside and square up for that sealant? I bet you kids want to get out of here."

"*That's* an understatement," Everleigh muttered.

The mechanic charitably pretended not to hear her.

•••••••••••••••••••••••••••••••

Soon, they arrived at their home for the foreseeable future. The A-frame was set on a rocky jut of land overlooking the ocean.

Thick vines climbed the yellow-stained siding like they were trying to swallow the house, and black shutters on the windows snapped open and closed in the wind. The roof was completely lost to the fog. A sign out front said "Welcome to Blackwater Lookout Bed-and-Breakfast!" in looping cursive script.

Beacon's lips twitched from the effort to keep the smile pasted on his face.

"This looks great and everything," he said, "but do you think there's someplace a little more . . . modern we can stay?"

"This is the only hotel in town," their dad said. He parked the car next to an ancient blue truck with wood paneling on the side that Beacon had only ever seen in '80s movies. "The lady on the phone said we were lucky to get rooms at all."

"Yeah, because tourism is obviously booming here," Everleigh deadpanned.

There were no cars. There were no people. There were no neighbors for miles. It looked like you could go days without ever having contact with another person, if you wanted. It was so different from LA, where you couldn't step out of your front door without bumping into someone.

"It's just temporary while we do some house hunting," their dad said. "A couple of those places we found online looked very promising."

"I'm sure it will be fine," Beacon said without much conviction.

A thickset woman with ruddy cheeks and wiry gray Brillo Pad hair came out of the front doors. She shielded her face and scowled down at the family, the wind sucking her apron away from her body.

"That must be Donna," their dad said.

"Donna seems like a blast," Everleigh replied.

"Who are ye?" Donna called over the wind. Beacon didn't know whether to be annoyed at Everleigh's rudeness or respect her honesty, because really, there was nothing to be happy about here. He'd been trying to be optimistic for his dad's sake, but it was getting hard. Couldn't he have found anyplace better for their fresh start? He didn't see anything appealing about this town. It was as if their dad had thrown a dart at a map and said, "Driftwood Harbor it is!"

"Malcolm McCullough," their dad said. "And these are my kids, Beacon and Everleigh."

For a minute, Donna looked as if she was going to turn them away, and Beacon got hopeful that they would have to leave after all. A whole sequence played out in his head. They wouldn't find anywhere else to stay in town, so they'd be forced to leave entirely, and once they did, they would decide to never come back. Maybe they'd move to Hawaii instead. Canada, even. He wasn't picky.

But then Donna gave a curt nod and said, "Welcome to Blackwater."

"Welcome to Blackwater, my butt," Everleigh said under her breath.

Beacon and Everleigh followed their dad into the inn.

Happily, the inside was a lot cheerier than the outside. The walls were made up of knotted-wood paneling, and there were overstuffed couches set around a stone hearth that had a crackling fire inside. It smelled like baking, which was another improvement over the outside, which smelled like fish.

"You kids must be hungry," Donna said. "I'll get the oven going."

"Oh, it's okay," their dad said. "That's very kind of you, but we had a bite to eat at that Home Sweet Home diner on the highway. The kids ate their weight in crinkle-cut fries. I think we'd all just like to get some sleep."

"Very well," Donna said. Her mouth pursed as if she'd sucked on a sour candy. Beacon made a mental note never to refuse her cooking.

They followed her brisk footsteps through the inn.

"I suppose you'll be wanting the bigger room for yourself?" she said to their dad, gesturing to a large bedroom on the main floor. She raised her eyebrows, as if challenging him to disagree.

"Well, yes," he stuttered.

"I figured," she said. "I'll let you get settled in. Kids, follow me."

She led them up a set of narrow, winding stairs to the second floor.

"The bedroom at the end of the hall is free, but one of you will need to stay here." She used a hook from the hall closet to reach up and unlatch a door in the ceiling. She pulled down a set of accordion stairs that led up into the darkness.

"It's not ideal," Donna said, "but we're tight on space."

Beacon peered warily into the attic, then at his sister. Everleigh crossed her arms and lifted her chin. It was a look he knew all too well. She was prepared to argue to the death until she got what she wanted.

Beacon sighed. "I guess I'll take the attic bedroom."

He hiked his backpack over his shoulder, then gripped both sides of the steep wooden ladder and climbed up. When he got to the top, he poked his head into the room. Pale moonlight slanted in from a small window in the corner, but otherwise, it was completely dark. He couldn't even see his hand when he waved it in front of his face.

"Light switch is on the wall!" Donna called from below.

"Okay!" Beacon replied shakily.

He gulped, climbing up farther, wondering idly if he'd somehow walked into a trap. Maybe this woman wasn't really an innkeeper. Maybe she was a serial killer, and this hotel was just a clever ruse so she could lure unsuspecting families into her death trap.

He'd been halfway expecting chains and bloodstains, but when he flicked on the light switch, he was happy to find a queen-size bed with a patchwork quilt and a braided rug thrown down over the wooden floor. The peaked ceiling was so low in spots, he couldn't stand upright near the walls, but other than that, it wasn't so bad after all. In fact, it would be nice to have this space away from the rest of his family and Donna.

That's what he told himself as he emptied his belongings into the dresser, changed into his pajamas, and climbed underneath the covers.

He closed his eyes and tried to sleep, but the old house creaked and groaned. Outside, the ocean bashed against the rocks in a rhythmic roar and crash.

A memory came flooding back. The Halloween before Jasper died, his older brother had had a bunch of his friends over to marathon scary movies. Jasper invited the twins to watch, and Everleigh had immediately plopped down onto the couch. Even though Beacon actually wanted to go trick-or-treating, he'd wanted to seem cool, and Everleigh and Jasper were always spending so much time together fixing cars and talking about cars and poring over car magazines that he sometimes felt left out. So he'd joined his sister and the older kids, who were in the middle of a movie about an evil clown who lived in the sewers. Beacon couldn't sleep for weeks after that, and even though he was eleven, he'd crawled into his dad's bed every night. Every day, he'd lived in fear of Everleigh finding out. If she did, he'd never hear the end of it.

One night, as he was trekking to his dad's room, he ran into Jasper, who was in the hall on the way to the bathroom. Jasper asked what he was doing up, and Beacon admitted that he hadn't been able to sleep ever since that movie with the evil clown. Jasper's face had grown serious, and even though Beacon knew Jasper wouldn't make fun of him, he'd gotten embarrassed. But then Jasper told him to wait right there. He came back a minute later, wielding Beacon's Little League baseball bat.

"Come on, little brother," he said, all business. Then he'd stormed into Beacon's room and flicked on the light. He yelled at the empty room that he was here, he wasn't scared, and he was ready to fight anyone who messed with his brother. Then he hit his chest like a caveman and spit into the garbage. It was so ridiculous that Beacon couldn't help laughing. Soon, they were both keeled over. Everleigh came in moments later, blearily rubbing her eyes, and their dad wasn't far behind, wielding his own baseball bat like he was going to strike an intruder. But neither Beacon nor Jasper could get control of their laughter long enough to explain what had actually happened, so eventually their dad and sister both got annoyed and went back to bed, leaving Beacon and Jasper wiping their tears. Evil clowns never seemed so scary after that.

But Jasper wasn't here now.

It took him a while, but Beacon finally drifted off to sleep.

That night, he dreamed of the ocean. He stood on a ledge of sharp rocks. The wind howled in his ears, and huge, angry waves crashed against his feet. But somehow, Beacon stayed dry. He bent down and touched the water. Suddenly he was tumbling through the ocean, and then the dream changed, and he was standing on the seafloor, the muted roar of the wind still loud in his ears. Jasper lay on a bed of bright green coral, his pale white hands clasped over his stomach. Fish darted around his body, flashes of silver and scales. Beacon called his brother's name over the thunderous scream of the water. Jasper's chest heaved, as if he were trying to speak. Beacon stepped closer to hear what his brother would say. Then Jasper's mouth gaped open wide, and a big black fish swam out of his mouth.

Beacon screamed.

....

He woke with a start. His cheeks were wet, and his body was drenched in cold sweat. His heart pounded against his chest.

The room was dark, and for a minute, Beacon forgot where he was. Outside, the wind shrieked against the windowpanes. Branches from a nearby tree scritched over the rain-splattered glass and made ugly, sharp shadows dance across the walls. His nightmare trickled away, and memories of the previous day came flooding back—the car wreck, the junkyard, the bedroom in the attic. He was in Driftwood Harbor. This was Blackwater Lookout. And something had woken him up.

Beacon pulled the covers up to his chin. It was just the storm, he told himself. He closed his eyes. But it was no use. He was wide-awake now.

He whipped off the covers and sat up. A gust of chilly air sent goose bumps racing up his back. He set his feet onto the cold wood floor, feeling exactly like those idiots in horror movies who hear a noise and go investigating even though you know it's a terrible idea.

One peek, he told himself. Just to make sure it was the trees that had woken him up. Then he could go back to bed.

The floor creaked and groaned as he crept toward the window. He peered outside, through the frosty glass.

Without all the lights and smog of the city, he could actually see the stars. They shone above, illuminating the angry black waves that battered the rocky shore below. He squinted into the dark, but he couldn't see anything wrong.

And then a lighthouse beacon trailed lazily over the ocean, and he caught something in the water. Or rather, *someone* in the water.

Beacon gasped, and the person in the water whirled around, almost as if hearing him. Her hair was plastered against her head, but he recognized the bright blond curls and blue-and-gold varsity jacket instantly.

Their eyes connected for a brief moment. And then a huge wave reared up and swallowed Jane's body whole.

3

Beacon slammed his hands against the glass. For a horrible second, he was frozen with panic. He watched the waves ebb and flow, waiting for the girl to reappear, for a hand to reach out through the water. But Jane never came back up. She was going to drown.

Beacon jerked into action, skidding across the room and landing on his knees. He threw open the trapdoor.

"Help!" he screamed. He nearly lost his footing twice scrambling down the ladder. When he was near the bottom, he jumped the last four steps, landing hard and sending a shock wave of pain up his legs.

Everleigh blearily pushed open the door at the end of the hall. Strands of dark hair were pulled loose from her ponytail and stuck to her cheeks, which were flushed through with pink. She blinked and shielded her face against the pale light in the hall as if she were a vampire.

"There's someone in the water," Beacon said between gasps of breath.

He didn't wait to see what she would say. He ran down the hall, then thundered down the steps two at a time.

"Beacon, wait!" Everleigh called.

But he didn't stop.

He careened through the darkened inn to a back door off the kitchen. He unlatched the dead bolt and leaped down the steps into the cold, stormy night.

The rain blew in diagonal sheets, battering the shore. He hadn't taken the time to put on shoes, and rocks and pebbles dug into his bare feet. He hardly felt it as he ran toward the water. But when he got close, Beacon stopped dead.

The ocean churned like a black sludge vortex. Mountainous waves crashed against the shore like hungry monsters destroying everything in their path. Wind blew a thick, briny mist across his face and soaked through his pajamas.

There was no way Jane could get back on her own.

He had to go in.

Beacon took a hesitant step forward. The icy water slapped his shins, and he gasped at the shocking cold. His legs were as heavy as cinder blocks, freezing him in place. He knew he needed to be fast, but he kept thinking of Jasper. Thinking of that night.

He gave his head a hard shake and forced his body to move. He had to help her. He was her only hope.

Beacon was only knee-deep when a powerful wave knocked him off his feet. He fell hard, swallowing a mouthful of salty water.

There was a terrifying moment when panic overtook him and he flailed helplessly. But then he managed to push himself up to his feet. He stood stalled at the mouth of the ocean, coughing and gagging, dwarfed in the shadow of the waves.

He needed to go farther. He needed to try harder. But he couldn't make his legs move. All he could think about was how water just like this had stolen the life from his brother.

But she was out there, and she needed his help.

He took another step, but someone grabbed his arm and yanked hard. Beacon stumbled backward, pulled onto the shore like a misbehaving toddler being dragged out of a grocery store. He was dumped unceremoniously onto a long rock slab. Everleigh stood over him, her face twisted into a mask of rage.

"What were you *thinking?*" she screamed over the sound of the waves.

"I need to help her," Beacon said.

"You're not going to be helping anyone if you're dead."

The back door flew open and their dad rushed out.

"Police are on their . . ." His words died on his lips when he saw the twins, drenched on the rock slab. "What are you doing? Why are you so wet? Please don't tell me you went in there." His eyes were as round as saucers and his lip trembled. Beacon was suddenly back to that night, the night they got the news. The sound of his dad's choked breathing made his chest squeeze hard, as if it had a cramp.

"I'm sorry, I—"

"Of course we didn't go in the water," Everleigh interrupted. She yanked Beacon up. "We stood on the shore to get a better look and got blasted by a wave. It knocked Beaks off his feet, but that's it."

The lie came out so deftly that it had a ring of truth. Beacon didn't dare look at his sister and give it away.

"Okay, well, let's get you inside and into dry clothes," their dad said. "You shouldn't be out here."

He hustled them inside. Beacon went upstairs and changed into a pair of clean, dry sweatpants and a hoodie. When he came back down, Donna was making tea like lives depended on it, briskly pouring steaming water into sturdy-looking mugs.

Everleigh sat at the kitchen table. She twisted her hands together and looked out anxiously at the lone fire truck and volunteer rescue workers rushing to and fro, siren lights reflecting off the ocean. Beacon knew what she was thinking about. *Who* she was thinking about.

He sat next to his sister. Together, they watched through the foggy, rain-splattered window as chaos unfolded outside. Rain hit the window like it was trying to wash the house away, but somehow the room felt deadly quiet.

After a year, Beacon still wasn't used to the silence. For the first couple of months after Jasper had died, he'd been too torn up with grief to notice much of anything going on around him. But then the casseroles stopped coming, and the visitors left, and it was just him and Everleigh and their dad, and the quiet that ate up everything made you think about all the things you didn't want to think about and feel all the things you didn't want to feel. It had been like he was living inside of a tomb. He'd started spending as much time away from home as possible so he could escape the ugly truth that Jasper was gone.

Everleigh, on the other hand, rarely left the house. If she wasn't in her room, she was in the garage, working on the car, the way she used to with Jasper. Beacon often wondered if she was punishing herself. If she thought she didn't deserve to forget, not even for a little while. Not after what happened.

The door burst open suddenly, and their dad and two officers in shiny wet jackets came in on a blast of cold air. The kids popped up from their chairs as the officers took off their hats and rubbed warmth back into their hands.

"Sheriff Nugent, Deputy Steele," Donna said icily.

"Donna," the one with the dark bushy mustache and bulbous red nose said with equal animosity. He wiped a smudge of dirt off the faded gold star on the lapel of his jacket. He must be the sheriff.

"May we come in?" the one with the graying red hair and beard said. Deputy Steele.

Donna looked as if she was thinking about saying no. There was obviously some kind of history between Donna and the law enforcement here, and it didn't make Beacon feel better about his living arrangements. After a long pause, she finally opened the door wider and ushered them into the kitchen, reluctantly pressing coffee mugs into their hands.

"Bless you, Donna," Sheriff Nugent said.

"Real kind," Deputy Steele said.

"Well?" Beacon asked impatiently.

The sheriff raised a thick eyebrow—he clearly wasn't happy about answering to a kid, especially one who'd used that tone.

"It's too dark and the water's too angry," he finally replied. "We're going to have to send a team out tomorrow morning."

"What?" Beacon cried. "It'll be too late then!"

"I'm sorry, son. It's all we can do."

Beacon sank down into his chair. If only he'd been quicker. Louder. A better swimmer. Why had he hesitated? He should have done everything possible to save Jane.

He buried his face in his hands. Long minutes passed. A century, maybe.

A ring pierced the tense silence. The sheriff pulled a blocky cell phone out of his pocket.

"Sheriff Nugent," he said. There was a long pause, then: "What? Are you sure? Well . . . that is certainly surprising, but I'm glad to hear it. Thank you. We'll see you at church on Sunday. Bye now." He ended the call.

"That was Deputy Raycroft," Sheriff Nugent said, tucking his phone back into his pocket. "He was just at the Middleton residence."

Beacon sat up.

"Jane is in bed sleeping. Just like she has been all night."

4

"B-but that's impossible," Beacon said.

"Robert saw her for himself." The sheriff slapped on his cap, as if he was getting ready to leave.

"No," Beacon said firmly, standing up. "It was Jane. I saw her Gold Stars jacket. She looked *right at* me."

"Tell us what happened again," the second officer said.

Beacon recounted the story, making sure not to leave out any details. But this time, the sheriff's eyes narrowed as Beacon spoke, and he and the deputy exchanged a knowing look.

"You say she heard you gasp, all the way from in your bedroom? Over the wind and rain and waves, and through a couple inches of window glass to boot?" the sheriff said.

Beacon felt himself shrink. "I know how it sounds."

"Listen," their dad said. "It's late, you're in a new place—I'll bet the house was making all sorts of weird sounds, right? You probably had a bad dream."

"It was real," Beacon insisted.

"Maybe it was someone else you saw, then?" his dad suggested. "A different Gold Stars kid." He looked at the sheriff.

"We'll find out soon enough if that's the case," the sheriff said. Although, it was clear he didn't think that would happen.

"We'll have a deputy check missing persons until we can get back out tomorrow," Deputy Steele said.

"Bless you, officers," Donna said.

"Sorry about the disturbance," his dad added, flitting a glance Beacon's way.

They were acting as if he wasn't even there. Acting like he was *stupid*. Nobody believed him. But he'd been wide-awake when he heard that scream.

"There *was* someone out there!" Beacon cried.

Everyone was looking at him with the most infuriating pity all over their faces—everyone but the sheriff, who eyed him with something closer to contempt.

Beacon stormed out of the room. He was halfway up the stairs when he heard his dad say, "I'm sorry, this isn't like him. His brother died recently."

Fury swelled inside him.

Ever since Jasper died, it seemed like all of Beacon's behaviors were automatically attributed to grief. Fight with Everleigh? "Anger is a normal stage of grief." Bad mood? "It's normal to feel depressed after losing a loved one."

It made Beacon want to scream.

Wasn't he allowed to have any legitimate feelings anymore, without having everyone making it all about his "trauma"?

He stomped up the stairs into his new attic bedroom and flopped down onto the bed. He was confused and angry and humiliated, and he just wanted the ground to open up and swallow him whole.

There was a creak behind him. He glanced up to see Everleigh poking her head through the hole in the floor.

"Go away," he said before burying his face back in the mattress. But of course, his sister didn't listen. She crossed the room and dropped heavily onto the end of his bed. Beacon jammed a pillow over his head so that she wouldn't see the tears threatening his lashes.

"Get it over with," he said gruffly. "I'm an idiot, a wimp, a liar."

He felt a hand clamp onto his shoulder.

"I believe you."

"Very funny," Beacon mumbled angrily.

"I'm not joking," Everleigh said. "I don't know what happened, but I know *you*. You're not a liar, and I don't think you imagined it."

Beacon rolled over and sat up. He waited for his sister to burst out laughing and say "Gotcha!" But she didn't.

"So what now?" Beacon said.

Everleigh shrugged, a whole-body gesture. "Now we go to bed."

"But someone's out there, and no one's helping. Maybe it's not

Jane—I guess it's possible it was someone else—but it was a person out there."

"If someone was out there, they're already dead," Everleigh said.

The words were a sucker punch to his gut, but it was true. It only took minutes without oxygen for someone to start losing brain function. Ten minutes and they'd be dead. He knew this better than anyone. But still. It didn't seem right. Just going to bed when someone was floating in the ocean.

"They'll find whoever it is soon enough," Everleigh said. "We just have to be patient."

It was too bad patience wasn't Beacon's strong suit.

••••••••••••••••••••••••••••••

The next morning, Beacon awoke to the smell of coffee and fried eggs. Bright sunshine slanted across his comforter, making the attic bedroom look warm and cozy and inviting, and not at all like a horror movie waiting to happen. Last night seemed very far away.

He heard clattering and the murmur of voices coming from the kitchen, so he pulled on a pair of jeans and a T-shirt and climbed downstairs. Everything was so bright and weird and different that for a moment, he half expected to see his brother standing at the stove, plucking eggs directly out of the frying pan while his dad pretended to be annoyed and swatted him away. Jasper could get away with anything. It was impossible to be mad at him.

Beacon walked into the kitchen, but of course, his brother wasn't there. Donna pushed eggs around a sputtering skillet, while his dad sat at the table and stared at a newspaper called the *Seagazer*, which he assumed was Driftwood Harbor's version of the *L.A. Times*. Beacon took a seat across from him, but his dad didn't look up. He'd probably been staring at the same page for the last ten minutes, if history was any indication.

His dad thought he had Beacon fooled with his twitchy smiles and positive attitude, but Beacon knew that he still kept Jasper's cell phone in service more than a year after his death, just so he could hear his voice on the voice mail. Beacon saw him lying on Jasper's bed late at night when he thought no one else was awake. He saw the keys left in the refrigerator, heard the grocery clerk calling after them that they had forgotten to pay. He saw the school recede in the rearview mirror as his dad missed their stop for the millionth time, lost in thought. He was hurting, too. Probably as badly as Everleigh. Maybe worse.

He guessed Driftwood Harbor wasn't going to be everyone's miracle cure after all.

Outside the huge window, sunlight glistened off the clear blue water. The sea lapped gently against the rocky shore.

"Morning," Beacon said.

His dad jolted. "Oh, hey, Beaks. Didn't see you there." He flashed Beacon a smile.

"Shouldn't the rescue crews be here already?" Beacon asked.

His dad looked away and fiddled with the handle of his coffee cup. Beacon's heart sank like a stone. He knew what his dad was going to say.

"They've canceled the search."

"What about the girl?" Beacon said.

"No one's reported anyone missing."

"It's a very small community," Donna added from the stove. "If anyone were missing, we'd know about it by now."

"But . . . I know what I saw," he said quietly. At least he thought he did. He'd been so sure last night, but maybe they were right. Maybe it was a dream.

He tried to tell himself that it was good news that no one was missing, but it didn't make him feel any better.

"Hungry?" Donna asked without looking over.

"Yes, please," Beacon said. He fell into a seat across from his dad, who was already wearing a pressed black suit and a striped tie. If Beacon hadn't seen him wearing regrettable pajamas last night, he would have wondered if he'd slept in the suit. He suspected his dad might be a tad bit overdressed for his new job. He couldn't imagine anyone here wearing suits and ties to work, even if it was still a branch of the Centers for Disease Control, where he'd worked back in LA.

Donna placed a plate of eggs and toast in front of each of them.

"Oh," his dad said, staring at his plate. There was a ring of black around the whites of the fried eggs, and the toast was charred so badly, Beacon was pretty sure he could use it as a weapon. By comparison, Beacon's plate looked ready for close-ups.

"Cooked it a bit long," Donna said. She stared hard at his dad, as if daring him to complain.

"That's no problem," his dad said. He forced a smile and picked up a piece of toast.

"Thank you," Beacon said. Donna gave a curt nod before she went back to work, banging dishes in the sink. Beacon pushed his food around the plate. All of the drama was sitting like a lead ball in his stomach. The thought of food made him a little sick.

"Where's Everleigh?" he asked after a while.

"Went into town," his dad said. He was using the edge of his fork to try to cut his eggs, but they just slid around the plate.

"What? This early?" Beacon said.

"She was up before sunrise. Said she wanted to check things out," he said, gritting his teeth and sawing at his eggs with a steak knife.

That didn't sound like Everleigh at all. She routinely had to be pried out of bed with the Jaws of Life.

Then Beacon remembered the car at the junkyard. She'd definitely gone down to Murray's.

That was just great. She'd be there all day.

"I'm going to check out some houses today before work if you'd like to come along," his dad offered.

"You're working already?"

"Victor runs a tight ship. So are you going to come house hunting? I've just got to stop off at the post office and make a quick trip to the bank first."

Sounded riveting.

"I think I'll just play around on my board," Beacon said.

"You sure?" his dad asked, raising his brows.

"Sure."

"Well, okay. School tomorrow," he said.

As if he'd somehow forgotten.

Beacon was skeptical that there were enough kids in this town to form a school, let alone a single class. He would have to see it to believe it.

He had a sudden, intense longing for his home in LA. For his friends and familiarity. But there was no use thinking about that. Home was all the way across the country, far out of reach. He was here now. He might as well make the best of it.

Beacon found his skateboard in the trunk of the car. Just holding his old Habitat board, with its blue and white pinstripes and coiled serpent in the center, made him feel better. Beacon had been skateboarding since he was seven, and the board was almost as old.

He'd gotten a handful of newer ones since then, for birthdays and Christmas, but this one was still his favorite. The perfect amount of concave and pop, and it somehow never wore out, no matter how hard he rode it.

He did some ollies and kick flips in the driveway for a while, but then he got bored and decided to go find Everleigh.

One good thing about living in such a puny town was that it was very easy to find your way around. He wouldn't need to ask his dad for a ride anywhere, either, or brave public transit. That's what he told himself as he rode down the empty, pitted roads. He didn't bother keeping to the side. There was no point.

It didn't take him long to find the main square, which consisted of a handful of buildings that branched off into four different directions. He spotted a bright turquoise bait shop, a long and low grocery store made out of dark red brick, a yellow stucco diner with old-fashioned steel stools he could see through the big windows, and off in the distance, the towering stone church. Residents walked up and down the cobbled streets.

It looked just like the postcards he'd found online before the move. Even though it was kind of charming, the idea that this was all there was made him a bit panicky. In LA, there was no shortage of things to do, exotic foods to try, and people to meet. It was as if the world had been reduced to black-and-white, when he'd been living in full color before.

He followed the road that skirted along the pier until he reached Murray's Auto Body.

He ducked inside, blinking against the dust motes floating in the thin beams of light.

"Out back," a gruff voice said.

Beacon scanned the room and found Mr. Murray flipping through a magazine with his oily boots up on the desk.

"Okay, thanks," Beacon said.

He found Everleigh in the junkyard. Or, at least he found her torso. She was buried beneath the Mercury Cougar from her ribs up. The car was already a hundred times more impressive since his sister had gotten her hands on it. She'd washed off all the layers of dust and grime, and beneath it was a vibrant, teal-green muscle car that looked just like the ones old people buffed in their driveways but never actually drove.

Beacon hopped onto the hood of an old Beetle next to the Cougar.

"How's it going?" he asked.

"Awful," Everleigh said without missing a beat. "Whoever owned this car probably never gave it a tune-up in his entire life."

"Or *her* entire life," Beacon said.

She rolled out from under the car. There was grease smeared under her eyes.

"A girl wouldn't be that dumb." She got up and wiped her hands on her sweatpants.

"Mr. Murray doesn't mind you doing all this?" Beacon said, gesturing at the shiny car.

She made a noise like *psshh*. "He's lucky I offered. He'll be able to sell this thing for over Bluebook once I'm done with it."

"*Are* you done with it?" he asked hopefully. "I was thinking we could explore the town. I saw a weird store called Tonkin's Bait Shop and Antiques. There was a cat plate in the window."

"Not even close," Everleigh said.

Beacon's shoulders dropped, even though he'd kind of known she was going to say that. "Can't you take a break?"

"I have way too much to do here. We start school tomorrow, so this might be my last chance to get lots of work in. It's not easy refurbishing a car, you know."

Beacon sighed. He almost mentioned how she never went to school anyway, so he didn't see why that mattered. But he could tell he wasn't about to change her mind anytime soon, so he didn't bother. The thought of checking out the bait shop by himself didn't seem half as appealing.

"Sorry, Beaks," Everleigh said. "Check back in an hour."

"Great. Awesome." Beacon hopped off the car, but he froze when he spotted a head of bright blond, almost white hair through a gap in the wire fence. His heart lodged in his throat. Jane weaved down the cobbled sidewalk with three other kids in Gold Stars jackets. Tinkling laughter floated on the breeze.

"Where are you going?" Everleigh asked distantly as she watched him vault over the fence. But Beacon didn't stop to answer his sister. He had to see her. He had to see for himself.

Beacon raced up the sidewalk and grabbed Jane's shoulder. She snapped around, yanking her arm away with the most affronted look on her face.

"Do you *mind?*" she spat.

Beacon opened his mouth, but no words came out. He stared at the girl and her perfect curled hair and expertly applied lip gloss. She didn't look the least bit as if she'd been struggling for her life mere hours before.

Jane stared back at him. Her bright blue eyes flared with anger.

"What's the problem out here?" Everleigh asked, jogging up.

"What's *his* problem?" Jane said. "He practically attacked me!"

A Gold Star with sleek black hair down to her chin nodded in agreement.

"We should report him to the police," the boy from yesterday with the wiry black curls—Nixon—said. Perry, the jockish one, started to pull out a phone, but Jane stayed him with a hand.

"I-I'm sorry," Beacon finally managed. "I thought . . ." His words trailed off. He didn't really know what he'd thought. Jane was here. She was fine, and he was obviously wrong about what he'd seen in the ocean.

"I know what you thought," Jane said, crossing her arms.

"Because I was woken up in the middle of the night by a sheriff's deputy."

"Pardon me," Everleigh said, without an ounce of apology in her tone. "The next time he sees someone drowning in the ocean he'll just roll over and go back to bed."

"Your brother sees people who aren't there all the time?" Jane said. "Maybe he should get that checked out."

Nixon bit off a snicker, while the rest of the Gold Stars just stared. Beacon wondered what had happened to their great manners. If only his dad could see them now.

"Unless you have any other death hoaxes you'd like to accuse me of, we'd like to get back to our shopping," Jane said. The four students turned around and walked away without so much as a backward glance at Beacon and Everleigh.

"What a weirdo," he heard Nixon mutter.

A creeping, prickling heat climbed up Beacon's cheeks. He watched their retreating backs, the blue-and-gold logo on their jackets shining dully in the pale afternoon sunlight. The same jacket he could have *sworn* he saw on Jane last night in the water.

Everleigh put a hand on Beacon's shoulder. "Don't worry about them. They're a bunch of small-minded losers. Come on. I'll go to that bait shop with you."

"I *know* she was in the water," Beacon said.

When she didn't answer, Beacon turned to his sister. Everleigh was pointedly not meeting his eyes.

"What?" he said defensively.

"Nothing," she said.

"What happened to *I believe you*, and *You're not a liar?*" Beacon demanded.

"I do, and you're not," she said. "But—"

"But what?"

She sighed and rubbed her forehead, smearing around the grease on her face. "Beaks, I know you're embarrassed about what happened, but it's okay . . ."

Beacon ground his jaw. He'd had enough.

"Come back, Beaks! Where are you going?" Everleigh called.

Beacon stormed down the street with his skateboard tucked up under his arm. He was sick of everyone treating him like he was crazy. Sick of everyone babying him. And okay, maybe he was a little embarrassed, too.

He trudged past the pier, the cool, salty air blowing off the water and bringing with it the distinct smell of fish.

He hated fish. To be perfectly honest, he didn't really like lobster, either.

The water lapped against the wooden support beams as fishermen called orders to one another in thick, guttural accents. He walked past tiny clapboard-sided houses separated by larger and larger fields of tall yellow grass hemmed in by barbed wire fencing. He'd never seen so many wide-open spaces before, without any people in sight. It seemed like a giant waste of land, if you asked him.

Beacon walked for so long that eventually, he realized he'd left the ocean path behind. He was in the middle of a forest of tightly packed trees.

Beacon's eyes darted around him, his heart beating in his ears.

How did he get here? Wherever here even was. He remembered walking along the path . . . but not to here.

Yesterday's storm had stripped some of the trees, and leaves and bark and twigs were scattered across the forest floor. The ground was damp and squishy, like walking on a wet sponge. A mist wove through the trees, dampness and decay heavy in the air.

How come he didn't remember walking into the forest?

He'd just been lost in thought, he decided. He'd been doing that lately—daydreaming for hours. Although *daydreaming* seemed too pretty a word for it. Mulling things over was more like it. Agonizing over the past. How things were. How it could have been now if just one small thing had been done differently. If he'd chosen path A instead of path B.

His mind was a super fun place this year.

That had to have been what happened. He'd just been too wrapped up in his own head to notice how long and how far he'd walked.

Beacon spun in a slow circle, leaves crunching under his shoes.

The sound ricocheted through the trees.

He realized it was quiet. Too quiet. No birdsong. No crickets. No rustling branches as squirrels jumped from tree to tree.

His insides knotted up tight.

Suddenly there was a flash of movement in the woods.

Beacon gasped and scanned the forest. Darkness wove through the tangle of trees, as if the forest devoured light.

It was nothing, he told himself. Probably just a squirrel or a deer. His dad had said they had lots of them out here.

Or a bear, Beacon thought darkly, remembering what Everleigh had said the other day—paws the size of dinner plates and claws like Wolverine.

A twig snapped, and adrenaline shot through his body. He whirled in a circle, trying to find the source of the sound.

Nothing. No one.

He held out his skateboard like a weapon, taking slow, careful steps back, away from the trees. Or at least he thought he did. He didn't know which way was out. Everywhere he looked was forest and more forest. Shadows and darkness.

"Wh-who's there?" Beacon asked. His voice sounded high and strange to his own ears, setting his pulse on edge.

No answer. Just the sound of weak, dead trees groaning in the wind.

Beacon swallowed.

"Whoever's out there, come out now, or—or else!"

Another flicker of movement. Beacon yelped and swung with the figure, trying to keep it in his sights. But it was gone again. Lost in the shadows.

Beacon took a shaky step back. Then another.

He turned around to run.

And slammed right into a person.

5

Beacon stumbled back into the dirt. As soon as he hit the ground, he shot back up, taking a defensive stance with his skateboard. The other kid pushed himself to his feet and picked up some sort of electronic device that looked like a radio from the fallen leaves.

"Watch where you're going!" the boy said indignantly, wiping dirt off his device.

Beacon's fear slipped a fraction as anger took its place.

"Me? You're the one following me through the woods like a creep!"

"I wasn't following you! I was just . . . seeing what you were up to. I don't usually come across anyone else out here."

Beacon's tense shoulders melted. He lowered his skateboard/weapon.

"Well, you could have said something before I practically had an aneurysm."

He took a better look at the boy. He wore a pair of huge leather goggles like the ones pilots used to wear, and his red hair was parted in the middle and flattened against his head with more hair gel than he'd seen on even the smarmiest of TV weather personalities. His white lab coat, worn over a suit at least two sizes too big, rippled in the stagnant breeze.

The boy pushed his goggles onto his forehead, revealing deep impressions across his freckled cheeks from where the plastic had dug in. The goggles, Beacon realized—was this the "creature" with the gigantic eyes he'd seen in the woods last night when the car broke down?

The boy slid on a pair of wire-framed glasses and eyed Beacon from head to toe, finally settling his gaze on the skateboard tucked under his arm.

"So who are you?" the boy asked.

"Beacon McCullough," Beacon said warily. "I'm new to town. Who are you?"

"Arthur Newell," the other boy said after a lengthy pause. "So what *are* you doing out here?"

Beacon's hackles rose at the boy's tone. He had just as much of a right to be in these woods as him. He didn't own them.

"I didn't know I wasn't allowed to take a walk in the woods."

"A walk in the woods with a skateboard?" Arthur said.

"I skateboarded to get to the woods. And you're one to talk, with those weird goggles and . . . whatever that thing is," he said, gesturing at the device in the boy's hands.

"These weird goggles have night-vision capability," Arthur said.

"Really?" Beacon had to admit, that was cool.

The boy puffed out his chest. "Made them myself."

"And what's that?" Beacon nodded at the radio thingy.

"It's an ARD," Arthur said, as if that explained everything.

"Oh, an ARD. Say no more," Beacon said.

"An alien radiofrequency detector," the boy said.

"Alien?" Beacon raised his eyebrows.

"That's what I said."

"So, you, like, believe in them or something?" Beacon asked.

"Yeah, I do. Go ahead and laugh," Arthur said.

"I wasn't going to laugh."

Okay, he was. In fact, his lips twitched at the effort to rein it in. Arthur scowled, then turned around and began stalking away through the woods, tramping over twigs and leaves and thwacking aside branches. Beacon panicked. He'd finally found someone to hang out with, and even if the boy was weird, he didn't really want to be alone out here.

"Wait!" Beacon called, tripping after him. "I wasn't making fun of you. It was just surprising is all."

Arthur didn't even slow down.

"So aliens, huh?" Beacon said, trying to coax him into speaking.

"As a matter of fact, I'm the president of YAT—Youth Searching for Alien Truth," Arthur said boldly.

"Wouldn't that be YSAT?" Beacon said. "You know, Youth *Searching* for Alien Truth?"

The boy glared at him over his shoulder. "It's YAT."

"Okay, okay." Beacon raised his hands in defense.

Satisfied, the boy kept walking. Beacon watched him disappear into the trees, then sighed, gripped his board, and chased after him.

"Wait up!" Beacon was out of breath by the time he caught up to Arthur. "So you think they're out here, in the woods?"

"I'm not ruling it out," Arthur said. "There's strange electromagnetic activity in the area. I've been trying to study it."

"Like *what* kind of activity?"

"Like cars breaking down for no reason," Arthur said. "Stuff like that." He gave Beacon a knowing look.

"That was you? Watching us from the woods?"

He didn't deny it. Beacon repressed a shudder.

"So you think our car broke down . . . because of aliens?" Beacon asked.

"No, definitely not," Arthur said. "Was probably just a coincidence. Same as the last dozen cars."

The hairs on Beacon's neck stood on end. "The radiator was broken," he said weakly.

"Okay."

"It just needed sealant."

"Awesome." Arthur tramped ahead.

Beacon chased after him. "Wait up, where are you going?"

"Home," Arthur said.

"You . . . live in the forest?" Beacon said uneasily.

"Yep, inside a tree. I like to be close to my squirrel friends."

Beacon stuttered a step.

"This is a shortcut, idiot," Arthur said.

(Well, he hadn't actually said "idiot," but it was implied from his tone.)

Soon, they came up to a house in the woods. The white siding was stained yellow, and the cedar shingles stuck up in places like wonky teeth. The roof had collapsed on itself so that the whole place looked a bit like a rotten smile.

Arthur climbed up the wobbly wooden front steps and whipped open the screen door.

"That you, Arthur?" a croaky voice called from inside the house. A woman with a puff of white hair and glassy, unfocused eyes came to the door.

"Hi, Grams," Arthur said.

"I heard you talking," she said. "Is there someone here?"

"Hi," Beacon said, stepping forward. "My name's Beacon. I'm new to town."

"Beacon—oh, how delightful!" the woman crowed. Her lined face lit up. Arthur's ears turned pink, and he rubbed the back of his neck. Beacon got the distinct impression he didn't get company very often.

"Well, are you going to invite your guest inside or just make him stand in the yard?" the woman said.

Beacon looked at Arthur.

"You wanna come in?" Arthur asked grudgingly.

Beacon knew he shouldn't go inside strangers' houses. He also knew what a pity invite was. But he said thank you and ambled up to the house.

"How about I make you two some sandwiches?" the woman said as Beacon entered.

Beacon's stomach rumbled at the thought of food. He realized it had been forever since his last good meal.

"We're not hungry, Grams, but thanks," Arthur said. "We'll be in my room."

"Okay, honey. Did you remember to take your Keppra?"

Arthur's cheeks tinged pink. "Yes, Grams."

"On time? Because you know what happens if you're late."

"I took it on time," Arthur said, and now there was no hiding how red his face was.

Oblivious, his grandma smiled widely. "Okay, well you have fun with *your friend*."

Arthur practically bolted. Beacon followed him down a short, narrow corridor. He had the urge to ask Arthur what would happen if he didn't take that medication on time, but he thought it was better to let Arthur tell him himself, if he wanted to.

Arthur's room was impossibly small, with a neatly made twin bed pushed up against one wall, and a pine desk against the other, which was brimming with circuit boards and wires and test tubes and beakers and a microscope that looked like it was straight out of the 1940s, not to mention the piles of books and journals arranged in neat, color-coded stacks. There wasn't a single poster on the clean white walls. The place looked more like a science lab than a kid's bedroom.

"This is my headquarters," Arthur said.

Beacon wandered over to the desk and peered through the microscope. Tiny bugs skittered across the surface of the slide. He reeled back, cringing.

"Got this from the school," Arthur said proudly, resting his hand on the microscope. "Can you believe they were just going to throw it away?"

Beacon reached out to touch a vial of brightly colored yellow liquid.

"I wouldn't touch that, unless you want to get your finger melted off," Arthur said. Beacon quickly snapped his fingers away.

"I'm kidding," Arthur said. "But . . . maybe don't touch it, just in case." He quickly screwed a cap onto the vial.

"What's this?" Beacon pointed to a big metal drum with a bare lightbulb sticking out of its top.

"That's the prototype for the ARD."

"The alien radiofrequency detector?" Beacon said.

"Yep. It's come a long way since then. I modeled the recent design off an old electromagnetic field meter my dad had in the garage from when he worked for the power company. They used it to diagnose problems with electrical wiring and power lines on the highway. Stuff like that. I figured it made sense to apply that technology to the ARD, and I was right. The signals are off the charts in the forest. I was obviously way off base with the old model."

"Obviously." Beacon was done touring the room and plopped down on the end of Arthur's bed. "So you really think aliens exist, then?"

"I know they do," Arthur replied confidently.

"Have you ever . . ."

"Had a close encounter?" he finished for him. "I wish."

"Then how do you know for sure?" Beacon asked. "If you've never even seen one."

"The universe is so huge," Arthur said. "Scientists think it could host up to 130 million galaxies. What are the odds that out of all those millions, we're the only planet that supports life? We've already discovered planets with the right conditions in our own galaxy. The rest is too far away for us to travel to or contact, but that doesn't mean they don't exist."

Beacon had to admit, it made a certain amount of sense.

"What made you so interested in all this?" Beacon asked.

"What do you mean—don't tell me you don't know about *the incident*," Arthur said.

"That thing from the 1970s or whatever?" Beacon said. "I read something about that."

"That thing or whatever just happens to be one of the most important UFO discoveries since Roswell."

"Neat," Beacon said. "I think I've heard of that one, too."

Arthur rubbed his forehead.

"All right, if you're going to be living here, you better have more information than that." He sat across from Beacon on the bed. "So in 1967, a large object crashed into the water by the pier. The entire town saw it. They mounted this big rescue attempt, but they couldn't find a single trace of the ship."

Arthur was staring at Beacon as if he was expecting a huge reaction.

"Wow, that's wild," Beacon said unconvincingly.

"Dozens of people saw this craft crash into the water *right there on the harbor*," he said, pointing toward the wall, or, Beacon presumed, the ocean beyond it. "And yet they couldn't find anything? Not even a tiny piece of the craft? Not a single nut, bolt, or screw? No floating debris?"

Okay, so that did seem a little weird.

"They closed the case, but a few years later an official government report was leaked where they called the craft a UFO."

A chill crept over Beacon like a fog on the harbor.

"Doesn't UFO just mean unidentified flying object?" Beacon said, playing devil's advocate.

"Technically," Arthur admitted. "But they'd never called any other supposed sightings a UFO before. But that's not even the best part." He was leaning toward Beacon, his blue eyes sparkling behind his glasses. "So there was a naval search after the crash, right? And they said they couldn't find anything? But satellites followed something moving through the water, all the way from Driftwood Harbor, through the Atlantic Ocean, until it disappeared off their radar entirely near Russia!"

"What does that mean?" Beacon asked.

"I think—a lot of people think," he corrected himself, "that whatever crashed into the water that night drove far enough away that it wouldn't be spotted and then resurfaced and flew back to wherever it came from."

"That sounds a little out-there," Beacon said.

"Then you tell me what other explanation there could be."

He didn't have a good answer for that.

"Well, if aliens are real," Beacon said, "why don't more people know about it?"

"They don't want us to know. Think about it—there would be mass hysteria. Everyone would be panicking about a full-scale alien takeover."

"Is that what you think is going to happen?" Beacon asked.

"Almost certainly."

There was a prickly silence as Beacon digested all this information.

"So, do you want to join?" Arthur asked after a while.

"Join what?" Beacon said.

"YAT," Arthur replied, as if it were obvious.

"Oh, no, thank you," Beacon said. "Aliens aren't really my thing."

"Right, of course." Arthur turned around quickly and pretended to be busy fiddling with something on his desk. "Just thought I'd ask."

Beacon thought he might have blown things with Arthur, when the boy turned around and said, "So what is your kind of thing, then?"

"Skateboarding, mostly," Beacon said, lifting up his board awkwardly. "Listening to music. Hanging out with friends. That kind of stuff."

"I've never skateboarded in my life. Is it hard?" Arthur asked.

"At first. But it's also fun. I could show you?" Beacon offered.

"Oh, no. I wouldn't be good at it."

"Well, you won't know until you try, right?"

"Uh, maybe some other time," Arthur said.

"Okay." Beacon slumped back onto the bed, searching for

something to say. "So you live with your grandma?"

"Yeah, ever since my parents died when I was eight."

He said it so boldly, as if it were just a fact. Which, of course, it was. But death was a subject Beacon's family tiptoed around. The elephant in the room everyone pretended they didn't see.

"How—how did they die?" Beacon said. He felt himself go hot all over saying the words aloud. But if Arthur noticed, he didn't mention it.

"Car accident. We were leaving this cattle-ranching expo. It was raining and dark, and there's this big stretch of highway that wraps around the mountain where you can't see much up ahead. All I remember is going to sleep in the back of the car and waking up in a hospital bed with Grams there." He shrugged limply, though Beacon could see the brightness in his eyes. "They died on the scene."

"I'm so sorry," Beacon said.

It felt kind of weird to be the one delivering the apology. He was so used to being on the receiving end. Being the one to shrug awkwardly, look away, and mumble a "thank you." Was "thank you" even the right response? Beacon never really knew.

It seemed like he had more in common with Arthur than he thought.

"My brother died last year," Beacon found himself saying. He'd never said the words out loud before. Not bluntly, anyway. He always found a way to get around saying the *D* word, as if by not saying he was dead, it would make it less true.

"He drowned," Beacon said. The other *D* word.

Now that he'd said it, he couldn't stop. The rest of the story just came pouring out like a dam had broken inside him.

"We were on this family trip up at Big Bear, a couple hours from home," he continued. "We'd rented this apartment a few streets away from the beach instead of staying in the hotel where we usually do. To save money or whatever. We were kind of annoyed about that because our usual place was right on the beach, and that meant we had to pack up early for supper and stuff, and I dunno, somewhere along the line I guess we got the idea to sneak out at night and go swimming."

He could still hear Everleigh's whispery voice as if it'd been yesterday. *Come on, Beaks. Dad will never know. It'll be fun!* He could see Jasper's eyes, shining with excitement in the dark. Smell the sunscreen on his skin. The smell would forever make him ill.

Arthur hadn't said anything yet. Beacon wondered what he was thinking but couldn't bear to look up and see his reaction.

"The waves were huge," Beacon continued. "Jasper said we should go back, but Everleigh dived in."

Don't be such babies! Her delighted laughter tinkled in Beacon's ears, making a shiver ghost over his back.

"She didn't come back up right away. There was a strong current, I guess. Jasper dived in after her. Everleigh ended up swimming back on her own, but . . ." Beacon shook his head. "The Coast Guard didn't find him until three hours later. By then it was too late."

He'd never told anyone the story. His chest felt tight and fluttery. He peeked up, expecting Arthur to ask him why he hadn't gone after them, too, to accuse him of being weak and afraid, but Arthur just said, "That's awful." He didn't seem the least bit bothered that Beacon had only known him for about five minutes before he'd unloaded his entire life story on him, either.

"Yeah," Beacon agreed. "That's why we're here. For a new start, I guess. Everything in LA reminded us of him. Our dad wanted to go somewhere he'd never been. I think that's why my sister hates this place so much. Because it's like we left him behind, you know? Like we're trying to forget about him or something."

Arthur nodded. After a minute, he said, "So where's your mom?"

"Died when I was a year old. Embolism. I don't even remember her, so it's not as bad as losing Jasper. I know that sounds bad."

"No, it makes sense," Arthur said. "Can't miss someone you've never met."

"Exactly," Beacon said. Although it wasn't the full truth. He did miss the thought of her. Of what it might be like to have a mom. Which qualities he had that might have come from her, besides the color of his eyes.

He didn't think he could have said any of this stuff to his friends back home. Sure, they'd all acted super sorry for him after Jasper died. But it didn't take long for them to seem annoyed that he wasn't himself again yet. As if he'd had a certain amount of approved time to grieve, and after that, his sadness was just annoying. So he'd pushed all the hurt deep down and put on a happy face. Everyone liked it better that way. Liked *him* better that way.

But nothing seemed to faze Arthur. He didn't seem to care what anyone thought about him. At first Beacon had thought that he was weird, but now he was starting to think they could be great friends.

A mosquito buzzed around Arthur's ear. He slapped it, then went over to the window and yanked down the pane. "Bugs get pretty bad out here," he said.

Beacon squinted past Arthur at the pink light outside the window, then looked at his watch. His heart dropped.

"What time is it?" Maybe his watch was broken, he thought, even though that didn't explain the sunset outside the window.

Arthur looked at his own watch. "Six fifteen. Why?"

Six fifteen. At night. Beacon felt light-headed. It was breakfast when he'd gone out in search of Everleigh. He'd spent way more time walking in the woods than he'd thought.

"I gotta go," Beacon said, jumping off the bed. "I was supposed to be back for dinner already." He grabbed his skateboard and flew out the door. He pulled out his cell and dialed his dad's number, but the call wouldn't go through. Zero bars of reception. Great. He jammed his phone back into his pocket and picked up his pace.

It was much darker on the way back, and even though Arthur had pointed him in the right direction, all the alien talk didn't help his trek back through the woods. He jumped at shadows and gasped at the sound of twigs and leaves crunching under his own feet. Before moving to Driftwood Harbor, Beacon had only been inside a forest once, on a school trip. It had been full daylight, and he'd been surrounded by twenty other chattering students and his teacher. He hadn't realized then how creepy a forest could be. Or just how masochistic hikers were for enjoying it.

By the time he finally found the road, full night had come. Streetlamps cast pale yellow circles of light onto the gravel. He could barely see the outlines of the town up ahead through the thick, soupy fog. And where was everyone? The town was so quiet. Yet he had the eerie feeling he was being watched, like a bug under Arthur's microscope. Every nerve in his body felt electrified. When the peaked roof of Blackwater Lookout came into view, it was only the last scrap of his pride that stopped him from breaking out into a run.

He glanced at his watch: 7:00 p.m. He was in so much trouble. Maybe Canada was a good idea after all. In fact, he could hitchhike there now.

Beacon stepped inside quietly. Maybe he could make it to his room before anyone noticed.

"Beacon?" his dad said, popping his head around the corner. "I was getting worried." There was a deep line carved into his forehead.

Beacon felt terrible. He knew better than to disappear after what happened with Jasper. He knew that his dad would jump to the worst conclusions.

"Sorry. I lost track of time."

He wanted to explain about the weird loss of time, but he knew that would only make him look like he was making up excuses.

"I tried to call, but there was no reception," Beacon said.

"Donna said service could be hit or miss around here . . . ," his dad said. He frowned, instead of giving Beacon the usual lectures about responsibility. "Well, wash up. We're already sitting down for dinner."

,,,,,,,,,,,,,,,,,,,,,,,,,,,,,,,,,,

Everleigh was sitting at the table when Beacon followed his dad into the kitchen. He was glad to see his sister there, even if she did look like she'd rather be anywhere else. Some days she never left her bedroom at all. Those were bad days.

He dropped his bag and board by the door and took a seat.

Donna glanced over from the stove. "Ah, the prodigal son returns," she said.

Whatever that meant.

She joined them at the table. There was a two-second pause, where they weren't sure if they should say grace or sacrifice a fish or whatever it was mariners did before meals. But then Donna dived in for a dinner roll, and everyone else followed suit.

"So, how was everyone's first full day in Driftwood?" their dad asked. "Everleigh, I hope you didn't spend all day underneath the hood of that car. And yes, I know about that," he added.

"Not all day," she said defensively.

"Yeah, she took bathroom breaks," Beacon muttered. Everleigh opened her mouth to show Beacon her chewed-up food. Gross.

"And how about you, Beaks?" his dad asked.

Beacon scooped some creamy mashed potatoes onto his plate. (Turns out Blackwater Lookout Bed-and-Breakfast was going to be a Bed, Breakfast, Lunch, and Dinner place until they got their own house.)

"I met a boy named Arthur in the woods today," Beacon said.

"In the woods?" their dad repeated. "What were you doing there?"

"I went for a walk. Anyway, Arthur said he's the president of this alien conspiracy club called YAT. He was carrying around a device to detect frequencies or something."

Beacon's dad choked on his mashed potatoes.

"What a freak," Everleigh said around a mouthful of food.

"Everleigh!" their dad said once he'd managed to swallow his bite and wipe his mouth. "We don't call people freaks."

Everleigh rolled her eyes and chewed on a lobster tail.

"He's actually pretty cool," Beacon said. "He built all this stuff, like night-vision goggles, and he knows a ton about the weird crash that happened in the harbor here in 1967. Some of it is pretty interesting."

"A bunch of silly nonsense," Donna said.

"I'm with her," Everleigh said, scraping food onto her fork.

"Arthur said tons of people saw the craft go down. Dozens of separate reports. But they never found any trace of it," Beacon said.

"Craft? Did you join his club, or what?" Everleigh said.

"No!" Beacon felt his cheeks get pink. "I just think it's interesting is all."

"If you ask me, it's a bunch of hooey," Donna said. "The old boys were probably drinking at the tavern when they said they saw that 'craft.' Dollars to doughnuts nothing happened. Giant waste of time. That boy should find a new hobby."

"I agree with Donna," their dad said. "Beacon, promise me you won't go creeping around through the woods again. You could have gotten hurt."

"I wasn't 'creeping around,' Dad!"

"It's dangerous, and I don't like it. Promise me, Beacon."

Beacon rolled his eyes. "Okay, whatever."

"Whatever what?"

"No creeping around in the woods."

His dad stared at him for a moment, as if he were going to make him pinkie swear or something. Beacon wished he'd never brought up Arthur or his stupid club.

Donna set down her fork and wiped her thin lips with a napkin. "Does anyone want pie?" she asked, and Beacon was glad the conversation was over.

....

After dinner, the family played a game of Scrabble in front of the fireplace. Even his sister joined in, instead of retreating to her room to listen to music and wallow in self-pity. It should have been a great night. But Beacon was somewhere else. He lost the third game in a row, and not by a small margin.

"Thinking about your first day of school tomorrow?" his dad asked.

"I think he's thinking about *aliens*," Everleigh said, doing jazz hands.

Beacon rolled his eyes.

But the truth was, he *was* thinking about them. He couldn't *stop* thinking about them. Everything didn't add up. Arthur had said there were dozens of separate reports about the crash. They couldn't have all been drunk that night, despite what Donna had said. The government had even confirmed a crash in the leaked documents. So why was she brushing it off? And then there was Jane and the sea, and how quickly the sheriff had closed the case. Not to mention the car breaking down exactly where Arthur said other cars broke down all the time, and the freaky time loss in the woods. He couldn't shake the feeling that there was something not right going on in Driftwood Harbor.

A computer was open for use by guests at the inn, but Beacon waited until everyone went to bed before creeping down the hall to use it. He'd already taken enough heat about the alien talk at dinner. The last thing he needed was for anyone to find out he was researching the incident.

The computer was dusty and archaic, shaped like a box, like the old TVs you saw only at yard sales. He pressed the clunky power switch, and yellow light glowed dimly from the screen, illuminating the dark room.

He pulled out the chair tucked underneath the desk. The old wood creaked as he sat. He went stiff, waiting to hear movement in the house or to see a light flick on in the hallway. But everything was quiet and dark. Everything but his heart, which crashed as hard as the water against the cliffs outside.

With clammy hands, he dragged the old mouse across the pad and brought up the search engine. He'd looked up Driftwood Harbor before, but that was back when he thought the world was a bit more straightforward than it was looking tonight.

He typed *Driftwood Harbor UFO incident* into the browser.

Then he waited.

And waited.

And waited.

Beacon was pretty sure he could run back to LA and fire up his desktop before the page loaded.

Finally, the results appeared. He opened the Wikipedia page.

On the night of October 16, 1967, at about 11:20 p.m. Eastern Standard Time, multiple independent witnesses reported seeing an object crash into the waters of Driftwood Harbor, Maine.

The initial report was made by local resident Paul Gephart. Driving through Driftwood Harbor, on Highway 3, he spotted a large object descending into the waters off the harbor. Gephart contacted the Coast Guard detachment in Portsmouth.

A sharp scratching noise made Beacon jump. He wheeled around, only to realize it was just a tree scraping against the window. Jagged shadows danced on the walls. He blew out an uneasy breath, then huddled into himself for comfort.

US Coast Guard quickly arrived at the scene. Concerned for survivors, they launched a rescue mission, but the object began to sink and quickly disappeared from view. No survivors, bodies, or debris were ever discovered, and by the next morning, the Federal Aviation Administration (FAA) had determined that all commercial, private, and military aircraft along the Eastern Seaboard were accounted for.

It didn't make sense. The water must have been shallow by the harbor. If something crashed there, they should have been able to locate pieces of the craft. But nothing? Not a single trace?

Beacon closed Wikipedia and scrolled through the search engine results, bypassing anything that looked a little too official. He wasn't interested in what the government had to say about it. He finally opened a website called buried-truth.org.

On October 16, 1967, local residents of Driftwood Harbor saw unusual lights in the sky before they descended toward the icy waters of the harbor.

There was a large subtitle in Comic Sans font that said **EVIDENCE!!!!** with a bulleted list underneath. Beacon leaned forward eagerly.

- *Object Floats on Water: As if seeing the falling craft weren't shocking enough, witnesses were left gaping when instead of crashing into the water, the object floated on top of it. In a chance encounter, local police deputy Donalda Pound had also witnessed the event. According to Pound's testimony, she reported seeing a yellow light moving over the water. Several times over the course of the event, the strange vessel submerged under water, only to reappear again farther from shore. When the Coast Guard attempted to respond to the apparent emergency, the craft could not be located. It had disappeared!*

- *Russian Submarine: Divers performed an extensive search of the area. When they didn't find a single piece of debris to prove there had been any craft in the water, the case was closed. However, a*

Russian submarine was seen in the harbor the night of the crash. What was it doing there???!!! What aren't they telling us?

- *Satellite Imaging: Satellite imaging from the night of the crash shows two objects moving underwater at a high rate of speed, from the shores of Driftwood Harbor all the way to Russian waters, where they disappeared entirely. What was happening under there that they don't want us to know???!!!*

- *CONCLUSION: The military launched an investigation and located the craft underwater. While doing surveillance on the craft and plotting their next move, a second vessel appeared. During this time, Russia sent their own submarine to investigate. But before either government could get their personnel anywhere near the vessels, the two UFOs surfaced and disappeared into the skies!!!*

That seemed like a bit of a stretch. Beacon didn't really know what to believe anymore.

He scrolled down, skimming over old newspaper articles and official documents. Finally, he squinted at an ancient black-and-white photo of a police officer.

Cold wrapped around Beacon's body like icy shackles.

She's younger in the picture, her gray hair dark and smooth, and she was wearing a peaked cap and police uniform instead of an apron, but Beacon would recognize Donna's pale eyes and cleft chin anywhere. He read the caption: "Driftwood Harbor Police Deputy Donalda Pound."

Donna was Deputy Donalda Pound.

"What are you doing?"

Beacon gasped at the voice.

He whirled around.

Donna was standing in the doorway.

6

Beacon froze as Donna narrowed her eyes on him, paralyzed in the chair. She wore a tattered housecoat thrown haphazardly over a pair of satiny pajamas with fish all over them, and her steel-wool hair was up in curlers. Somehow, that made the whole thing more frightening than if she'd been wearing chain mail.

"I said what are you doing?" she asked, her voice pitched low and even. Sharp shadows played over her face.

Beacon swallowed. He fought to find a good excuse, but his brain seized up. "I was just, just—"

She started toward him. He quickly closed the browser with shaky fingers, but the computer reacted slowly to his commands. The page remained frozen on buried-truth.org, and the picture of Donna.

She crossed the room in two impossibly quick strides and leaned over Beacon's shoulder, just as the window closed to the desktop home page.

"About to do some homework," Beacon finished lamely.

"Homework," she repeated.

Beacon instantly realized his mistake. He started at his new school tomorrow.

"From back home," he amended. "An online assignment."

Donna stared at him. She was so close that he could see the little dark hairs on her chin that older ladies sometimes got. His heart raced so hard, he could feel it in his ears. There was no way she didn't hear it.

"It's late," Donna finally said. "Go to bed."

Beacon scrambled up. He wanted to ask Donna—Donalda, whatever her real name was—what she'd really seen that night. He wanted to ask her why she no longer worked for the sheriff's office, and why she owned this inn instead. He wanted to ask her *so many* things. But more than all that, he just wanted to get away.

He walked down the hall on gelatin legs, as if he'd been on a boat for days and now the ground ashore felt like the rolling sea. His muscles twitched with the impulse to run, though he knew that would only make him look guilty. But when he got to the second floor, he couldn't take it anymore. He raced down the hall and up the accordion stairs. When he finally reached his room, he rolled the dresser over the trapdoor, then jumped onto his bed, climbed under the covers, and pulled them up to his chin, his heart banging against his rib cage like it was trying to escape.

••••••••••••••••••••••••••••••••

Beacon was already awake when his alarm clock went off the next morning. He'd barely slept, jumping at every creak and groan of the old house. All he could think about was Donna, and why she'd changed her attitude about the UFO crash so drastically. She'd obviously thought it was real back in 1967, but now she was calling it all a bunch of hooey and accusing the other witnesses of being drunks. Why hadn't she mentioned she'd seen the crash? Why wasn't she a police deputy anymore? What was she hiding?

He wasn't entirely sure he wanted to know the answers to his questions.

Beacon got ready for school. He spent an embarrassing amount of time styling his curls in an artful swoop before realizing he looked like a peacock and giving up. He ran his fingers messily through his hair until the locks sprung back into their usual soft curls.

He came downstairs wearing his brand-new jeans and a blue-and-white-striped sweatshirt that he'd gotten because it reminded him of his Habitat board.

One good thing about moving to a whole new city—scratch that, a whole new town—was that the twins' dad had bought them entirely new wardrobes out of guilt. (Well, he'd said it was because the weather was different here by the water, but the twins knew better.)

Beacon hadn't thought he would be this nervous for his first day of school. He wasn't *super* popular back home, but he had friends, and the mean kids mostly left him alone. A middle-of-the-pack kind of guy. But now that the day was here, he felt like there was a giant squid swimming around in his stomach. It didn't help that he knew word about him must have spread like wildfire already, thanks to the Gold Stars. Everyone would know him as the weird kid from LA before he even set foot inside the school. He couldn't even eat the breakfast Donna had waiting for him that morning, even though it was French toast (his favorite) and one of the only meals he could rely on to not be made out of fish products. His food avoidance only partially was because he still wasn't sure he could trust her. To be on the safe side, he'd decided to keep a good ten feet between them at all times. He nibbled his toast from the safety of the doorway, claiming that a backache from the new bed made it hard for him to sit.

"Everleigh, we're going to be late!" his dad yelled upstairs. For the third time. "And don't even think about pulling the sick card, because we're not doing that here."

"I'm coming, I'm coming."

Everleigh trudged down the stairs, defiantly sporting her ratty jean overalls with the hole in the knee over a white T-shirt, despite having a whole slew of new clothes to choose from. Her brown hair was pulled back into a messy ponytail that Beacon couldn't be entirely sure she hadn't slept in. She obviously wasn't the least bit worried about starting at a new school. Even before the accident, Everleigh never cared what anyone thought about her. Sometimes he wished he could be like his sister. Those were dark times.

Everleigh breezed into the kitchen, snatched up the brown paper bag marked *Everleigh* off the counter, and said, "Are we going, or what?"

Their dad pressed his lips into a line, but Everleigh was going to school mostly without a fight, and he knew when to pick his battles, so they just piled into the car.

The routine felt familiar, but all wrong. They'd never done a first day of school without Jasper before. It seemed dumb to just realize it now, but his brother would never get any older. They would turn thirteen, fourteen, fifteen, have birthday parties, and hit milestones. Who knew, maybe they'd even get married and have kids of their own one day. They would do it all without him, while Jasper stayed frozen in time, forever sixteen.

The school was a ten-minute drive along the highway that wrapped around the ocean. Beacon had been expecting a one-room shack, but the school turned out to be a normal, redbrick building with an American flag rippling on a grassy quad. A bunch of kids milled around out front. At first, Beacon thought they were in uniform, but then he realized that they were just dressed formally. The kids wore polo shirts and pleated skirts and pants. He suddenly felt underdressed in his new sweatshirt and jeans.

Their dad shifted the car into park in the big roundabout in front of the school and unbuckled his seat belt.

"Whoa, there, cowboy," Everleigh said, putting out a hand. "What do you think you're doing?"

"I'm coming inside," he said, as if it were obvious.

"Uh, no, you're not," Everleigh said.

"Why not?" he asked.

"Walking into school with your dad?" She raised her eyebrows so high, they got lost in her hairline.

"Sorry, Dad," Beacon said, "but Everleigh has a point."

"But what about your schedule?" their dad said. "You don't even know who your teacher is yet."

"We can find the principal's office on our own," Everleigh said.

"You sure?" he asked uncertainly.

"*Sure*," they both said a little more forcefully than necessary.

"Well . . . okay," he said after a pause. "Remember you'll need to take the bus home after school. I'll be at work, and I don't think I'll be able to make it back on time. It's Brown bus #33. Just ask a teacher if you can't find it. And you know how to contact me if there are any issues. You have your cell phones, right?"

"Yes. We'll be fine, Dad," Everleigh said.

He looked to Beacon for confirmation, and he nodded.

"Okay, then . . . well, have a great day!"

Everleigh climbed out of the car and swung her backpack over her shoulder, and Beacon rushed to jump out after her. Their dad waved happily as he sputtered away, then honked the horn.

"Oh my god," Everleigh muttered.

If they didn't have an audience before, they definitely did now. Dozens of pairs of eyes followed them as they crossed the quad toward the school. Beacon felt his face flush with warmth.

"Why is everyone staring?" Everleigh said out of the side of her mouth. "And why is everyone so quiet?"

Beacon hadn't noticed it before, but his sister was right—there were no peals of laughter, no gossipy throngs, no one tossing a football across the quad. Just kids standing in small groups, chatting politely with one another. Watching them.

"I don't know," Beacon whispered back. "But it's weird."

Inside the school was the same eerie quiet. The silence followed them through the halls, lingering in the air like a heavy blanket. Their sneakers squeaked loudly as they walked. Everywhere they went, heads turned at the sound.

"Um, this is creepy," Everleigh said.

"Cosigned," Beacon said.

The twins went straight to the office. The secretary handed them their welcome packages, and Beacon and Everleigh pulled out their schedules.

"Mrs. Miller," Beacon said, at the same time as Everleigh said, "Mr. Pembroke."

They weren't in the same class.

Disappointment coursed through him. But Everleigh didn't seem fazed.

The bell rang.

"Off to the races," Everleigh sighed. She shrugged her backpack farther up her shoulders and set off down the hall as if she owned the place.

Beacon stood stalled in the middle of the hall, the map from his greeting packet hanging limply in his hand. He was kind of regretting not taking his dad up on his offer to show him into the school.

He pushed through the flood of kids like a fish swimming against the tide and eventually found his classroom right as the second bell was ringing.

"You must be Beckon McCullough," the teacher said, bungling his name.

"Beacon," he corrected.

"That's right," she said. "Welcome to Driftwood Harbor Academy. Here we have some of the finest faculty and students in the country, and we're very pleased to have you join us."

He very much doubted that. She didn't sound pleased at all—she spoke as if she were reading from a script.

There were two types of teachers back in LA: the older ones, who wore unflattering clothes from the '80s, and the young, hip twenty-somethings, who dressed embarrassingly like teenagers and tried to be cool. Mrs. Miller was neither of those. She *looked* young, but she dressed as if she were ready to go to a funeral. Black dress, black stockings, and shiny black heels that clicked loudly when she walked. Her nose was sharp and hooked, like a bird's beak.

"This week we're reading *The Yearling* by Marjorie Kinnan Rawlings." She handed Beacon an ancient-looking paperback with an illustration of a boy caressing a baby deer on the cover. It couldn't have been published any more recently than the 1600s. "Seating is assigned alphabetically, and I've rearranged the students' desks to accommodate you. You will be seated there for the remainder of the year."

Beacon followed her finger to an empty desk by the window. Instantly, he recognized one of the Gold Stars seated in the spot next to his. The boy with the tightly coiled dark curls. Nixon.

Nixon stared at him through heavy-lidded eyes. If Nixon hadn't already hated him after the encounter in the street with Jane yesterday, Beacon guessed he did now after the new seating arrangement.

That was just great.

He took his seat next to Nixon.

"We will begin," Mrs. Miller said.

Beacon was used to how things worked at his school in LA, where the teacher would have to call for order several times while clapping her hands and looking extremely harassed as someone flew a paper airplane past her head. But he could see there would be none of that here. When she spoke, the entire class fell instantly silent. All the students sat perfectly upright with their hands clasped neatly on the desks, as if they were actually eager to learn.

Beacon never thought he'd find himself longing for someone to make a loud fart sound with their mouth, but here he was.

"Please open your books to page sixty-one," Mrs. Miller said.

Beacon looked at the side of Nixon's head. Maybe the seating arrangement would be a good thing. He could clear things up with the Gold Stars and get back on a good footing.

"Hey," Beacon whispered to Nixon.

The boy slid a glance his way, and Beacon gave a little salute that Nixon didn't return.

"I met you the other day. In the junkyard, after our car broke down?"

Beacon left out the part about their second meeting in front of the junkyard. No need to remind anyone about that.

Nixon looked at him for a solid thirty seconds before responding.

"I remember," he said flatly.

"Oh. Okay. Cool."

Of course he did, Beacon thought. He was probably the first new person in Driftwood Harbor in the last decade. Great job, idiot.

He should have let it go, but for some reason, Nixon's cool attitude only made him want to try harder to make him like him.

"Boring, am I right?" Beacon whispered, gesturing at the

paperback Mrs. Miller was reading from as if she were reciting a grocery list.

The kid frowned at Beacon.

"*The Yearling* is a classic," he said.

Strike two.

"Oh. Yeah, I know that. We were just reading *The Hunger Games* in LA is all."

"Well, you're not in LA anymore," Nixon said.

As if he needed to be reminded of that.

"Look, I'm sorry about the new seats," Beacon said. "I didn't know she was going to do that. I can ask to move if it bothers you that much."

"Would you like to share something with the class, Beacon?" Mrs. Miller said. Everyone in the class swiveled to look at him.

"No," he said, sinking in his chair.

The teacher returned to her lesson. Beacon sighed and peered out the window. The clouds sat low and threatening, the air still like a held breath. The occasional rivulet of rain burst through and spit across the window.

A beep overheard jolted him from his thoughts. Static filled the classroom before a clear female voice spoke from a speaker in the corner of the room.

"Would Beacon and Everleigh McCullough please report to the principal's office?"

The students once again swiveled to face him. If this were back home, they would have been oohing and snickering under their breath, but the students here just looked at him with unreadable, wooden expressions. Beacon shoved back his chair and grabbed the hall pass dangling from Mrs. Miller's fingers. He set off down the empty corridor.

After a moment, a set of sneakers squeaked behind him.

"Beaks!"

Everleigh jogged over.

"What do you think this is about?" she asked.

"No idea," Beacon said.

"What if it's about Dad?"

Beacon hadn't even thought of that. He frowned.

The secretary took a long moment to finish clacking away at her computer before she finally looked up.

"Beacon and Everleigh?" she asked.

They nodded. She led the twins to an office behind the desk. The name plaque on the door read "Nurse Allen." Beacon could see the silhouettes of two people moving inside the room.

When the door swung open, Beacon was surprised to see Jane. She did a double take at the twins, then quickly pasted on a smile and smoothed a hand over the front of her button-down shirt. That's when Beacon noticed a quarter-size bloodstain on the white fabric.

"Thank you, Nurse Allen," Jane said, turning back to the other person in the room. "I feel better already."

"Great. We'll see you in church on Sunday," the woman said. "Give my regards to your mothers."

Beacon frowned at Jane's retreating body. Why was her shirt bloody? But the question disappeared as Nurse Allen beckoned the twins into the room.

The woman was as tall as a basketball player, her wide-set shoulders testing the limits of her scrub top. She wore her shiny dark hair curled crisply around her pointed chin and sprayed with enough product that it looked as if she could walk through a hurricane and come out looking exactly the same. She was smiling, her veiny hands clasped around a big key ring.

"Thank you for coming down," she said. "Sorry to interrupt you in the middle of class."

The nurse began talking about the gloomy northern climate and low vitamin D levels as she flipped through the key ring, then jabbed a small gold key into a lockbox behind her desk.

"Is my dad okay?" Everleigh interrupted.

The nurse squinted at her as if she'd suddenly sprouted a second head.

"Why wouldn't he be?" she said. She had a syringe in her hand. Everleigh blinked at her.

"You're here for a vitamin injection," the nurse said. "Mandated by the school board. Every child in the district receives one."

"A vitamin injection," Everleigh repeated slowly. Beacon could practically see the wave of relief wash over his sister. Meanwhile, panic ignited in his belly like kindling.

"What happened to Flintstones gummies?" Beacon squeaked. "Isn't there a pill we could take?"

"The injection is much more effective," the nurse said.

She motioned for Everleigh to sit in the chair and then started flicking air bubbles out of the syringe. Beacon took a quick step back.

He *hated* needles. Once, when he and Everleigh were eight and Jasper was twelve, their dad had taken them to a pharmacy to get free flu shots. It had taken their dad and three pharmacy techs to hold Beacon down. A startled shopper had even called the police, thinking that he was being abused. Yeah, it was just as embarrassing as it sounded.

Beacon knew that it was unreasonable—that it only hurt for a second, and that he was too old to be scared of something so silly. But logic never seemed to matter when it came to needles.

Tension grew in his face as his breathing became more rapid and shallow.

"This will sting," the nurse was saying as she wiped his sister's shoulder with an alcohol swab. "Stay still."

Everleigh flinched as the nurse injected her with the syringe, but she quickly pasted on a smile that Beacon knew was for his benefit.

"That was easy!" she said, rolling her T-shirt sleeve back down and jumping out of the chair. Her aggressive optimism only made him panic worse. If she was trying to hide how bad it was, it must have been *really* painful.

"Your turn, Beacon," the nurse said.

He looked at the chair, still swiveling from how quickly Everleigh had vacated it. His sister gave him a supportive squeeze of the shoulder.

"Relax," Everleigh whispered.

But Beacon couldn't relax.

He could see the nurse talking, could see Everleigh rubbing the crease between her eyebrows, but he couldn't seem to make his body move toward the chair. Before he knew it, he was out of the office and running down the hall, the lockers flashing past in a blur of green. He didn't stop running until he was outside.

The cold air blasted his senses, clearing some of the fog from his brain. He sat on the base of the flagpole in the quad, gasping for breath as adrenaline pumped through his body like he'd just run a marathon.

He was going to be in so much trouble. Why couldn't he just take the shot like a normal person? As if he needed any more reasons for the kids here to think he was weird.

Above him, the storm that had been threatening all morning blew in fast. The flag rippled, whipping and snapping tightly like the sail of a ship. Bloated, slate-gray clouds moved across the sky with unnatural speed.

The double doors of the school burst open.

Beacon stood up quickly, but it was just Everleigh who ran out.

"There you are," she said, jogging to catch up to him. "I looked everywhere for you."

"Is she coming?" Beacon asked, looking over her shoulder.

"No. I told her you were feeling sick today. You're off the hook for now."

Beacon sighed with relief and fell back to his perch like a limp jellyfish. Everleigh sat next to him.

"Don't tell Dad, okay?" Beacon said.

"I'm not a snitch," she said. After a long pause, she added, "But you're going to have to do the shot tomorrow, or they'll call home."

"I know," he said.

There would be no avoiding it. The thought made Beacon's stomach lock up tight. He knew he wouldn't feel better until it was over with, in the distant past. He wondered idly if his dad had known about the injection, and resentment burned in his belly, even though he wouldn't have gone to school if he'd had any warning. He could think up any number of illnesses on short notice.

"Ten thirty tomorrow," Everleigh said. "She made me promise."

Beacon nodded numbly.

"Come on," Everleigh said, nudging him with her shoulder.

"Let's go inside before it starts pouring."

She got up, then sucked air through her teeth and grabbed her head.

"You okay?" Beacon asked, squinting up at his sister.

"Yeah, just a bit dizzy. Got up too fast, I guess." She shook her head a few times. "Get back to class before that nurse comes looking for you." Then she punched him in the shoulder so hard, he hissed and bounded away.

7

Beacon didn't see Everleigh at lunch. He called and texted her, but she didn't reply. He looked for her at her locker, in the caf, and outside of her classroom—he even asked a stranger to check for her inside the girls' bathroom, just in case she was hiding in there. The girl looked at him as if he were nuts, which didn't do wonders for his reputation. But his sister was nowhere to be found.

Sure, they hadn't made any concrete plans to meet up. Yes, Everleigh had cut too much class to keep track of, faked sick at least twice per week, and basically used every excuse in the book to not go to school. But Beacon had just assumed they would be spending the lunch hour together, since it was their first day and they didn't know anyone except for Arthur, and Beacon hadn't seen him in the caf either.

For a minute, he panicked that something had happened to his sister, but then he realized that she'd obviously just gone back to the body shop to work on the car.

Irritation bubbled inside his veins. He walked back to his locker and sank to the floor, peeling off the plastic wrap from the egg salad sandwich Donna had packed for him. At least out here, there wouldn't be anyone to make fun of him about the smell.

He lifted the sandwich to his mouth, when the bell rang. Lunch was over.

Great. Thanks a lot, Everleigh.

Beacon was still low-key angry when the final bell rang at the end of the day. He packed up his stuff and waited for Everleigh by the row of big orange school buses lined up in the gravel parking lot.

He scanned the quad for Everleigh's swishy ponytail and busted overalls, but he didn't see her anywhere. He didn't really want to walk onto the bus by himself, but soon, the engines rumbled and he got worried they were going to leave without him.

Beacon got on and took a seat at the front. He stared out the window, red in the face, his fingers clenched into fists. He hardly saw the ocean as it passed in a hazy blur, the windows rattling with every small bump in the rutted pavement.

As soon as the bus rolled to a stop in front of the inn, he stormed down the steps and up the driveway.

He was all set to tell his dad that Everleigh was at the junkyard, that she'd ditched him at lunch, and that she'd ruined his first day at school. But when he walked through the front door of Blackwater Lookout, he was shocked to see Everleigh sitting at the kitchen table with their dad, calmly unfolding a napkin into her lap. Donna bustled around, making some type of fish dinner, based on the smell.

"Hi, Beacon! How was your day?" Everleigh asked cheerily.

For a moment, he was too baffled to speak.

"Beacon, your sister is asking you a question," his dad said.

"Where were you?" Beacon finally managed.

"I got a ride home," Everleigh said, completely unperturbed by Beacon's obvious anger.

"A ride home? With who?" he snapped. "And why didn't you tell me?"

"I'm sorry. You're right, I should have let you know. I feel terrible for making you worry."

"Don't be a jerk," Beacon said.

"I wasn't. I apologized." She smiled politely. Sometimes she could be so sarcastic.

"And what about lunch?" Beacon said. "Where were you then? Why didn't you answer when I called?"

"All right, that's enough," their dad said. "Beacon, go wash up and join us. Donna was kind enough to offer making an early dinner because Victor wants me back at work for a late shift."

Donna grunted.

Beacon was so stunned, he didn't even have the brain space to complain about his dad working in the evening. His sister had royally screwed him over, and she was going to get away with it.

He stormed out of the room to wash his hands.

A few minutes later, he was sitting around the table with Donna and his family, steam wafting up from the plates of noodles covered in shrimp.

"So, how was your first day at school?" their dad asked.

"It was great!" Everleigh said. "I met a lot of really nice kids, and the teachers were so helpful with the transition. I think I'm going to like this place after all."

Beacon's fork paused midbite. His sister might have gotten away with being sarcastic with him, but there was no way his dad was going to let it fly.

But when he looked at his sister, she was twisting pasta around her fork with a contented smile on her face.

The sound of Donna's fork stabbing her plate came into hyperfocus.

"That's fantastic," their dad said. "And, you, Beacon?"

"It was just awesome," he said, taking a note out of his sister's playbook. "Really, such a treat."

"Beacon, don't you think you should tell Dad about the incident in the nurse's office today?" Everleigh said.

Beacon's mouth fell open in outrage. She'd promised! She'd said she wasn't a snitch!

Beacon had covered for Everleigh too many times to count. He couldn't *believe* she was ratting him out now.

"What happened in the nurse's office?" their dad asked.

"Nothing," Beacon gritted out through his teeth, making "shut up" eyes at his sister. "Just a misunderstanding."

"I wouldn't say it was nothing," Everleigh said, tilting her head at Beacon in admonishment.

"Everleigh!" Beacon cried.

"What? I think it's important to tell the truth." She turned to their dad. "Beacon refused his mandatory vitamin injection today. He ran out of the office, and the nurse was quite upset."

"Beacon, is this true?" their dad said.

He shrunk in his chair. There was a beat of silence where the only sound was the scrape of utensils on china as Donna twirled her pasta.

"You know how much I hate needles," Beacon said finally.

"*Beacon.*" Their dad stretched out the word like it had about ten syllables. Donna sighed heavily.

"Well, did Everleigh tell you she skipped school at lunch to go to the junkyard?" Beacon asked.

Their dad looked at her. Beacon smiled smugly, but Everleigh didn't look the least bit nervous.

"That's not true," she said. "I had lunch at Jane Middleton's house."

"Jane?" Beacon said. "As in, Jane from the Gold Stars?"

"Yes. She lives near the school. Her moms made us soup and sandwiches."

"How nice!" their dad said. "It's great to see you making friends."

"How nice?" Beacon stuttered on the words. It was as if he was in some sort of alternate reality where nothing made sense. "She ditched me on our first day. I looked for her everywhere and ate lunch alone!"

"Everleigh, you really should have told your brother where you were going," their dad said.

"I know. I'm sorry about that, Beacon," Everleigh said. "It won't happen again."

"Well, that was a very nice apology," their dad said. "Right, Beaks?"

"Whatever happened to Jane being a freak?" he answered.

"Beacon!" their dad said.

"What? She said it!" He pointed an accusing finger at his sister.

"I regret that," Everleigh said primly. "And I would appreciate it if you didn't denigrate her character. Jane is a nice girl. You need to consider how your words can be harmful to others."

"That's very well said," their dad said, as if this wasn't totally and completely out of character.

Everleigh glowed with pride at the compliment.

Beacon ground his jaw. He didn't know what kind of game his sister was playing. He also didn't know what *denigrate* meant. But there was no way she was being sincere. He didn't understand how his dad couldn't see right through it.

"May I be excused?" Everleigh said. "Jane invited me to a Gold Stars meeting, and I'd like to check it out. It starts in fifteen minutes."

Okay, this had to be a joke.

Everleigh used to be a master prankster, back before, when anything seemed funny. They would get into epic prank wars with Jasper—covering Jasper's entire car in Post-it notes, replacing the filling in the doughnuts in the fridge with mayo, signing each other up for weird newsletters using each other's e-mail addresses. Everleigh always came out on top. This had to be what was going on.

Only something was missing. Instead of a mischievous glint in her eye, Everleigh stared blankly as she waited for their dad's response. She seemed . . . vacant, somehow. Like the lights were on but nobody was home.

"Yes, you may be excused," their dad said. "Just be back by eight."

"Thank you, Dad. Donna, this was a wonderful meal." Everleigh pushed back her chair and stood up, folding her napkin onto the table. Beacon's mouth dropped open.

Everleigh was wearing a skirt. She still sported the plain white T-shirt she'd worn to school that morning, but now, instead of the overalls, she wore it under a dark pink dress with a ballerina skirt that skimmed her knees.

For a solid ten seconds, Beacon just stared.

"Are you . . . wearing a dress?" he finally managed.

In all his twelve years, he'd seen his sister in a dress exactly once. They were seven years old, and their dad had taken all three of the kids shopping for something to wear to their great uncle Larry's funeral. After some serious complaining, Everleigh had marched into the changing room with the black dress the saleswoman had picked out and slammed the door so hard, it almost rattled off the hinges. When she came out a few minutes later, she was sweating, her ponytail was slumped next to her ear like ice cream dripping off a cone, and she was huffing with her hands balled into fists. She looked like a demonic linebacker going to prom.

"I would rather be dead than wear this dress," she'd announced. Then she slammed back into the changing room.

She never wore a dress again.

"Jane lent it to me," Everleigh said now.

"Okay, what does Jane have on you?" Beacon said. "Did you hide a body together?"

"That's not funny," Everleigh said.

"I think it looks very nice," their dad said, wiping his mouth with his napkin. "Don't you agree, Donna?"

"Very pretty," she grumbled without looking up from her plate. She looked as if she'd rather be anywhere else but here. Beacon could relate.

"This is going too far," Beacon said. "You're freaking me out.

You win. You're the prank master. Just stop it."

"Prank?" Everleigh quirked her eyebrows. "What are you talking about?"

"This is a joke," he said.

Everleigh looked at Beacon as if he were a complicated math equation she couldn't figure out. She shook her head.

"Anyway, I'm going to head to the meeting now," Everleigh said to their dad.

"Have fun," he said.

She took her dirty dishes to the sink, and then whisked out of the kitchen. In the other room, they could hear the front door thump closed behind her.

Beacon looked from his dad to Donna, who were both pointedly looking away from him.

"Seriously?" Beacon said. "No one's going to say *anything* about that?"

"Beacon, you're not being very kind," his dad said.

"You don't think any of that was weird?" Beacon gestured at the vacated spot where his sister had been sitting.

"It was different," his dad conceded. "But I'm glad she's making an effort to make this place home. And I think it's nice she's making friends."

As if Everleigh had ever gone out of her way to do that before. Even when Jasper was still alive, she'd been the farthest thing from a social butterfly. She'd had one friend, Anna, and she'd had Jasper and Beacon. She hadn't needed anyone else, or so she'd said. Afterward, it was as if she were specifically trying to repel people. Anna had tried for a while—calling, texting, dropping by, and trying pathetically to lure her out to do this or that—but there was only so much she could do before even she had to take the hint. Everleigh had said she wanted to be alone, but Beacon knew the full truth: She just didn't want to let anyone get close again, in case she lost them, too.

"When has Everleigh shown even the slightest interest in volunteer work?" Beacon asked, changing tack. He could tell he wasn't getting anywhere talking about Jane.

"Sure, she hasn't been particularly interested in philanthropy in the past, but it's never too late to start. You should think about it, too. It sounds like a very nice group."

There it was again. That *nice* word.

"What about the dress?" Beacon said, floundering.

"I thought it looked—"

"Nice?" Beacon said.

His dad nodded.

"It looked weird!" Beacon cried. "Everleigh wears jeans. Old jeans. With holes. And when did she even have time to borrow clothes from Jane anyway?"

"She probably got it at lunch," his dad said. "Look, I know this must seem unusual, Beaks, but remember that this is what we were hoping for by moving here. That the change in scenery would make a difference for our family. Everleigh has had a hard time making connections ever since . . . ever since," he said simply. "It's great that she's opening up. Let's not make her feel uncomfortable about it."

A strange, distancing feeling overcame Beacon's body. It was as if he were watching actors pretending to be his family instead of having dinner with his real dad and sister.

"I'm happy if she wants to open up," Beacon said, "but this is all so sudden. It doesn't make any sense."

"I'm sure you'll make friends soon, too," his dad said gently.

"I *have* made a friend."

"Well, that's great. Then you have no reason to be jealous."

"I'm not jealous!"

Fury roiled through him. His dad wasn't even listening to him.

Beacon scraped back his chair.

"Where are you going?" his dad asked.

"Out," he snapped.

"Where?"

But Beacon was already out the door.

He ran. Down the long, twisting driveway of Blackwater Lookout. Through the meadow of overgrown, soggy grass and over the bubbling creek. Past a run-down cemetery full of cracked, crumbling gravestones and into the woods, twisting with dark shadows and menace. He didn't stop until he was on Arthur Newell's front steps. He knocked three times, then gripped the old wooden railing as he panted for breath. The door swung open.

"I didn't know where else to go," Beacon gasped between ragged breaths. He squinted at Arthur, and Arthur whipped off the hood of the fuzzy brown one-piece pajamas he was wearing.

"It's Chewbacca," Arthur explained, even though Beacon hadn't asked.

"Arthur, is that someone at the door?" Arthur's grandmother called from inside the house.

"It's Beacon!" Arthur yelled back so loudly that his voice cracked.

"Oh! Beacon! How nice!" his grandma replied.

"Can we talk?" Beacon whispered urgently. *"Alone?"*

Arthur pushed the door open wider.

"Does your friend want a snack?" his grandmother asked, coming to the door. "I can make some tuna sandwiches."

"Thanks, Grams, but we have important, uh, school stuff to talk about," Arthur said.

The boys quickly retreated to Arthur's room. The moment the door closed behind them, Arthur spun on him and said, "Okay, spill. You're acting really weird, and coming from me, that's saying something."

Beacon sat on the bed, his heart racing almost as fast as his thoughts. He didn't even know where to start.

"Something is going on with my sister. She's being really . . . good," he said, struggling to explain all the changes he'd seen in Everleigh tonight. "Just yesterday she was making fun of Jane and her Gold Star minions and now she's going to one of their meetings, saying things like 'wonderful' to describe her meal, and asking to be excused from the table."

"Hmmm," Arthur said, pursing his lips pensively. He slid a notebook off his desk, opened it to a fresh page, and poised a pen over the pad. "Tell me about the events leading up to this change."

Old Beacon would have laughed at the way Arthur was acting, as if he were an investigator on one of the weekly crime shows his dad liked to watch. And it *was* a little hard to take him seriously in his furry pajamas. But mostly he was just glad someone was finally listening to him.

"I don't know. She was normal yesterday and this morning at breakfast, too. Then we were called down to the office to get the vitamin injections."

"I heard about that," Arthur said. "You freaked out over the needle or something, right?"

"Hey! How did you know that?" he said.

"Small town. Word gets around fast."

"Well, I didn't freak out," Beacon said indignantly. "I just . . . delayed the injection until tomorrow." He lifted his chin.

"Okay, whatever," Arthur said as if he didn't believe him one bit.

"So what happened during the injections?"

"Nothing, really. Everleigh seemed normal in the nurse's office. I didn't see her again until we got back to Blackwater Lookout after school. That's when she started acting weird. Like, *a totally different person* weird. At first I thought she was joking around, but now I don't know. She seemed really serious. I've never seen her behave this way before. It's really freaking me out. And the worst part is, no one cares. Everyone's acting like it's no big deal."

"Interesting." Arthur tilted his head, his eyebrows rising above his glasses.

"What?" Beacon asked.

"So the changes happened right after the injection?"

"Not right after," Beacon said. "I talked to her five minutes later, and she seemed normal. Well actually, she did get dizzy. It came on suddenly."

"Does she usually get dizzy?" Arthur asked.

"Not really. But she was just running through the halls. Maybe it was from that?"

"Or maybe it was a side effect of the injection," Arthur said. "Maybe *all of this* is a side effect of the injection. She went into that office normal and came out different. It's *got* to be it. There's got to be something in that shot!"

"Why would the school do that?" Beacon said. He wanted answers, but he was having a hard time believing the nurse was an evil mastermind. He wondered if he'd made a big mistake asking the president of YAT for advice about this. "It just doesn't make any sense. Why would anyone want to change Everleigh?"

"Haven't you noticed anything strange about the kids here in Driftwood?" Arthur asked. He pinned Beacon with a look that made him shift uneasily. He remembered the kids in class, their perfect postures and obedience. He remembered Nixon shutting down all his jokes, and the eerie silence of the classroom and halls. But he just figured that it was different out here. That being raised in isolation, away from the big city and all the pressures that came with it, made the kids better.

"Every single kid is an A student," Arthur went on. "No one talks back. No one misbehaves. Almost everyone is a member of the Gold Stars." His eyes narrowed at the mention of the volunteer group.

"Are *you* in it?" Beacon asked.

"I don't want to be in their dumb club," Arthur said defensively. From the way Arthur's cheeks tinged pink, Beacon got the distinct impression there was more to the story.

"The kids here are perfect," Arthur said, bringing the conversation back on track. "And the same thing happened to Perry."

"The Gold Star?" Beacon asked, remembering the wide-set boy with the spiky blond hair.

"His family moved to town last summer. From New York or

something. Supposedly he was getting into a lot of trouble back at home. There was a rumor online that he'd been to juvie—something about a church burning down."

"Whoa," Beacon said.

"Yeah. Well, within a week, he was on the football team and volunteering with the Gold Stars. You can't tell me it's because of the lobster and fresh air."

Beacon felt his blood turn to frost.

"I've been investigating this ever since, but I didn't put it together about the vitamin injection," Arthur said. "But now that it's happened twice, and within the first week of school? That can't be a coincidence."

"Okay," Beacon said, playing along. "But what about you? Didn't you get the injection, too?"

"Everyone gets it," Arthur said. "It's mandatory."

"Then how come you're normal?"

Well, relatively normal, anyway.

"I don't know," Arthur said, shrugging. "Maybe it didn't work on me?"

That reason seemed flimsy.

"All I know is that I've always felt different from everyone else here," Arthur said. "Maybe this is the reason."

"But why?" Beacon asked. "Who's doing this? What's going on here?"

"I don't know. But there's definitely a conspiracy happening here. We just can't ignore all this evidence."

Yesterday, Beacon would have told Arthur he was out of his mind. And he still wasn't totally putting that option off the table. But right now, his theory didn't seem so wild. There *was* something wrong with his sister. Something wrong with this whole town. And Arthur was the only other person who seemed to notice or care.

So Beacon sat up straighter and threw his shoulders back.

"I want to join YAT," he announced.

Arthur beamed. "I thought you'd never ask."

8

Beacon felt better already. He wasn't just sitting around, doing nothing. He was being proactive.

"So should we call a meeting, then?" Beacon said.

"Sure."

"When?" he asked.

"Why not right now?" Arthur said. "Unless you're busy."

"No. Now is great!"

Excitement leaped through Beacon like a school of silvery fish jumping the waves. They were going to get the best minds in conspiracy theories together and figure everthing out. He couldn't wait to hear what everyone had to say about this.

Arthur pulled on a lab coat over his fuzzy pajamas. Then he took out a different spiral notebook and opened it to the first page, writing *YAT Files: The Case of the Freak Sister Mutation* across the top in big, blocky script, then underlining it twice.

"Any ideas where to start?" Arthur said.

"Wait, we're starting already?" Beacon asked.

"Why not?" Arthur said.

"Shouldn't we wait for everyone else to get here?"

"Like who?"

A sinking feeling washed over him.

"Please tell me you're not the only member of YAT," Beacon said slowly.

"Of course not." After a long pause, Arthur added, "There's you now, too."

Beacon mashed his palm into his forehead.

"What did you expect?" Arthur said defensively. "It's an alien conspiracy club. People aren't exactly lining up at the door to join. But don't worry. I've done hundreds of top secret missions. We're going to get down to the bottom of this. Now let's get started. First, you'll need to start monitoring your sister's behavior. Note any differences, big or small. We don't know what's important, so just write everything down."

Beacon nodded. He could do that.

Arthur wrote *Observe sister* on the list.

"Any other ideas?" Arthur poised his pen over the paper.

Beacon twisted up his mouth, thinking hard. He wanted to be helpful.

"This all started with the injection, right? So we need to figure out what's in it."

"Awesome idea!" Arthur said. "We need to get our hands on a

syringe so we can figure out what's in the formulation."

"The nurse keeps the syringes in a lockbox behind her desk," Beacon said. "Maybe we can break inside somehow and take one?"

"Easy, tiger," Arthur said. "I don't exactly want to get arrested."

"I thought you said you've done hundreds of top secret missions," Beacon said.

"I have." He adjusted his lab coat haughtily around his Chewbacca one-piece. "Just not the kind where police are involved."

Beacon didn't exactly have experience in this area, either. The worst thing he'd ever done was eat a sour candy from the grocery store without paying. And even then he'd told the cashier out of guilt. But this was his sister. He had to do something. He needed to get that needle. But how?

"The key to the lockbox is on a big key ring Nurse Allen keeps in her pocket," Beacon said. "Even if we could somehow break into the school after hours, we wouldn't be able to get into that box without the key."

"Oh, good. More B and E," Arthur said. "I was worried there wouldn't be enough in this plan."

Beacon's confidence that the YAT club would solve all of his problems began to dwindle.

"Unless . . . ," Arthur said.

"What?" Beacon said, sitting up straighter.

"You're not going to like it."

"Just tell me!"

Arthur leaned forward. "Okay, so you said you missed your injection yesterday, right? And Nurse Allen wants you to go back tomorrow?"

"Yeah . . . ," Beacon said warily.

"So you go back, only when you're in the office, you steal the syringe!"

"And how do you think I'll manage that without her noticing?" Beacon asked.

"I'll stage a distraction. Then while Nurse Allen is out of the room, you'll replace her syringe with a placebo and stick the vitamin injection in your bag."

"A placebo?" Beacon said.

"A fake. A syringe full of saline. I can even get us a syringe to use. My grandma is diabetic!" He said it with way more enthusiasm than was strictly necessary. "She has a ton of insulin syringes. We can clean one out. It might not be exactly the same, but it just has to look close enough that Nurse Allen wouldn't notice at first glance. It's a perfect plan!"

"Yeah, maybe for you," Beacon said. "What if your distraction doesn't work?"

"Trust me, it will. One sign of a seizure, and my teacher will be screaming for the nurse."

He said it as if he had personal experience. Beacon thought

of Arthur's grandma asking if he'd taken his medication. Arthur answered the question that was balanced on the tip of Beacon's tongue.

"I have epilepsy. Ever since the car accident. Brain damage, I guess."

"Oh," Beacon said. "I'm sorry."

"Don't be," Arthur said. "If I take my meds, I'm fine. I haven't had a seizure in, like, six months or something. Seriously, don't look at me like that. I'm not sick."

"Okay, but do you think it's safe to fake a seizure?" Beacon asked. "Won't they, like, try to do CPR on you or something?"

Arthur laughed. "No. They'll just turn me on my side to make sure I don't swallow my tongue or suck back puke or whatever. So long as I keep it under five minutes, they don't have to give me any meds or anything like that, either. It'll be fine."

Even though Beacon was less certain about the ethics of this plan, he was happy that Arthur had trusted him with this information. It felt like they'd just become a bit closer.

"What about if Nurse Allen *does* notice it's a different syringe?" Beacon said. "What if your distraction doesn't work? What if Nurse Allen doesn't leave? Then I'll have to get the vitamin injection anyway."

"That's not going to happen," Arthur said. "Besides, you have to get the shot either way, right? The school isn't going to let you go back without it, and your dad will flip if you're suspended. So this is win-win. You get Nurse Allen off your back, but you get to stay Beacon. Unless of course you want to become a Gold Star lemming . . ."

Beacon released a heavy sigh.

Arthur was right. Still, that didn't mean he had to like it. Beacon was a good kid. He was used to following the rules. It was Everleigh who took risks and got into trouble, who made things harder for their dad. But he didn't see what other choice he had. He'd already lost enough. He wasn't about to lose Everleigh, too.

"Fine," Beacon said. "I'll do it.

"Perfect," Arthur said. "Operation Jungle Avalanche is underway."

"Jungle Avalanche?" Beacon quirked an eyebrow.

"It's a code name," Arthur explained.

"Okay, but why Jungle Avalanche?"

"Because it sounds cool," Arthur said. "And because I'm the president of YAT. Now are you in or out?" He stuck out his hand.

Beacon hesitated before he took it.

"I'm in."

....

It was already full dark by the time Beacon got home later that night. He hadn't meant to be out so late. In fact, he could have sworn he'd only been at Arthur's for an hour, tops. But when he'd glanced up from their notebook, it was 9:00 p.m. He told himself that he'd just been too caught up in all the YAT stuff to notice how dark it was getting. That was so much easier to swallow than the growing sense that something wasn't right about the passage of time here. Or with him. That was a problem a little bigger than the YAT club was going to solve.

He braced himself for an argument about storming out of the house the way he had, and for coming home so late. It had seemed so right in the moment, but now he just felt bad. His entire family was cracking, and he was the only one holding it together. He couldn't lose it now.

When he stepped inside, he found his dad sitting in the big orange recliner in the living room with his feet kicked up and a pile of binders and papers scattered around him. A fire crackled and popped in the hearth.

"Where's Everleigh?" Beacon asked carefully.

"Bed. Donna just went up not long ago, too."

"Okay . . . ," Beacon said.

His dad smiled.

Beacon wasn't an idiot—he knew a bone when one was being tossed to him. He needed to get out of his dad's sight *stat* before he changed his mind about Beacon being in trouble. But when he turned for the stairs, his dad said, "Come and have a seat."

Beacon cringed before schlepping over to the couch.

"How are you doing?" his dad asked. He was using his TV dad/ therapist voice, and Beacon withered up inside.

"Good," Beacon said.

"How are you *really* doing?" he said meaningfully.

Beacon shifted uncomfortably.

"Good, Dad. Everything is fine." He pasted on a smile.

"It's okay. I want you to tell me the truth," his dad said gently.

Beacon almost said it all—everything that he was feeling. That he resented having to be good all the time because Everleigh acted out so much. That he was entitled to be sad, too, and that he wasn't okay, not even a little bit. But when he opened his mouth, he ended up saying, "This place is weird."

"It's very different from LA," his dad agreed.

"No. I mean, yes, it is," he said. "But it's just—strange. There's something off about the people here." He was struggling to put his feelings into concrete terms and not entirely sure how much he should say. "I just get an eerie vibe. I don't know."

"You're upset about your sister," his dad said.

"You don't think this is all out of character for her?" Beacon asked.

It had been a year and thirteen days since Jasper died. A year since he'd had his sister. There were times it seemed like maybe she was getting better—she'd smile in the old way she used to that would make the skin at the corner of her eyes crinkle, or laugh from deep inside her belly instead of the loud, theatrical sound she'd been doing lately. But then she'd frown before becoming angrier than ever, then stomp up to her room and stay there for days blasting music. That was the thing about grief. It was a monster that lurked in the shadows. Whenever you thought you'd escaped it, whenever you stepped into the light, it was right there with sharp claws and teeth, dragging you back. It didn't let go.

"It is a bit out of character, sure," his dad said. "But it's a good out of character, don't you think? Your sister has had a really rough go of it this last year. I think getting out of LA might have given her the permission she needed to start moving forward and being happy."

"I guess," Beacon said. "But there's other things, too. I just feel like everyone is watching me. Like—like I'm an animal in a zoo exhibit or something."

It wasn't anything he could really put his finger on. Just a stare caught out of the corner of his eye. A scratch in a corridor when he thought he was alone.

He almost mentioned how he'd found himself in the woods without knowing how he got there, but he stopped himself. It would only make his dad decide not to let him wander around on his own. This place was bad enough without being confined to the inn, and he needed his freedom if he was going to be doing an investigation.

"You're the new kid," his dad said. "I imagine Driftwood Harbor doesn't get a whole lot of turnover. You're interesting to them right now. Once they get used to you, they'll start treating you normally, and it won't be so weird."

"Yeah, you're probably right," Beacon lied. He was a bit disappointed his dad had brushed off his concerns. But what had he expected? That he would order the kids to pack up their stuff this instant and go back home, all based on a weird feeling and the fact that his sister had made friends too quickly?

"Thanks for the talk, Dad," Beacon said.

"Anytime."

His dad cuffed him on the shoulder, and Beacon went up to his room.

••••••••••••••••••••••••••••••••

The next morning, Everleigh came downstairs wearing makeup. Now Beacon knew things were really serious.

Everleigh smiled pleasantly, her thumbs hooked underneath her backpack straps as she watched the school bus rumble down the road toward the inn. Meanwhile, Beacon's stomach churned like the sea. He felt as if anyone who looked at him could see straight through his canvas backpack to the stolen insulin syringe in the front pocket.

This was a bad idea.

"There's the bus!" Everleigh said brightly.

"Boy, nothing gets past you," Beacon said, repeating his sister's joke from the other day. He slid a glance at her, waiting for her to call him a copycat and to tell him to get his own jokes—to just be normal Everleigh—but instead she hiked her bag up her shoulders as the bus ground to a halt in front of them and climbed jauntily up the steps. He'd never seen her this eager to go to school. Beacon made a mental note to update his notebook about her behavior and followed her onto the bus.

"Everleigh!"

Jane waved from the back of the bus, and Everleigh beelined for her. Beacon suddenly remembered the spot of blood on Jane's shirt yesterday and her strange reaction at seeing the twins. But she looked totally fine today.

From the second seat from the front, Arthur waved Beacon over with a brisk gesture meant not to be seen by anyone else. Beacon was relieved to see his friend, wearing a faded blue argyle sweater at least two sizes too big underneath his lab coat. Beacon sat down next to him and pulled his bag onto his lap.

"Hey," Beacon said.

There was a round of controlled laughter from the back seat as the bus jolted away from the inn. Arthur darted a glance behind him, then quickly snapped his gaze away. For someone who claimed to have done hundreds of top secret missions, he might as well have been wearing a neon sign that said "We're up to no good."

"Did you remember the stuff?" Arthur whispered.

"Of course," Beacon said.

"Are you okay?" Arthur asked. "You're all sweaty."

"I'm fine." Beacon swiped his forearm across his brow; it came away wet. "So you remember the plan?"

"No, I got amnesia overnight," Arthur said. "Yes, I remember."

"You can't be late, okay? Ten thirty."

"Honestly, you're starting to insult me," Arthur said.

Ten minutes later, the bus rolled up to Driftwood Harbor Academy. The brakes squealed as the driver put the vehicle in park. Outside, students converged toward the doors like gulls on a discarded meal.

It was game on.

9

Beacon didn't hear a word the first hour of class. He knew they were working on math, his strongest subject, but all he could think about was the nurse aggressively flicking air bubbles out of a cartoonishly large needle. He tried to remind himself about everything that Arthur had said—that this was the best plan, that it was the only way to find out what they'd done to his sister, and that Nurse Allen was going to give him the shot no matter what—but all of that seemed very far away.

The clock counted down like a bomb about to detonate. Ten more minutes.

Would Nurse Allen be able to see his guilt? Would she look at him and instantly know he was causing trouble? What if she asked to see inside his bag? What if she caught him in the act and he was suspended or expelled? *Or worse,* he thought with a horrified rush, *what if they call the police?*

He thought of his dad's angry face, and all the blood left his head in one hot rush.

"Beacon?" Mrs. Miller's voice broke through his thoughts. Everyone was looking at him.

"The answer for x?" she repeated.

Beacon mumbled a number, and his teacher shook her head as the students stared at him blankly—somehow, that was worse than if they'd laughed. He sank into his chair.

Just then, there was a knock at the door.

"Sorry to interrupt," Jane said, standing primly in the doorway. "I have a note for you."

She held out a slip of paper for the teacher. Mrs. Miller scanned the words, then looked at Beacon. His heart leaped into his throat.

"Beacon, the nurse would like to see you in her office," she said.

Beacon's eyes snapped to the clock. No. This wasn't right. It was too early.

"Thank you, Jane," Mrs. Miller said. Jane nodded and left the classroom. But not before smiling at Beacon.

Mrs. Miller dangled a hall pass from her hand.

"My appointment isn't until ten thirty," Beacon said weakly.

Mrs. Miller looked at the clock, then raised her eyebrows. "It's 10:21. I think that's close enough."

Beacon thought about refusing her, but he could tell from Mrs. Miller's stern expression that it wouldn't go over well. He got up and shouldered his bag, then grabbed the hall pass. This wasn't good. Arthur was prepared for ten thirty. They'd planned everything around hearing an announcement asking for Beacon to go to the office, like yesterday. Arthur would have no way of knowing he'd been called down early.

Outside the classroom, the halls were deserted. His sneakers *squeak-squeak-squeak*ed on the shiny tile floor. He walked as slowly as possible without stopping completely and stalled twice at water fountains to take long slurps of water. But it was a short hall. The principal's office loomed. He was about to duck into the bathroom for a few minutes when Nurse Allen stepped out and spotted him.

"Beacon!" She waved him over with a brisk, authoritative gesture.

"I need to use the bathroom," he said quickly.

"And you can," she said, "right after your vitamin injection. No more stalling."

There was nothing to do now but walk over.

He forced his legs to move toward the nurse, his body locked up tight. His eyes found the clock on the wall. 10:24. Was it close enough?

"Glad to see you're feeling better," Nurse Allen said as she closed the door behind him. The keys jangled loudly as she walked to the lockbox, selecting the small gold key. He gulped as she turned the key, then pulled out the syringe. It had become the size of a rocket ship in his head, and he was slightly surprised when the needle looked small enough to snap in two if you grabbed it the wrong way.

"Have a seat," she said, nodding at the chair. Next to it was a metal tray topped with alcohol swabs and cotton balls. They might as well have been torture devices, given how fast his heart raced.

Beacon didn't move.

"We're not going to have more funny business today, are we?" she asked.

Beacon shook his head and shuffled to the chair. He sat down and gripped the armrests with sweaty fingers.

10:26.

"Can you tell me about the possible side effects of the injection?" Beacon asked.

The nurse raised an eyebrow.

"I like to be informed," he said. "You know. Like HIPAA guidelines?"

He had no idea what HIPAA was, but he'd heard his dad mention it when he was shopping for a new health insurance plan, and he thought it sounded legit.

He must have been on the right track, because the nurse said, "Redness and swelling at the injection site. That's about it."

She picked up the syringe. Panic shot through him.

"What's the incidence of adverse reactions?" he asked in a squeaky voice.

"You're going to be fine," she said. "Now, if you could just roll up your sleeve."

Beacon's eyes shot up from the needle to the door. Where was Arthur?

"Beacon?" The nurse's voice had ground to an angry edge. There was a tiny drop of liquid sitting suspended on the tip of the needle. Beacon swallowed hard and started slowly rolling up his shirtsleeve.

Come on, Arthur! Where are you?

He rolled the shirtsleeve with clumsy, fumbling fingers, pretending to get the fabric stuck to stall for time. After a minute, Nurse Allen huffed and yanked the sleeve up over his shoulder, stabilizing his arm with her big, veiny hand. Beacon yelped and squeezed his eyes shut. His breaths came in sharp bursts, his forehead drenched in sweat, the thump of his heart vibrating in his ears.

The door burst open, and the secretary rushed in. "We need you," she announced breathlessly. "Someone's having a seizure."

A tidal wave of relief washed over him. He had to bite back the hallelujah that almost slipped from his lips.

Nurse Allen paused, looking at Beacon's arm. He used the moment of hesitation to yank his shoulder out of her grip and roll down his sleeve.

"I'll be back," she said, stabbing him in place with a finger. "Don't go *anywhere*."

She burst out of the room with the secretary, leaving the door to the office hanging wide open.

Now that she was gone, Beacon's body went into survival mode. All he wanted to do was get out of there, as far away from the needle as possible. But this was his chance. He wasn't going to get another one—if he tried to pull this trick again, she'd be onto him for sure.

He unzipped his backpack and reached into the interior pocket for the insulin syringe.

Arthur had stolen it from his grandmother's medicine cabinet the night before and filled it with saline solution. Up close and side by side, the syringes looked nothing alike. They were roughly the same size, but the printing on the side of the insulin syringe was orange, and on the vitamin injection, blue. If the nurse paid an iota of attention, she would see that something was off. But Beacon didn't have any other options right now. She could be back any second.

He swapped out the needles, stuffing the stolen syringe into the bottom of his bag, then burying it underneath a pile of schoolbooks. He darted a glance at the doorway. The office area was empty; even the old secretary was gone, probably calling in reinforcements to help with Arthur's "seizure."

He'd done it.

Beacon blew out a slow breath.

A minute passed. Two.

He could have stolen the syringe twice over with how much time he had.

His eyes floated over to the gray filing cabinet underneath the window. He never would have considered it before, but his success with the syringe bolstered his confidence. He got up and wandered closer to the cabinet, then casually reached down and tested the handle. The drawer slid open easily. A rush of adrenaline fizzed through his body. Students' names were stretched out across the top tabs of the files. He scanned quickly and found the one marked *McCullough, E,* then with one last glance at the doorway, he yanked it out and opened it wide on the top of the other files. He pulled his cell phone out of his pocket and snapped a picture of the file, then he shoved it back inside.

He was still alone—he could hardly believe it. He knew he was pushing his luck, but when was he going to get another chance like this? He scanned the files again, first looking for his own name, then when he didn't find anything (did Nurse Allen have his file out for this appointment?), looking for Arthur's. He'd love to impress his new friend with a picture of his file. He spotted *Newell, A.* He quickly slid out the folder and took a pic.

He still had time.

Who else was there? Jane! What was her last name again? Middleson or Middleton or something like that. He skipped to the *M* section, but there was no one with a name even close to the one he remembered. Maybe he'd heard wrong. Then he saw the name *Sims, N.* That had to be Nixon—he was sure he'd heard Mrs. Miller call Nixon "Mr. Sims" that morning. He snatched out the file and opened it up. The thing was huge—like fifteen pages. He riffled through the folder, snapping pictures of each page.

Footsteps and voices rounded the corner. Beacon went stiff, before he jolted into action and scrambled to rearrange the papers back inside the folder. He shoved the file inside the cabinet, kneed the drawer closed, and jumped into his seat. The chair was still swiveling underneath him as Nurse Allen stepped into the room. Her dark eyes narrowed on him, then fell to his hands. Beacon realized he was still holding his cell phone.

"What are you doing?" Nurse Allen asked. The calm, even tenor of her voice was even more chilling than if she'd yelled at him.

The cell was frozen in Beacon's hands. His heart banged so hard, the beats blended together. "I was just—"

"Give that to me," she barked.

He quickly bashed buttons, but she yanked the phone out of his hand.

"Zombie Apocalypse Countdown?" she said, squinting at the screen.

"Sorry," Beacon said. "I got bored waiting."

There was a loaded pause before she said, "We have a strict No Cell Phone policy on school property."

"I didn't know," Beacon said. "It won't happen again. Sorry."

She twisted up her mouth. Beacon worried that she might look through his phone more carefully and find out the truth, but then she just said, "It better not," and shoved the phone back at him. He quickly stowed it in his pocket. Then before he knew what was happening, she had his shirtsleeve rolled up and his shoulder wiped with alcohol.

"Wait!" Beacon yelled, jumping back. The chair bumped into the windowsill behind him, but she tracked his movements, following him with the syringe. The needle jabbed into his shoulder. He felt the cool slip of liquid into his muscle.

"See, that was easy, wasn't it?" Nurse Allen said.

He fainted.

▸▸▸▸▸▸▸▸▸▸▸▸▸▸▸▸▸▸▸▸▸▸▸▸▸▸▸▸▸▸

By lunch, the entire school knew about Beacon's fainting incident. A Gold Star he'd never seen before had even stopped him in the hall to ask how he was doing. It was all he could do not to shout "I forgot to eat breakfast!" for the millionth time.

So much for confidentiality.

He spotted Arthur stuffing his books into his locker.

"Great idea," Beacon said by way of hello. "I was about two seconds away from becoming a Gold Star."

Arthur cast a furtive glance around, then closed his locker and leaned in.

"Did you get it?"

Beacon nodded.

"Oh my God. Oh my God, oh my God, *oh my God.*"

"Shhh!" Beacon hissed.

"Where is it?" Arthur asked. His eyes were bulging out of their sockets.

"In my bag."

"Oh my God."

"And I got pictures, too," Beacon said. "Of a bunch of student files."

"*What?*" Arthur's voice came out a choked squeak. Beacon didn't know whether to be happy that he'd impressed his friend or insulted he was so surprised.

"Come on, let's go to the quad," Arthur said. "I know a good spot."

Beacon followed Arthur outside, then around the giant sports field, where students were playing a game of soccer. Arthur sat against the fence, under the shade of a giant pine tree. He spread out a workbook and some papers in front of him. "So it looks like we're studying," he explained.

Beacon sat next to him.

"So?" Arthur was practically vibrating with excitement. He tugged at Beacon's backpack, trying to get inside before he even got it off his shoulders. Because that didn't look sketchy at all.

Beacon unzipped his bag and slipped his hand underneath the

pile of schoolbooks. He pulled out the syringe and slid it discreetly to Arthur, who handled it as if it were some kind of holy relic before putting it in his own backpack.

"Wow," Arthur breathed. "You actually did it."

"I told you I did."

"But you actually *actually* did it!"

Okay, now he was just being rude.

"What now?" Beacon asked.

"We can put it under a microscope. Run a few lab tests—pH, stability, viscosity. And we can compare it against info online. See if it's any different from real vitamin injections."

"That's it?" Beacon asked. "How can any of that prove it changes people?"

"It can prove that the vitamin injection isn't what they say it is—at least I hope it can. And I don't feel comfortable testing on animals. Unless you can find a willing subject, that doesn't leave us with a whole lot of options. Incoming! And then you just carry the two," Arthur said loudly, pointing dramatically at a workbook as a pair of students approached. They gave Beacon and Arthur a weird look before resuming their conversation and walking past.

"You can never be too careful," Arthur whispered to Beacon out of the side of his mouth.

Beacon flipped the book so that it wasn't upside down. "Agreed."

He pulled out the salmon sandwich Donna had packed him

against his will and peeled off the plastic wrap.

"What about the pictures?" Arthur asked.

Beacon brought up a picture on his phone, leaning in with Arthur as he munched on the sandwich (which, fine, was pretty good). He'd tried to look at the photo earlier, underneath his desk, but Nixon kept glancing over at him and he couldn't trust the Gold Star not to tell on him and get the phone confiscated.

He scanned the single printed page of blocky computer script. At the top of the page was the name *Everleigh McCullough*, and beneath it was a number: *Participant 1258BYZ*.

"Participant?" Beacon said. "That's kind of weird."

"Super weird," Arthur said. "Why not student or even patient?"

They kept reading.

Healthy female with a non-concerning history, save for recurring ear infections around 12–14 months old and a tonsillectomy at 9 years old, which was tolerated well. Allergy to tree nuts and Elastoplast. Significant mood changes in the last year, reportedly beginning after the death of the participant's older brother. Defiance, back talk, sarcasm, and limit-testing behaviors noted to be increasing in frequency and severity.

"How do they know all this stuff?" Beacon said, feeling light-headed.

"They must have talked to your dad."

Beacon hadn't considered that, but his dad *had* been in contact with the school. He guessed it made a certain amount of sense that the school would want to have any relevant medical information about its students, but ear infections at a year old? Talking back to your dad? Why did Nurse Allen need that information?

He wondered what he would have found in his own file. Relentlessly optimistic. Nervous and scattered. On the verge of a nervous breakdown.

"Look at this," Arthur said, pointing.

Next to *C27H4403* was a handwritten note that read: *Left arm, tolerated well, no reactions.*

"That must be the vitamin injection," Beacon said.

"That's the formula for Calcitrol," Arthur said.

"What's that?"

"The active form of vitamin D."

"That's it?" Beacon said.

"Well, they're not just going to write 'Formulation for the transition into a Stepford Wife' are they?"

"What's a Stepford Wife?" Beacon asked around a mouthful of food.

"Trust me, you don't even want to know. I watch a lot of old movies with my grandma. Okay, let's see Nixon's."

Beacon swiped to the next picture.

"Hey, that's my file!" Arthur said.

"I thought you'd want to see it," Beacon said. Though now that he was looking at the file, and the long list of seizures and medical complications listed inside, he was second-guessing himself. Arthur's cheeks were red as a tomato.

"Let's skip to Nixon's," Beacon said. He quickly swiped to the next picture, and they both leaned in again.

"Whoa," they both said together.

Nixon had had the injection *dozens* of times.

"Okay, that is one hundred percent verifiably weird," Arthur said. "Why would he have been given the same injection so many times?"

"Maybe his vitamin D levels are really low?" Beacon said, playing devil's advocate.

"Or maybe the injection isn't what they say it is," Arthur said.

Beacon had to agree. It was too weird.

"Look—'repeat episode of erratic, oppositional behavior,'" Arthur muttered, reading a note listed on the file. "Are you sure this is Nixon's file?"

"His name's right at the top," Beacon said. "Look—there it is again," he said. Another note about Nixon's behavior.

"I knew there was something up with those Gold Stars," Arthur said triumphantly. "Now I have proof. I just wish you'd had time to get pictures of a few more of their files. Now *that* would be some evidence." His eyes glimmered.

"What's the deal with you and the Gold Stars?" Beacon asked.

"There is no deal," Arthur said stiffly.

"Did they kick you out or something?" Beacon pushed.

Arthur snorted. "They'd have to have let me in first." Arthur's eyes popped wide, as if he hadn't meant to say that part out loud. He cleared his throat.

"What happened?" Beacon asked.

"I dunno," Arthur said, shrugging heavily. "Jane just said they were full. But then they added Nixon and Perry, and now your sister. I guess they just didn't want me."

Why wouldn't they want Arthur? He'd seen his bedroom— there was no way a kid that obsessed with science didn't have killer grades. Beacon guessed it was possible they just didn't think he was "cool" enough, but for some reason, that didn't feel like the truth.

"Do you think it's because you're immune to the injection or something?" Beacon asked.

Arthur's eyebrows scrunched up in thought, as if he'd never considered that before.

"Heads up!" someone called.

A soccer ball hurtled through the air. Arthur blocked his face dramatically, even though the ball landed at least three feet away from him. A student ran over. Not just any student, but Beacon's sister.

Everleigh sported a pair of knee-high socks and satiny soccer shorts.

"Hey, Beacon! How are you?" she asked breathlessly. "I heard you fainted."

"What are you wearing?" he asked, ignoring her question.

"I joined the soccer team!" she said brightly.

A whistle blew, and she looked over her shoulder.

"Gotta go! See you at bedtime." She kicked the soccer ball back toward the field, then chased after it.

"Bedtime?" Beacon called. "Where are you going? What about the bus?"

"I'm going to Jane's after school," she said, running backward. "We have a Gold Stars meeting at seven and we need to get a few things ready." Then she spun around and trotted off, her ponytail bouncing behind her.

Beacon watched Everleigh run nimbly around the field, high-fiving her teammates after scoring a goal. He hardly recognized her. In fact, he was having a hard time remembering all the stuff he would need to add to the notebook about her weird behavior. Arthur had said to write down whatever was different: He might as well just write *everything*.

Of course Beacon wanted Everleigh to be better. He didn't want her to keep wallowing in her room and pushing everyone away, like she'd done for the past year. He didn't want to keep watching her wear her guilt like a badge of shame she'd be stuck with for the rest of her life. But he also wanted his sister to be his sister. And this wasn't Everleigh.

He had to do something.

A thought popped into his head. It seemed so obvious that he couldn't believe he hadn't come up with it before. The plan formed quickly, and a sly smile crossed his face.

"What?" Arthur said.

"I have an idea."

10

The church sat at the top of a sloping lawn overlooking the sea. There were towers and turrets and huge patches of moss clinging to the ancient stone walls. Beacon would have thought it was a castle if it wasn't for the cross rising into the thick, dark clouds.

According to Jane, the Gold Stars held their meetings here. So after dinner, he and Arthur had met up on the main road and headed for the church.

"What now?" Arthur said. They were hidden behind the gnarled trunk of a tree twenty feet away from the church. Arthur's bike and Beacon's skateboard were lying in the grass as they watched the church through a pair of binoculars they passed back and forth. So far, they'd discovered that there were only a few casement windows on the ground level, and the glass was so thick, you could see only smears of color moving around inside.

Beacon felt the weight of disappointment like a ten-ton truck on his shoulders. This had been his idea, his mission, and it was failing before it even started.

Branches creaked and swayed above them in the howling winds.

"We have to go inside," Beacon said.

"What if we get caught?" Arthur said.

"Then . . . then we say I'm here to get my sister."

"That seems like a bad idea," Arthur said.

Beacon thought so, too, but he wouldn't admit it.

"Don't be such a wimp," he said, echoing his sister's words. But he wasn't his sister, and he just felt like a jerk for saying it.

Just then, the church bells pealed, sending a flock of pigeons above them cooing and flapping into the sky. Beacon yelped and ducked, covering his head with both hands.

Arthur raised his eyebrows over his glasses. Beacon quickly rearranged his shirt and ran his fingers through his thick brown hair.

"Let's just do this."

Arthur stowed his binoculars in his backpack, then hiked the bag up his shoulders and tightened the straps.

"Operation Moonlight Serenade is underway," he said.

Beacon knew better than to ask what that meant.

Beacon and Arthur stepped out from behind the tree. Ducking low, they jogged up the hill until they reached the crumbling front steps of the old church. The boys exchanged a glance before Beacon climbed up to the top and grabbed the door handle. He twisted it slowly. The heavy wooden doors broke open, the sound echoing around the high ceilings of the church. Beacon cringed at the loud noise, but when no one appeared, he stepped warily inside.

Pale gray light shone through the stained glass windows, casting an eerie glow onto wooden pews covered in faded red velvet. It smelled like incense and dusty old prayer books.

Beacon had been in a church exactly once. It had been full then—standing room only. That's what happens when a sixteen-year-old dies.

"Where is everyone?" Beacon whispered. He could have been sure that Jane said they held their meetings here. She'd pointed right at this place that first day in the junkyard.

"Probably in the basement," Arthur whispered. "There's a rec room people use for meetings and stuff like that. Look, there's a door back there." He nodded toward a door tucked all the way in the corner.

They stole down the narrow aisle between the pews, their tiptoeing footsteps deafening on the cold stone.

Beacon could hardly believe he was doing this. For half a second, he thought, *Wait until I tell Everleigh about this.* But then he remembered that he couldn't tell Everleigh. She would only rat him out to their dad.

He felt an unexpected twinge of sadness inside his gut. He'd never really thought that he and Everleigh were particularly close. Not like it was on TV, anyway, where twins had a special connection, finished each other's sentences, and were basically glued at the hip.

Beacon and Everleigh argued and bickered from sunup to sundown, covering everything from which TV show to watch to who got to sit in the front seat on the way to visit their grandma in the nursing home. But they had been friends, Beacon realized. Maybe even best friends. He couldn't think of anyone else he'd want to tell his deepest secrets to, or anyone who knew him half as well as Everleigh. And now she was gone—here, but gone.

Well, Beacon wasn't going to let that happen. He'd already lost his brother. He couldn't lose his sister, too.

They reached the door. Through it was a narrow set of stairs that led into darkness.

"I guess the cemetery was taken," Arthur said thinly.

"It's just a basement. There's nothing to be scared of." Beacon said it with more confidence than he felt.

He reached for the light switch, but Arthur said, "No! Someone could see."

"Right. Good point." Beacon lowered his hands, wiping his clammy palms on his jeans.

"Like you said, it's just a basement," Arthur said. "Nothing to be scared of, right?"

Beacon nodded and boldly stepped through the door.

Despite his pep talk, dread crawled up his spine the deeper they went into the bowels of the church. The stairs seemed to go on forever, the air taking on an impossibly colder, mustier scent.

Finally, they reached the bottom. A long hallway with faded red carpeting stretched out into shadows. There was a single, bare lightbulb flickering from the low ceiling that reminded him of an old horror film his dad liked, where a set of dead twins haunted an old, creepy hotel.

He shook his head hard. That was definitely *not* what he should be thinking about right now.

"Which one do they hold the meetings in?" Beacon whispered, looking at the doors set into either side of the hall. They were all closed.

"I don't know," Arthur said. "I've never been down here before."

"Haven't you lived here all your life?" Beacon said.

"So? I'm Jewish!"

"Well, how do we know which one they're in?" Beacon asked.

Arthur twisted up his mouth. "We'll just listen at the doors. It can't be—"

His words were cut short as footsteps sounded from the stairwell.

The boys gasped and looked around for someplace to hide. Without knowing which room the Gold Stars were in, they could walk through any one of these doors and straight into their meeting.

The footsteps grew louder. Shadows moved on the wall at the end of the corridor. Any moment they would be caught.

Beacon grabbed Arthur's arm and pulled him through the first door he could reach. Miraculously, it was unlocked, and the boys stumbled inside a dark room. Light from the hall reflected off a stainless steel refrigerator. There was a toaster and coffee maker on the counter, and chairs rested upside down on a small table. They were in a kitchen.

The footsteps approached. There wasn't enough time to close the door without being noticed, so Beacon and Arthur squeezed behind the door and pressed themselves against the wall. Through the gap between the hinges, Beacon saw a flash of blue and gold and dark, tightly coiled hair.

"Thank you so much for helping," a female voice said. "I wouldn't have been able to carry these on my own."

"No problem. Happy to help," a boy replied.

Jane and Nixon. The Gold Stars walked down the hall with stacks of juice boxes and cookie packages in their arms.

Beacon's heart pounded like a war drum.

Nixon and Jane walked closer. Closer. Closer.

They were right in front of the door to the kitchen. If Beacon and Arthur were caught now, there would be no explaining why they were skulking around in the dark. And if they got caught, they'd lose their chance and never find out anything.

But the Gold Stars didn't notice them. They walked down the hall with purpose, chattering to each other.

They were safe.

Just then, a loud noise erupted inside the kitchen. It sounded like a cat yelping after someone had stepped on its tail.

Beacon's eyes flew wide open.

Nixon and Jane stopped.

"What was that?" Jane said.

"I don't know," Nixon replied. He cocked his ear as Arthur scrambled to shuck his backpack, which was emitting loud hisses and shrieks.

"Turn it off, turn it off!" Beacon mouthed at Arthur.

Arthur pulled out the ARD and frantically felt along its sides for the power switch. He flicked it off just as Nixon and Jane turned around.

"It was coming from in here," Nixon said.

The boys pulled back behind the door, making themselves as small and quiet as possible.

Nixon stepped into the doorway. Everything inside Beacon bunched up tight, his heart banging against his rib cage. Nixon scanned the kitchen. If he took another step into the room, he'd see Arthur's backpack on the floor. Two more and he'd see *them*.

Beacon didn't move. Didn't breathe.

Nixon frowned and took another step inside. Just then, there was a loud *thunk, thunk* noise from the refrigerator. Beacon recognized it as the sound his fridge back home in LA made when the ice maker dropped ice cubes into the tray. Nixon's forehead smoothed.

"Just the fridge," he said, walking out.

The boys stayed pressed behind the door until Nixon and Jane's footsteps faded. Then Beacon let out a huge, relieved breath. When they were certain Nixon was out of earshot, Beacon peered cautiously outside the room and just caught the door at the end of the hall as it closed behind the Gold Stars.

"What the heck?" Beacon snapped. "Why'd you bring that? You almost got us caught!"

"Don't you realize what just happened?" Arthur said. "The ARD went off."

"Yeah. And it almost ruined our investigation."

"No. You don't understand. The *alien radiofrequency detector* went off," he repeated more slowly. "In the presence of *Gold Stars*."

What Arthur was saying finally clicked. "Are you saying you think Nixon and Jane are aliens?" Beacon asked.

"No! Well, I'm not *not* saying they're aliens. It's never gone off like that before, and now it goes off when Gold Stars just happen to be walking past?"

Beacon's heart skipped into overdrive. It had to mean something.

"We need to get closer," Beacon said. "See if it goes off again."

"Are you out of your mind?" Arthur said. "We just barely escaped getting caught and you want to go *closer?*"

"What happened to all the '*alien radiofrequency detector went off*' stuff?" Beacon said, mimicking Arthur's excited tone. "Come on, we'll turn the volume way down. We have to test this. It's like you said—it's never gone off like that before. That *can't* be a coincidence. Aren't you curious?"

Arthur wavered. Beacon went in for the kill.

"Isn't the number one most important part of an experiment that it has to be replicable? If we can't repeat the experiment and get the same results every time, then we can't say for sure what caused the ARD to go off."

When Arthur released a heavy sigh, Beacon was really glad he'd had to endure his dad talking about experiments for twelve years at the dinner table.

"We'll just go a bit closer," Arthur said.

With Arthur trailing behind him, Beacon smiled, then peered around the door again. The hall was empty. He took a deep, steeling breath and walked out.

With each step they took, the ARD hissed and moaned. Arthur frantically turned down the volume, but the closer they got, the louder the noises became, until steam began spewing through the vents in the top of the machine and the unit vibrated in Arthur's hands like an angry raccoon he was trying to snuggle.

"Whoa!" Beacon whispered. "It's going berserk!"

Arthur switched off the machine. "We got what we need. Now, can we please get out of here?"

"Wait," Beacon said. "We haven't completed our operation yet."

"We got even more than we hoped for. We have proof now. Let's not push our luck. Besides, the door is closed." He nodded at the room where Jane and Nixon had disappeared. "I can't hear anything. Unless you want to walk right in there, I don't see what else we can do."

"So that's it, then, huh? You're too scared."

"I'm not scared! I'm just out of ideas is all. And do we really need to discuss this right outside the door?"

"You *are* scared," Beacon said.

"I am not," Arthur said firmly.

Beacon motioned to switch the ARD back on, and Arthur snapped the machine away.

Beacon gave him a knowing look.

"Fine, you come up with an idea for how we can listen in on this meeting, and I'm on board," Arthur said.

"Really?"

Arthur nodded.

Beacon's eyes drifted upward, closing in on the ceiling. Arthur followed his gaze to the ceiling tiles and began shaking his head.

"No. Uh-uh. You're not talking about—"

"I am. There were ceiling tiles just like that in my basement back home—there's got to be a ventilation shaft up there. We can crawl right over their meeting! They'd never even suspect it."

"Let's pretend that's not a terrible idea," Arthur said. "How would we even get up there? It's way too high." He shot a surreptitious glance at the meeting room door.

"The kitchen," Beacon said. "If we put a chair on top of that table, I'm sure we can reach."

"Oh yeah. That sounds like a fantastic idea," Arthur said sarcastically.

But Beacon was already jogging off toward the kitchen. Arthur watched him go, then sighed and followed. When he got to the room, Beacon had already pulled three chairs down and was flipping the fourth one right-side up on the tabletop.

"Steady the chair for me," Beacon said as he clambered up onto the table.

Arthur did as instructed, stabilizing the chair legs as Beacon climbed up onto the seat, then reached up and slid a ceiling tile aside. Dust drifted down, and Beacon waved it out of his eyes and fought back a cough. Then he shoved his head into the hole. Exposed pipes hung down from a narrow metal tunnel just big enough for a small human to fit inside.

"It's perfect," he said, his voice muffled. He reemerged with his face coated in a layer of grit. "I'm going in."

The chair legs squeaked and strained against Arthur's grip as Beacon wrestled himself up like a fish out of water.

"Hold the chair steady!" Beacon said.

"I am!" Arthur whispered. "Quit squirming so much."

Beacon climbed inelegantly into the shaft. The space was so

small, he was forced to crouch on all fours with his back to the hole he came up through.

"It's too tight to turn around," Beacon said. "You're going to have to get up on your own."

"Perfect," Arthur grumbled. "I've always wanted a broken leg."

Beacon frowned. A memory rushed back at him. Beacon and his friends had been at the Culver City Skate Park a couple of years ago when he'd fallen trying to do a rail slide. He didn't need a doctor to tell him that his leg was broken.

He'd been in so much pain, he could only remember a few bits and pieces of what happened next: the wail of sirens, the bumpy ambulance ride, his dad and Everleigh arriving out of nowhere, running alongside the stretcher as they wheeled him down the brightly lit hospital hallways, and the utter, sheer panic as the operating room loomed closer. Even though he'd had a bone sticking out of his leg, and even though his dad had reassured him they'd put him to sleep before they did anything to him, he was still paralyzed with fear at the thought of all those needles and scalpels slicing into his skin. He'd been contemplating throwing himself off the stretcher when he heard his brother's voice. Jasper yelled for them to wait and sprinted up to the stretcher.

"Did you remember to wear clean underwear?" he asked Beacon breathlessly.

Despite everything, Beacon had cracked a smile. Their grandma was always telling them to make sure they wore clean underwear in case they got into an accident. They thought that was so funny—as if dirty underwear was the biggest thing you had to worry about if you were seriously hurt.

His brother knew he was scared and wanted to make him laugh.

Beacon swallowed hard. He wondered when memories like this would stop punching him in the gut. If there would ever be a time he could think about his brother and it wouldn't make a pit open up in his stomach. Everyone said that time healed all wounds, but it had been a year since Jasper died, and he was still hurting.

Arthur clambered up into the shaft behind him.

"You okay?" Beacon asked as Arthur panted for breath.

"Never been better," Arthur got out between coughing fits. There was some fumbling, and then light shot through the tunnel.

"Ah!" Beacon cried, shielding his face.

"Sorry," Arthur said, moving the light. He'd shucked his backpack, which was scrunched up in front of him, and he held a small flashlight.

"Good thinking," Beacon said. "Slide the tile back over so no one gets suspicious."

"Because a single chair right-side up on the table isn't going to look suspicious at all," Arthur said. But he did as he was asked.

"Okay, let's get moving," Beacon said. "The room was at the end of the hall, so we have some ground to cover."

The boys shuffled forward on their hands and knees, a thin beam of light illuminating their path. They couldn't go very quickly without making too much noise, and progress was frustratingly slow. Beacon worried they would finally get to the end of the shaft only to discover that the meeting was already over. Or worse, that they'd get locked inside the church for the night. Visions of spending the night in the dark, creepy church swirled in his head.

He pushed himself to go faster. Finally, they heard muffled voices up ahead.

Arthur clicked off the flashlight, plunging them into darkness. They crawled forward a few more feet before Beacon slowed to a stop. He bent low and tilted his ear to the floor of the shaft, straining to hear. That was definitely a boy's voice he heard. And that one sounded like Jane. Wait, was that Everleigh?

He couldn't make out a thing!

"Squish over!" Arthur whispered.

Beacon made angry slashing gestures across his neck. Arthur gestured angrily back, making swirling motions around his ears, then crossing his forearms dramatically, until Beacon rolled his eyes and squished against the side of the shaft to make room for him. Arthur squeezed next to Beacon, like sardines in a can.

Beacon peeled back a tiny section of the ceiling tile. A sliver of light reflected into the metal passageway. They kept perfectly still, their ears cocked to the tiny gap in the tile.

"Does anyone else have a suggestion?" someone said.

That was *definitely* Jane. In fact, Beacon could see the top of her bright white curls from where he was crouched.

"We could do a bake sale," the girl with the sleek black hair from the other day said.

"We've done five bake sales this year," a boy said in a familiar voice that Beacon was sure belonged to Perry.

"And they've all been successes," the girl pointed out.

"That's true," Jane said. "And while everyone does love your famous shortbread cookies, Sumiko, I agree with Perry that something new and innovative would be fun."

Beacon didn't know what he'd been expecting, but it wasn't to overhear the fraught preparations for a fundraiser.

"I could do oil changes."

Everleigh!

Beacon's blood pressure spiked at the sound of his sister's voice.

"That's a fantastic idea, Evie."

"Yeah, Evie. We're so glad you decided to join us."

Evie?!

Oh, no . . .

There was almost nothing Everleigh hated more than when people called her cutesy nicknames.

Beacon cringed, waiting for Everleigh's inevitable flash of anger. But she only smiled politely.

"Well, what are the rest of us going to do while you do the oil changes?" Nixon asked.

Beacon's mounting dread was immediately eclipsed by anger. He didn't like the dismissive way Nixon was talking to his sister.

"I could show a few of you how it's done," Everleigh said. "And we could do car washes, too. Not just a regular wash, but detailing. People would pay good money for that."

Jane clapped her hands excitedly, and a murmur of support rose through the room.

"Well then, it's decided," Jane said. "Let's break for snacks."

The kids rose from around the table, a blur of gold and blue. Jane approached Everleigh, and the two of them walked to a small display table full of goodies against the wall, their conversation lost in polite chatter. Beacon watched his sister pick up a shortbread cookie and gingerly take a bite, instead of eating the whole thing in one shot, then belching obnoxiously, like she normally would. Jane picked up a cookie, too, and the two of them turned back for the table. As Jane walked, she placed the cookie in between two of the buttons on her shirt.

Beacon closed his eyes hard, then reopened them. Jane was wiping crumbs off the front of her shirt.

"Did you see that?" Beacon whispered, his heart banging hard.

"See what?" Arthur answered.

Beacon stared through the gap in the ceiling. There was no

logical reason why Jane would have put a cookie inside her shirt. Was he imagining things?

Beacon heard a crack.

Before he could even get a chance to figure out what caused the noise, Arthur whispered, "Uh-oh." And then the ceiling shaft gave out beneath them.

11

Beacon's stomach shot up as he went down. There was a deafening crash as he and Arthur landed hard in the middle of the boardroom table, papers and pens and pitchers of water flying everywhere. Gold Stars screamed and shielded their faces, leaping away from the chaos. Next to him, Arthur rolled up to sitting, groaning as he plucked a piece of broken shortbread cookie off the front of his shirt. For a moment, everyone stared at them in shock.

"*Beacon?*" Everleigh said.

"What the heck is going on?" Nixon said.

"Oh, hey!" Beacon fumbled to his knees and brushed dust off his jeans. "Looks like a great meeting you were having. Love the oil change idea. Very innovative." He hopped off the table, pain slicing through his leg from the fall. Next to him, Arthur quickly retrieved his flashlight and stuffed it inside his bag, next to the ARD. Then he slid off the table and readjusted his glasses.

"Well, don't let us interrupt you," Arthur said. He saluted, then moved toward the door.

"Wait!" Jane said. "What were you doing up there?"

"What was that machine in your backpack, Arthur?" Perry piped up. "Were you spying on us?"

"Spying? Of course not," Beacon said with a laugh. He opened the door.

"Wait a minute," Nixon said. "We want an explanation."

"You damaged church property," Sumiko chimed in. "Do you have any idea how much that will cost to repair?"

"Well?" Everleigh said. "What do you two have to say for yourselves?"

Beacon and Arthur looked at each other.

"Run!" Beacon yelled.

Arthur and Beacon bolted down the hall. They were going so fast that when they reached the end, they slammed into the wall before skittering up the stairs like dogs trying to run on hardwood floors. Footsteps pounded behind them.

"Stop them!" a voice boomed.

They burst out of the stairwell and tore across the nave of the church. In Beacon's peripheral vision, he could see kids in blue and yellow jackets skirting around the pews on both sides, trying to hem them in.

"Faster!" Beacon cried. He grabbed Arthur's arm and yanked him through the wooden front doors. Beacon shielded his face against the wind and squinted into the dark.

In LA, it was almost as bright at night as it was during the day, the city lit with streetlights and traffic and businesses open twenty-four hours. Here, the shadows of the trees blended seamlessly into the black sky, waves battering the rocky shore and drowning out all other sound.

The boys ran.

They were headed toward their skateboard and bike lying in the grass under the tree, but the Gold Stars were closing in fast. Nixon, Perry, Jane, a handful of kids he'd never seen before—even Everleigh was chasing after him with a hardened look on her face that sent a chill down Beacon's back. He'd seen that face before but never directed toward him. Sure, they argued. But it was all surface. Nothing ever came between them. And now here was his sister, chasing him like she meant to hurt him.

"Leave them!" Arthur called, pulling Beacon away from the skateboard and bike under the tree and toward the gravel road that twisted away from the church.

"I can't leave my board!" Beacon argued.

"You have to!"

Arthur was right. If they went to the tree first, they'd have to double back to reach the road. By then, they would be surrounded.

With one last pained look at his board, Beacon turned for the road.

Charcoal clouds chased them from above, the wind sending

vortexes of leaves and dirt swirling around them. The cold air shocked Beacon's throat as he pushed himself to go faster, faster, faster. He sent a furtive glance over his shoulder. Even with the detour, the Gold Stars were gaining on them.

"Why are they chasing us?" Beacon yelled.

"They want my ARD," Arthur gasped out.

"Why would they care about your ARD? How would they even know what it is?"

"Trust me, I saw the way Perry looked at it." Arthur gulped for air. "We have to split up. They'll come after me, but you'll have the machine."

"No way!" Beacon cried.

"We have to save the ARD. It's the only way."

They rounded a corner. Behind the cover of a woodshed, Arthur whipped off his backpack and pulled out the ARD. He shoved the machine at Beacon's chest. Beacon grunted, his shoulders dropping against the sudden and unexpected weight of the machine.

"Don't let them see it," Arthur said, zipping his bag. Then, before Beacon could argue, Arthur slipped on his backpack and made a hard left toward the ocean.

"Wait!" Beacon cried, but the boy was gone.

Beacon steeled his jaw, then tucked the ARD underneath his hoodie and ran in the opposite direction, back toward the church and his skateboard.

Beacon had expected to see a whole slew of pursuers, but when he looked, it was only Perry and Everleigh chasing after him. That meant that the rest of the Gold Stars had followed Arthur—maybe he was right about the ARD after all.

Well, they weren't getting it.

Beacon ran hard and fast, his muscles screaming in protest. He came up on the church from behind, only to find a tall white picket fence blocking in the property.

He hesitated briefly, unsure what to do. If he ran all the way around the fence to the road, there'd be a good chance Perry and Everleigh would catch up to him; and then it wouldn't matter if there were only two people after him and a million more after Arthur—they would get the ARD anyway.

Beacon made a split-second decision and put his head down, charging toward the fence. He vaulted it in one fluid motion, landing awkwardly on the side of his foot. His ankle rolled and he fell on his side, his head banging into the hard-packed grass. He stumbled up, pain shooting up his leg, his ear ringing and hot. He felt for the ARD inside his hoodie. It was safe.

Relief washed over him. But it was short-lived.

Through the buzzing in his ears, he heard the fence rattling behind him. Perry's spiky yellow hair crowned the top of the fence. Everleigh's painted fingernails gripped the wood.

Beacon was so tired and sore, all he wanted to do was find

somewhere to lie down for around a century. But he needed to keep moving. Distance was all that mattered right now.

He pushed past the pain and ran toward the tree. One hand cradling the ARD, he scooped up his board and ran in a big arc around the church. He was at the top of the hill. Before him was a sloping road that dipped dangerously toward the ocean.

Beacon dropped his board and hopped on, pushing off hard. He looked behind him; his pursuers were much closer than he'd expected. Everleigh pumped her arms hard, her ponytail flying out behind her. Perry's cheeks were stained red, and there was a fiery, grim determination in his eyes that make a spike of energy zip through him.

Beacon ducked low against the wind, willing his board to go faster. Perry surged forward and reached out, but his fingers only brushed Beacon's arm before Beacon finally gained momentum. Beacon flew down the hill. The cold wind whipped his cheeks, and a smile broke out on his face. He couldn't help it; he gave a jaunty wave as he sailed away from the kids.

But when he turned back around, the smile slid off his face.

Arthur was by the water, and he was surrounded. Beacon watched in mute horror as his friend ran left; a Gold Star blocked his path. Arthur turned right: another Gold Star. He backed up onto a thin, weathered pier that stretched out over the black water. Beacon had thought the harbor by the main square was the most disreputable he'd ever seen. But this one looked as if it were gasping for life. It was made out of rotten, sagging wood and was partially submerged in water. The shore was lined with razor-sharp rocks, churned mud, and garbage. He could just make out a sun-faded wooden sign staked into the grass that read "Deadman's Wharf."

Beacon was torn. He was supposed to get away and save the ARD, but he couldn't just leave Arthur.

Gritting his teeth, he headed for the water.

When he reached the end of the road, he hopped off his board, leaving it lurched in the grass, and then he clutched the ARD against his chest as he ran toward the pier.

"There's nowhere to go," he could hear Nixon saying as Beacon stepped onto the end of the dock. Still, Arthur backed up, sending panicked glances all around him. The pier didn't look stable enough to support a bird, let alone two twelve-year-old kids.

"Hey!" Beacon yelled. "Looking for this?"

He held up the ARD.

Nixon turned. Beacon saw the exact moment the Gold Star recognized the device. Nixon's eyes flashed, right before he charged down the dock like a defenseman chasing a quarterback. The dock creaked and swayed violently under his thundering steps, water spraying up all around him. Arthur put his arms out for balance. Even from a distance, Beacon could see the terror in his eyes.

Just then there was a loud snap.

"Arthur!" Beacon yelled.

Nixon dived for the shore.

Beacon cupped his hands around his mouth and yelled, "Get off the dock, Arthur!"

But it was too late.

Beacon watched helplessly as the pier split in half. The last thing he saw was Arthur's arms flailing as his feet left the dock. Then he disappeared into the water with a colossal splash.

12

Drowning wasn't anything like it was in the movies. Arthur didn't yell for help. He didn't splash in the water and flail his arms while people on shore scrambled to save him. He just . . . slipped under the water and never came back up.

"Arthur!" Beacon screamed.

He didn't make it a step before two Gold Stars grabbed him. Someone ripped the ARD out of his hands—Jane. She held up the machine.

"No!" Beacon cried, right as Jane smashed the device onto the rocks. It splintered in two, coils and screws flying everywhere. Nixon crushed the remains under his boot heel.

Beacon jerked against their grip like a fish flipping back and forth on the end of a hook, but he was caught. There were more of them now—at least a dozen Gold Stars penning him in. Their eyes were narrowed and sharp, their faces twisted into masks of anger. Everleigh and Perry jogged up. His sister didn't look remotely out of breath for having just chased him at top speed for the last ten minutes, or the least bit concerned that her brother was surrounded by a lot of angry kids.

"Let me go!" Beacon yelled. He cast an anxious look past the kids, to the water. The spot where Arthur went down rippled gently before the waves picked up again.

"He's going to drown!" Beacon said. "Everleigh, you can't let him drown!"

"Take him back to headquarters," Jane said calmly.

Beacon sent his sister a pleading look, but Everleigh just scowled at him like she didn't even recognize him. Whatever spark of hope he might have held that his sister hadn't been brainwashed went out as if it had been doused with a bucket of water.

The Gold Stars started dragging Beacon away.

"What's going on here?" A fisherman in chest waders shone a flashlight at the kids. The Gold Stars holding Beacon quickly let go of his arms. The fisherman stepped closer, his light dancing over the shore. The Gold Stars scattered in a burst of yellow and blue like fish darting away from a motorboat.

"There's a boy in the water!" Beacon screamed, pointing.

"What's that you say?" The fisherman cocked his head, putting a hand up to his ear.

"A kid is drowning!"

"I can call the authorities from my mobile," the fisherman said after a pause.

Beacon ground his jaw so hard he thought the bones might crack. Arthur didn't have time for that.

He ran to the edge of the pier, leaning over the remains of the weathered dock. Staring at the black water, memories flooded back to him. Pale skin. Blue lips. Blond hair swaying gently in the cold, cold water.

His body seized up. He searched the shore for the fisherman, but the man was gone.

No one was coming for Arthur. No one was going to save him.

Beacon hesitated. One second. Two.

And then he kicked off his shoes, whipped off his hoodie, and dived into the sea.

Cold sliced through his body. Gritty seawater stung his eyes. He strained against the blackness, looking for any sign of his friend, but all he could see were floating particles and the blur of his own chaotic movements in the murky water.

Right away, Beacon realized he should have taken off all his clothes. His jeans made every action feel weighted, as if he wore a lead suit. But it was too late now. He pushed himself down, digging deeper, despite everything in his body screaming at him to move up toward the surface, toward air. He couldn't see anything.

Finally, the lighthouse beacon passed over the surface of the water, and he saw a glimmer of white below. Could it be Arthur's lab coat? He plunged down, his head pounding, his chest tight, every cell in his body begging for oxygen.

Was it like this for Jasper? he wondered. The coroner had told their dad that his brother didn't struggle, that he'd hit his head on a rock and been knocked unconscious before water filled his lungs and he drowned. But Beacon had always wondered if that was just something he'd said out of kindness. He couldn't imagine the coroner telling his dad that Jasper's last moments had been filled with dread and panic and desperation, until oxygen deprivation stole all his thoughts and he faded away, floating like seaweed for hours until the rescue crews finally found his body.

Beacon needed to breathe.

With superhuman strength, he launched himself up. His head broke the surface and he was gasping, gulping, sucking in air. Pinpricks needled across his face as oxygen returned to his head in one big rush.

But Arthur was still down there.

With one last big breath, Beacon dived under again.

It was so dark, he couldn't see a thing. But then the lighthouse light roved over the water again, and he didn't see just a slice of white that could have been Arthur's lab coat. He saw *Arthur*. The boy was yanking on his lab coat, which was tangled up in a knot of seaweed that was growing through an old lobster trap covered in barnacles.

Just before the searchlight passed, Arthur looked up and met Beacon's eyes. He could have sworn the boy smiled before they were plunged back into darkness. But that couldn't be right. Beacon must have been seeing things. Lack of oxygen could do that to a person.

Beacon swam toward the spot where he saw his friend, pushing himself hard against the weight of the water and the growing pressure in his chest. Finally, his fingers bumped into something hard, and then he felt fingers clamp down on his shoulders.

Arthur.

He immediately went to work trying to untangle the boy. He wrenched on the seaweed, on the coat, on Arthur's arms, but no matter how hard he tried, he couldn't get his friend free. Finally, he yanked the coat off Arthur's shoulders. When he got it free, he grabbed Arthur around the middle and rocketed off the old trap with every ounce of his dwindling strength, half swimming, half floating to the surface.

Beacon's chest burned as if his lungs were on fire. They were moving too slowly. They weren't going to make it. But just when Beacon was about to breathe water, their heads finally broke the surface.

Choking and coughing, Beacon and Arthur splashed toward the pier, then clambered up onto the broken dock. They crawled over the wood, onto the cool, damp grass. Misty wind blew across them, but Beacon didn't even feel the cold.

The boys sat in the grass, breathing raggedly. For a solid minute, neither of them spoke. Beacon was glad that the fisherman had at least scared off the Gold Stars. There was no way Beacon and Arthur could outrun them in their current state.

Beacon wondered where the fisherman had gone. It was a good thing he hadn't waited for him to get help. Then Arthur definitely would have been dead. As it was, Beacon couldn't believe his friend was okay. He didn't know how it was possible. He'd been under for so long.

"The investigation is ruined," Arthur finally said. "They got the ARD, and now they know we're onto them. We'll never get any top secret info now. It's all over."

"A thank-you wouldn't kill you," Beacon said, swiping a sopping lock of hair out of his eye.

"Sorry," Arthur said. "I'm just disappointed. I spent a whole year working on that thing."

"At least you still have the prototype," Beacon said.

"I guess."

They sat in silence, the wind whistling through the wood of an old shed near the shore.

"Look, there's something I have to tell you," Arthur said, twisting to face Beacon. "Brace yourself, because it's going to sound a little out-there."

"More out-there than saying the Gold Stars are aliens?"

"Possibly," he said.

Beacon sat up straighter.

"When I was underwater, I held my breath for as long as I could, but then I just had to breathe and when I did . . . it didn't hurt or make me choke or anything. It was just normal, like breathing air."

Beacon stared at his friend, trying to make sense of what he'd just said.

"Are you saying that you can . . ."

"Breathe underwater?" Arthur finished for him. "Yes. I mean, I think so. I know it sounds nuts, but think about it, Beacon—I should be dead right now. But I'm not. I'm totally fine. You don't think that's weird?"

He did think it was weird. He remembered the way Arthur had looked at him as Beacon struggled to reach him, a vise clamping tight around Beacon's chest, pinching his airway. Arthur had looked calm. Patient. Comfortable, even. He hadn't imagined that smile. There was something very strange going on with the kids in Driftwood Harbor . . . and with Arthur, too.

He was suddenly afraid of his friend.

Don't be stupid, he told himself. *This is Arthur. He isn't dangerous.*

"Okay, let's just pretend that's possible," Beacon said thinly. "How come you didn't know this before?"

"I can't swim," he said. "I never go in the water. And I don't regularly go around testing to see if I have superpowers."

"Do you think this is related to what's going on with the Gold Stars?" Beacon asked.

Arthur started to answer, but a loud voice from behind them broke through.

"There they are!"

Beacon stiffened. When he turned, he saw Jane stabbing a finger right at them. Sheriff Nugent stood behind her. He walked toward the boys at a brisk, businesslike pace, the gold star on his jacket shining dully in the moonlight. Beacon stood up. Right as the sheriff raised his right arm and pointed a gun at him.

Beacon yelped, scrambling back and bumping into Arthur.

"Don't shoot!" Beacon said, putting his hands up. But the sheriff didn't stop. He trained his eyes on him, his aim never wavering.

Beacon turned around to run, but the sheriff fired. Beacon had just enough time to see two beams of blue light zap out of the end of the blocky barrel of the gun before everything went black.

13

It was the dream again, only it wasn't. Jasper was lying in bright, spongy coral, wrapped up in a prison of seaweed as fish flitted all around him. His eyes were open and he was looking right at Beacon, almost as if he were waiting for him.

Beacon tried to get closer, but no matter how quickly he swam, his brother stayed exactly the same distance away.

Jasper opened his mouth, his lips forming a perfect O.

"Beacon."

His brother's voice ghosted over the water.

••••••••••••••••••••••••••••••

Beacon woke to a slow beeping noise and the heavy smell of antiseptic. He blinked his eyes open. He was lying on his back. Bright white lights shone from spotlights hanging from the ceiling. There were wires taped all over his chest, trailing out from underneath the hospital gown that someone had changed him into.

Beacon pushed himself up. The sudden movement made blood leave his head in one big rush, and he had to take deep breaths until the faint feeling passed. But when the fog cleared, he thought he might pass out again. Scary-looking medical equipment that he didn't even want to begin to guess the use of sat next to his stretcher. A paper-thin computer monitor displayed his heart rate, breaths per minute, and oxygen saturation and beeped in time with his pulse. There were metal trays topped with scalpels and syringes and something that looked like a demented wine opener.

He was in some type of surgical suite.

Beacon leaped off the stretcher and spun in a circle on the cold concrete floor.

The room was circular. Half was lined with mirrors, while the other was covered with clean white cupboards. There was a desk area with a clipboard and papers on top and a leather chair tucked underneath. Next to it was a door. Beacon started toward it, but something else caught his attention first. A window. A single window, looking out into blackness. Movement flitted behind the glass. Beacon gasped, stepping back. It happened again, but this time, he saw what the movement was: a fish darting past the glass, into a patch of seaweed and coral.

He was underwater.

His breaths turned short and sharp, as if he were breathing through a straw.

What was happening? How did he get underwater?

He tried to think back. He remembered spying on the Gold Stars, being chased through the church and down to the water. He remembered Arthur nearly drowning and then . . . the sheriff shooting him. Only it hadn't been regular bullets that shot out of the gun, but snapping blue laser beams. But that didn't make sense. Had he dreamed that? Was he still sleeping now?

Beacon rubbed his eyes hard. When he blinked them open again, he was still inside the surgical suite.

Just then, he caught sight of his pale, skinny reflection in the wall of mirrors. He got the sudden, sinking feeling that the mirrors weren't mirrors at all, but one-way glass—the same kind that police officers use in interrogation rooms so they can see the suspects, but the suspects can't see them.

Beacon became uncomfortably aware of his heartbeat.

He had no idea where he was or how he got here; he just knew that he had to get away.

He ripped the wires off his chest, gasping at the bright, hot pain. The beeping stretched out, long and dull.

The door burst open.

Beacon leaped back, scrambling to put his body behind the stretcher. But he went still when he saw who had come in.

"Dad?"

His dad entered the room, smoothing down his red tie as he

quietly closed the door behind him.

"What are you doing here?" Beacon asked. "What am *I* doing here? What is this place?"

"Have a seat," his dad said. The calm tenor of his voice only made Beacon panic even more. Why wasn't his dad freaking out about this?

Maybe Beacon was dead, he decided. Yes. That made sense. The sheriff had shot him. He was in the afterlife now.

He'd thought it would be better than this. He'd thought he'd see Jasper.

"I imagine you're very confused." His dad perched on the end of the stretcher. He patted the spot next to him, but Beacon stayed standing.

"How did you know I was here?" Beacon asked.

"I work here," his dad responded.

"This is the CDC?" Beacon asked, looking around.

His dad shook his head. "No. I'm afraid I haven't been entirely truthful about why we moved to Driftwood Harbor."

Beacon shifted uncomfortably.

"I still work for the government," his dad continued, "but it's a different branch. The Central Intelligence Agency."

"The *CIA*?!" Beacon cried.

His dad grinned. "Pretty neat, huh?"

"What do you do for the CIA?" Beacon asked.

"It's top secret government information, but I've checked with Victor and received authorization to let you in on what's going on here. Can you keep a secret?"

Beacon wasn't entirely sure he wanted to hear what his dad had to say, but his dad didn't wait for him to answer.

"I'm helping to develop an antidote for a new strain of disease caused by climate change. It will help people—children especially—survive when sea levels rise. With what happened to Jasper, I thought it was important. It wasn't until I got here that I realized just how important this antidote really is."

"This antidote . . . is this the same injection they gave Everleigh at school? The one they tried to give me?" Beacon asked.

His dad nodded.

"Did you know they were going to give it to us?" Beacon asked. "How come you didn't tell us the truth about it?"

His dad didn't reply to him, just moved on. He did that sometimes when he thought Beacon was being especially childish, not dignifying his behavior with a response. It made Beacon furious.

"The CIA recruited me because of my work for the CDC," his dad continued. "They've gathered all the top people in infectious diseases to work on this. They need every brain they can if they're going to get this project up and running in time."

"What does any of that have to do with this place?" Beacon gestured around the suite. "Where are we? Why are we underwater?"

"I was getting to that. As you know, back in 1967, an aircraft landed in the harbor. Many people claimed it was an alien spacecraft. A UFO," he said, making air quotes. After a pause, he added, "And they were right."

Beacon's breath stalled in his chest. Of all the things he'd thought his dad might say, that wasn't it. He stood there, paralyzed, trying to remember how to breathe. Trying to make sense of it all.

"You're—you're saying aliens really do exist?"

His dad nodded. "I can see you're overwhelmed. I felt the same way on my first day of work."

Beacon swallowed, his heart beating too fast. "What happened after the crash?"

"Their spacecraft was irrevocably damaged. They lost all contact with their home planet. Without the right supplies, or the right technology or assistance, they had no way to get back home. They were essentially trapped. Can you imagine? Landing on a strange planet, with no way home? A planet full of people who would want you dead if they found out you existed? Humans haven't exactly been shining examples of empathy and tolerance over the millennia. If the public found out that aliens were walking among us, they wouldn't be in a hurry to invite them over for dinner, that's for sure."

"So they didn't fly home then?" Beacon said. "After they crashed in the water? I thought satellites saw two vessels move from here to Russia after the crash before they disappeared."

His dad laughed and shook his head. "You sure have done your research. That was the US military chasing off Russian vessels. We were protecting the ship. The UFO never left these waters."

"Oh," Beacon said. A thought suddenly occurred to him, and he went cold all over. "Am I inside the UFO right now?"

His dad nodded.

Beacon looked around, suddenly seeing the place in a whole new light. He'd never felt claustrophobic before now, but the walls suddenly seemed very close.

"So aliens have been on our planet since 1967 and no one knows about it?"

"Some people do. *You* know." His dad nudged him with his elbow and gave him a conspiratorial little smile that Beacon knew was supposed to placate him. It only made him feel like he might bring up his supper.

"The government has been helping them to adapt," he said. "Integrate into society. They've done remarkably well. I have trouble myself telling a Sov from a human."

"A Sov?" Beacon said.

"Short for Sovereign. They didn't have a name for themselves, but it turns out it was a royal ship of sorts that crashed. Someone started calling them the Sovereign, and it just stuck."

"So they look like us?" Beacon thought they'd be long and thin and pale with slits for a nose, the way aliens on TV always looked.

"They do now," his dad said. "In most ways. They don't like to show their natural form, and we don't press them to."

"What's that supposed to mean?" Beacon said warily.

"Their species is very unique. Normally, mutation takes place over the course of millions of years. But the Sov can adapt very quickly. Much more quickly than humans, or any other species on earth."

"So they can look however they want?" Beacon asked. He wasn't sure he liked that.

"Sure, I suppose," his dad said. "But they choose to blend in. It's easier that way."

"How do we know we can trust them?"

He had to assume that the Sov were smarter and more advanced than humans if they'd figured out intergalactic space travel. If they could blend right in with humans, what was stopping them from a total takeover?

"For one, it's been forty years since they landed here, and they haven't killed us yet. But also because they're helping us. A little exchange of favors."

"Helping us how?" Beacon asked.

His dad scratched the back of his neck. "I don't want to scare you."

"That ship has sailed," Beacon said.

His dad heaved a huge sigh and looked him in the eye. "I

mentioned the antidote is to help us survive when sea levels rise, right? Well, that's only half of the truth. There's an environmental . . . *threat* coming," he said, choosing his words very carefully. "Thanks to climate change, the planet's been warming more and more every year, and that's not going to stop. In fact, it's expected to increase exponentially with each passing year. The warmer the planet gets, the faster the rate of evaporation from the ocean, the more precipitation we see, and as the atmosphere gets warmer, it can hold more moisture, affecting the intensity of the precipitation—"

"Cut to the chase, Dad," Beacon interrupted.

"There's going to be a collection of weather events that will, quite frankly, devastate our planet," his dad said. "Storms, tsunamis, massive flooding all across the coastal regions."

Beacon felt the air get knocked out of him, as if he'd been punched in the gut.

"When?" he gasped out.

"Not tomorrow, or even next week or next year. It's not projected to hit for quite some time. But we're doing everything we can to be prepared for when it does."

Beacon pictured a giant wave swallowing Blackwater Lookout, and his chest tightened.

"What are we doing here if there's floods coming?" he asked, his voice high and strained. He waved his hands around. "Shouldn't we be moving inland? Ohio, Nebraska—why are we in *this* place?"

He could spit into the ocean from his bedroom window!

"That's where the antidote comes into play."

"How can this antidote possibly help us survive tsunamis?"

His dad raised his eyebrows, waiting for him to piece things together. He hated when his dad did that. It just made him feel stupid.

"I don't know. Are the Sov helping us to breathe underwater or something?" Beacon asked.

Unexpectedly, a smile crossed his dad's face.

"Really? How?" Beacon asked. "Is that why I'm in this gown?" He plucked at the flimsy green gown.

"It's a chemical compound, hidden inside the antidote," his dad said. "It alters our DNA makeup so that we don't require oxygen to live. The simplest way to think of it is this: You know how humans evolved from primates? Over the course of millions of years, our genes mutated to give us a survival advantage in our environment. Millions of years from now, we might have gills to help us survive our new water planet. But that won't help us now. People will die. A lot of people. But the Sov, they have this ability to mutate quickly. In seconds," he said, punctuating the statement with a brisk snap of his fingers that made Beacon jump.

"They're creating a formula based on their own genetic makeup that speeds up human mutation. I won't bore you with the finer details, but trust me when I say it's science like we've never seen it before."

"But . . . why?" Beacon asked. "Why are the Sov helping us?" Of all the wild stuff he'd heard, he knew that was a silly point to latch on to. But he just didn't get it. He couldn't see why a supersmart, advanced alien race would come all the way here from . . . wherever it was they came from . . . just to help. He'd seen enough sci-fi movies to know that aliens only came here for three reasons: to take over the planet, to make us their slaves, or for some human stew.

"I can see you're still suspicious," his dad said. "Let me try to explain. The Sov—they don't experience time the same way we do. Where humans can see the past and experience the present, the Sov can also see a bit of the future. Not all of it, not the little day-to-day things, but certain"—he frowned, searching for the right words— "calamitous events, are visible to them. That's how they know about the environmental disaster. But they're not helping us out of a simple sense of benevolence, although I truly do believe that is a factor, too—they're good people, Beacon. I mean, good creatures. You get the point." He smiled, as if he expected Beacon to laugh. Beacon didn't.

His dad cleared his throat.

"Further into the future—now, we're talking millennia here—the Sov will be at war. Another species will attack and raze their planet, leaving no survivors. In exchange for their help now, the Sov would like ours later."

Beacon didn't really see how humans could be of much help. The

Sov seemed so sophisticated. Compared to them, he really did feel like an ape.

"Think of how far humans have already come," his dad said, reading his mind. "Now think of just how much further a couple thousand years could take us—we'll be a pretty big asset then. At least the Sov seem to think so."

Beacon sat there, taking it all in. He and Arthur had guessed that the vitamin injections weren't what the school told them they were. But they never would have guessed this. Aliens in Driftwood Harbor? A government cover-up? Storms that would destroy the planet? An antidote that would help them to breathe underwater?

Everleigh could breathe underwater, he realized.

Beacon didn't know whether to find that cool or creepy.

All of a sudden, he thought of Jane's Gold Stars jacket shining brightly in the moonlight, right before she was toppled by a big, hungry wave. Of the way all the Gold Stars looked to her first, as if seeking approval.

"Jane Middleton is an alien, isn't she?"

"She is Sov," his dad confirmed.

Shock ricocheted through his body. And indignation.

"So it *was* her in the water that night?" Beacon said.

"I didn't know it at the time, but yes, it was her. She was on her way to the lab. Most of the Sov take the passages, but some of them prefer to go through the water."

"Who else is one of them? Are all the Gold Stars aliens?" Beacon asked.

"No, the rest of the kids are normal humans, just like you," his dad said. "Well, they do have one superhuman ability, thanks to the antidote."

He winked.

"Mutation won't solve all the problems, of course," his dad continued when Beacon didn't react the way he'd hoped. "There will be issues with agriculture, not to mention the economy. We've got a multitiered plan in place, and we're in preliminary preparations for underwater cities, just until the floods recede in a decade or two and we can rebuild."

A decade or two? Living in an underwater city? Now Beacon really did wonder if he was dreaming.

"Have you had this antidote?" Beacon asked.

His dad nodded. "We all have—everyone who works here. We're very lucky to be on the forefront of this. We won't get left behind."

"Did you take it by choice, or did they trick you, too? Force you to take it like they did to Everleigh—like they tried to do to me?"

"It was a choice. I'll admit, I didn't know the full extent of what the antidote did before we got here or how far along they were, but once the Sov showed me the truth, how could I not take it? How could I not let them give it to you? Knowing that I wouldn't lose you two the same way I lost Jasper. I couldn't say no."

"Does all this have anything to do with why Everleigh is acting so weird?" Beacon asked.

"One of the benefits of this program is that the injection causes participants to behave in a more regulated manner," his dad said. "The toxin dulls the part of the brain that encourages impulsivity and resistance, while promoting activity in the part of the brain responsible for benevolence and kindness. It's especially effective on children."

"Kindness?" Beacon said. "Is that why the Gold Stars chased me and Arthur like they wanted to kick our butts? Because they just wanted us to sign up for their bake sale?"

"The antidote isn't perfected yet," his dad said, and Beacon knew he must feel really guilty about everything when he didn't even say anything about his attitude. "Sometimes we have to give top-offs."

Nixon, he realized. That's why his file had been full of injections. Why they'd noted incidents of bad behavior.

"None of this seems right," Beacon said. "Maybe I wouldn't mind so much if Everleigh seemed like Everleigh, just nicer. But she's a completely different person. And you didn't even ask us if we were okay with this. Shouldn't we have a choice?"

"I feel badly about that," his dad admitted. "After what happened with your brother, I thought putting all this on you would be too much. I figured it might be easier if you didn't have to worry about any of that, at least for a while, until the shock of it all was less fresh.

I can see now that I was wrong. But it's not all bad, Beacon. Think about it—you'll be safe now. We'll all be safe now. You'll never have to worry about drowning. I'll never have to worry about losing another kid again." There was a crazed gleam in his dad's eyes that made Beacon feel off center, as if the world was shifting just slightly off its axis.

Beacon shook his head. "Dad, just how much of this do you really believe? Or is the antidote making you believe this?"

His dad frowned. "I don't know what you mean."

He grabbed something off the metal side table beside the stretcher. When he turned around again, Beacon saw what it was: a syringe. He backed up.

"Do not come near me with that!" Beacon said.

"Beacon, you're being unreasonable. This is for your own good." His dad slid off the stretcher and stepped closer. "This will only hurt for a second."

Beacon scrambled back, clattering into another tray. He hurried to put it between him and his dad. "What is this, Dad? Is this some kind of punishment?"

"What do you mean?" his dad said.

"For Jasper. He's dead, and it's because of us. We know that, and we're sorry we did it, okay? We're sorry we sneaked out, and we're sorry we went into the water that night. It was a stupid idea, and we're never going to stop wishing we hadn't done it. But you can't do this, Dad! You can't just rip us out of our home and take us across the country for some—some *freaky alien experiment*, okay?"

He'd screamed the last part.

"It's not your fault, Beacon," his dad said calmly. "It's neither of your faults."

Beacon was shaking his head. He wanted to plug his ears, block out the words. They weren't true.

"This isn't a punishment," his dad said, looking at the syringe. "Don't think of it like that. I just want you both to be successful in life, and this will help with that."

"Yeah, well, where was your antidote before, huh? We could have really used it last year. Then maybe Jasper would still be here."

There was a stunned silence, and Beacon wished he could take the words back. Just grab them from the air and stuff them back in his mouth.

He should have apologized, but he couldn't get the words out. He was so full of emotion—anger, sadness, guilt, confusion, terror—that he thought he might combust. So he did the only thing he knew how to do.

He ran.

"Wait!" his dad called. But he was already gone.

He barreled into a dimly lit control room. A dozen men and women wearing sleek wireless headsets and black suits jumped up from the ring of state-of-the-art computers circling the surgical suite, confirming his suspicion that the mirrors hadn't been mirrors at all, but windows.

"Stop him!" someone cried, pointing at Beacon.

Beacon ran. His bare feet slapped on the tile, his hospital gown flying out behind him. He didn't know where he was going. Everything looked the same, long stretches of immaculate white halls and polished tile floors. Finally, he turned a corner and saw a set of metal swinging doors up ahead. Maybe it was the exit.

He slammed through the doors and stuttered to a stop.

Dozens of people were seated around rows of gleaming stainless steel tables. It might have looked like a scene in any cafeteria, with pizza and french fries dipped in ketchup stretched all along the tables, except that the men and women weren't eating with their hands. He watched in mute horror as a large, gooey organ reached out from inside a man's chest, which looked as if it had been cracked in two, and closed around a hamburger; the food dissolved with a hiss of steam before the organ sank back into the chest cavity with a loud slurp. The man—the alien—wiped his chest with a napkin before buttoning up his shirt.

All at once Beacon remembered the bloodstain on Jane's shirt the day she stepped out of Nurse Allen's office, and the time he could have sworn he saw her slip a cookie under her shirt at the Gold Stars meeting. He hadn't been seeing things. She had been eating through her chest.

"They're like sea stars." Everleigh had appeared next to Beacon. She stood there, watching the aliens. "They evert their stomachs outside their bodies to eat. The digestive enzymes absorb the food, and the liquefied food is then absorbed through the body and transferred to other organs. Pretty neat."

"H-how do you know all this? Why are you here?" Beacon asked.

"Because I'm a Gold Star, of course," Everleigh answered proudly.

"I thought the Gold Stars were a youth group to promote social responsibility or whatever," he said.

"We are. And we're also youth ambassadors for the Sovereign. If you join us, you'll get to find out all about them, too. You can be a part of this incredible partnership."

Beacon backed up, bumping into the door. Right now, his twin sister seemed as alien to him as the creatures inside that cafeteria.

"Don't be scared, Beacon," Everleigh said. "They're here to help us, not hurt us." She offered him a sterile smile.

He turned around and ran. Down the corridor, through another set of doors. Down hallway after bleached white hallway, past people in headsets ordering him to stop.

He was careening down another nondescript corridor when a set of hands banged on the glass from behind one of the doors. He skidded to a stop and whirled around.

Arthur!

His friend smiled when he saw him, but his eyes were red and weary behind his glasses, which had a crack down the middle of one of the lenses and sat crooked on his nose. He looked like a ghost of himself. What had they done to him?

Beacon knew it seemed too good to be true that the aliens were helping them adapt. Why would they hurt Arthur? Kidnap Beacon? Brainwash kids?

Beacon tested the handle. Locked.

"The doors are electronic," Arthur said, his voice muted from the inches of thick door between them. "You aren't going to get it open like that."

That didn't stop Beacon from jerking the handle, then slamming his body against the door. He heaved and shoved at the thick metal with all his might. All he got out of it was a sore hip and bruised, stinging hands. A siren wailed overhead, and red light beamed across the white walls.

"Go," Arthur cried. "Get out while you can."

"I won't leave you," Beacon said.

"Don't be dumb," Arthur replied. "If you don't leave, then we'll both be trapped."

He didn't want Arthur to be right, but he was. If Beacon was caught, there would be no one to come after them. No one to save them. His own dad was complicit, and the rest of his family was on the other side of the continent. Arthur's grandma would report him missing eventually, but who knew what might have happened to them by then, if the police even found them at all. Sheriff Nugent had been the one to shoot him. He might be Sov, for all he knew. Leaving was the smart thing to do. But he couldn't just abandon his friend.

Beacon got an idea. He turned on his heel and raced around the corner. He remembered passing a fire hose not long ago. He just hoped he could find it in time.

He was running so fast, he skidded past the glass enclosure. He doubled back, panting for breath, staring at the thick, coiled hose locked behind the glass.

He may not be a genius like Arthur, but he *had* dropped his phone into the bathtub twice. If there was one thing he knew, it was that water fried electronics.

He pulled the sleeve of his hospital gown over his fist, then took a steely breath and punched the enclosure. A firework of glass rained down. He yelped and yanked his hand back, shaking his stinging fist. There were two gashes on his knuckles that he was sure would hurt a lot more when the adrenaline stopped pumping through his body.

He grabbed the end of the hose. Then he ran down the corridor, unspooling the coil as he did. He skidded up to Arthur's cell . . . just as Gold Stars rounded the corner. Jane's perfect blond curls bounced around her shoulders as she jerked to a stop and stabbed a manicured finger at Beacon.

"Stop right now!" she yelled.

Footsteps pounded the tile, and in moments, more Gold Stars appeared from the other direction.

He spun in a circle, but it was no use.

He was trapped.

14

"Put the hose down and your hands on your head," Nixon ordered.

Beacon narrowed his eyes and aimed the hose at the door.

He fired.

Water surged through the hose, inflating the tube with a speed and power that nearly blasted him off his feet. He struggled as it fishtailed in his grip like an angry serpent. Finally, he managed to point the hose right at the crack in the door. He doused the door in water, and sparks fizzed and popped from the gap in the metal.

"Stay out of the water!" Arthur yelled from inside. "You'll get electrocuted!"

Beacon leaped back from the growing puddle at his feet. Gold Stars thundered toward him in a clamor of squeaking boots.

"Stay back!" Beacon shouted.

But they didn't stop running.

One by one, they ran into the water like lemmings running off a cliff. And one by one, they all went down, twitching in the charged water. Nixon, Perry, Sumiko—they were all dead.

No. No, no, *no*. He had only meant to free Arthur. He hadn't meant to *kill them*.

What had he done? These kids weren't even Sov. They'd just been brainwashed like his sister had been.

That's when he saw the girl with the dark brown ponytail facedown in the water.

Beacon let out a noise somewhere between a scream and a sob. He dropped the hose.

"Everleigh."

He ran to his sister, falling to his knees just outside the pool of water. Tears stung his eyes. This couldn't be happening. Not again.

"Oh, Everleigh."

He reached out to touch her shoulder. But to his shock, his sister turned. Beacon gasped and skidded back.

"What the heck happened?" Everleigh asked, groaning as she got up.

"Everleigh! You're alive!"

"Of course I'm alive. Why wouldn't I be?" She looked around, as if seeing the craft for the first time. Then she glanced down at her outfit, and a repulsed look came over her face.

Perry stumbled to his feet. He swiped water off his Gold Stars jacket and shook out his spiky hair like a dog.

Nixon got up next. He winced and clutched his head.

"What's going on?" Perry asked him.

"I—I don't know," Nixon said.

Sumiko pushed herself up, wobbling slightly. She squinted at her surroundings as if trying to puzzle something out.

They didn't want him dead. They didn't want to trap him. They didn't even seem to remember why they'd been chasing him so desperately. The Gold Stars had somehow been snapped out of their mind-controlled state.

Beacon didn't get it.

But then he realized what had happened. The electronics. The water. Beacon had electrocuted the kids, and it had messed with their brains. It undid whatever the Sov's antidote had done to alter their brain waves so they would be complacent.

Thrilled, Beacon turned to the door.

"Arthur, we found a cure!"

But Arthur wasn't in the window. Beacon cupped his hands around his face and peered inside the room. Arthur was lying on the floor in front of his stretcher, clutching his stomach. His pale skin was practically see-through, and rivers of blue veins ran across his sweaty temples. He was lying in a puddle of water.

"Arthur!" Beacon cried. He reached for the handle, but Everleigh yanked his hand away.

"Do you have a death wish?" she snapped.

The air around the door fizzed and popped with electricity.

"But Arthur is hurt!" Beacon said.

Arthur's eyes flickered open, and a wave of relief washed over Beacon. Thank God—he wasn't dead.

"Get out of here," Arthur croaked.

"I'm so sorry—I didn't know it was going to electrocute you," Beacon said. "I was just trying to help."

"Don't worry about it," Arthur said. "If it wasn't for your stupidity, we wouldn't have found a cure." He managed a wry smile that Beacon couldn't return.

"Why is everyone just standing around?"

The clear, crisp voice made Beacon's back go straight. He turned to see Jane pushing herself up from the puddle. Water dripped from her drenched curls.

"Get him!" she commanded, pointing at Beacon.

For a moment, Beacon didn't get it—why was Jane acting like the same old Jane? But then he realized that she was Sov. She hadn't needed any injections, so the electrocution hadn't altered her personality.

No one moved.

"I said get him!" Jane screamed.

"But . . . why?" Sumiko said.

Elation coursed through Beacon. Jane didn't control them anymore!

"Come on, let's get out of here," Beacon said.

"But what about the others?" Everleigh looked at Perry, Sumiko, and Nixon. "We can't just leave them."

"Oh, yes we can."

Beacon wasn't about to sit around trying to figure out whether the other Gold Stars were on their side or not. All he cared about right now was saving his family. What was left of it.

"Fine. I guess I'll have to do the dirty work myself," Jane said darkly.

She smiled.

The mouth in her chest burst open through her shirt, emitting a shrieking scream through row upon row of razor-sharp yellow teeth.

Everleigh screamed.

"Run!" Beacon yelled.

He grabbed his sister's arm and yanked her down the hall. They took off, fists pumping, shoes squeaking on the tile. There was a series of cracks and clicks behind them. Then eight distinct, wet slaps as something hit the tile. Beacon didn't know what had made that sound, but he knew it wasn't something human.

The twins ran blindly, their breaths coming in hot, fast bursts. Finally, they reached an intersection of four corridors. Beacon peered down each one, then made a split-second decision and pulled Everleigh toward the one on the left. But Everleigh wrenched her arm back and shook her head.

"No, this way." She nodded at the corridor on the right.

Beacon narrowed his eyes at his sister. Had she been jolted back into a Gold Star? Was she luring him into a trap?

"Just trust me, Beaks," she said.

It could be a trick, but he didn't have time to overthink it. The slapping, slurping sounds were closing in on them.

They turned down the corridor on the right. But no matter how fast they went, the sounds only seemed to get closer. They were going to get caught.

Just as Beacon had this thought, his sister tugged him through a door. He had enough time to register that it was a janitor's closet, right before they were enveloped in darkness. Pale, dim light shone through slats in the door.

Beacon made himself as small as possible, trying to control the sounds of his labored breathing.

"Shhh," Everleigh whispered. "She's coming."

They froze, watching through the slats as the monster—Jane—shambled past. The thing moved over the tile like a wave of flesh. A tangled mess of tentacles and claws spilled out in all directions from its center, its skin the mottled, wet color of raw meat. The creature stopped in front of the janitor's closet, then stood up on two powerful tentacles, revealing its mouth on the underside of its body. Its jaws peeled open, and a thick, wet organ slid out from between its razor teeth, slithering low over the ground—scenting them. The kids held their breath, not daring to move. The organ slithered up to the closet. It rattled and croaked as it slid through the gap under the door, nearly touching Beacon's leg. He clamped a hand over his mouth, trying to suppress a scream.

After a long moment, the organ withdrew, and the monster slid past, slurping, slapping, leaving a gelatinous yellow slime in its wake.

They waited. And waited. When they were sure Jane was gone, Beacon blew out a harsh breath.

"Oh my God," he said.

"I'm going to need so much therapy after this," Everleigh replied.

"How come it didn't smell us?" Beacon asked, pushing himself up.

"The cleaning chemicals must have masked our scent," Everleigh said. "Come on, let's get out of here before she comes back."

Everleigh pushed the door open, and Beacon followed her out.

"Oh, and by the way, I forgive you," Everleigh said.

"For what?"

"For thinking I was trying to trap you earlier. And for the record, I heard you cry when you thought I was dead."

Beacon's cheeks blazed with heat. His sister was back.

"Let's just go," he said.

They tiptoed quickly down hall after hall, peering carefully around every corner. But everything looked the same. Were they going in circles?

"Any more helpful memories?" Beacon whispered.

A pained crease grew between Everleigh's eyebrows as she gazed searchingly down a hall—left or right?

"I think the exit's this way," she said uncertainly.

Beacon followed. But the corridor ended in a huge metal delivery-bay door, like the ones in old warehouses. There was no door handle, only a digital panel full of flashing lights with the faint outline of a hand.

Everleigh placed her palm over the print, and the panel emitted a deep beep. Access denied.

Beacon dug his fingers into his scalp, pacing the hall behind his sister. "We're going to be squid food."

"I'm sorry," Everleigh said. "This place is so big, and everything looks the same."

Suddenly a set of voices echoed from the other side of the metal, and the door began zooming up. The twins jumped back and flattened themselves against the wall.

Three men emerged, laughing boisterously and patting one another on the back. If any of them were to turn around, they would see the twins.

Instantly Beacon recognized one of the voices. Sheriff Nugent. The sheriff slung his thumbs into the strained belt loops of his pants.

The delivery-bay door began sliding down. Everleigh shot out her foot. The door paused, then began sliding up again, like the motion-sensor-activated doors of an elevator. Beacon held his breath, his whole body tensed as he waited for the men—or whatever they were—to turn around and notice. But they disappeared around the corner. Beacon couldn't believe his luck.

The twins ducked into the room.

"I *was* right," Everleigh said.

The room was filled with sleek silver eggs the size of cars. From where they were standing, Beacon could see two padded seats and a steering device that looked like the controller of a video game inside one of the crafts.

"Whoa," he whispered. "Are these alien ships?" He cautiously stepped closer.

"Pods," Everleigh said.

"Huh?"

"Jane was telling me about these in the caf earlier. Personal submarines that researchers use to go back and forth to the mainland when they don't want to use the tunnels." She jogged toward a pod. "Come on. Let's get out of here."

"What do you know about driving a submarine?" Beacon asked, following his sister.

"Nothing. But I know a lot about cars. How different can it be?"

Beacon peered into the window of a pod. A complicated panel of lights and dials glowed neon blue from the dash. From the looks of it, very different.

Everleigh climbed into the driver's seat. Beacon scoured the body of the pod for a handle when his hand passed over what looked like a motion sensor. The door made an elegant swoosh noise as it rose up instead of out, like a Lamborghini. He climbed in next to his sister.

She pressed a red button, and a hatch in the ceiling peeled open.

"Note to self, don't touch the red button while underwater," Everleigh said.

"You're really inspiring a lot of confidence in your abilities," Beacon said.

"You want to drive instead? Be my guest."

Beacon motioned zipping his lips.

Everleigh tried another button. Music blared through the speakers.

"Turn that off!" Beacon cried. Everleigh frantically bashed at buttons. Warm air blasted out of the vents, wipers slashed across the glass, and the lights on the panel dimmed, but the music remained very firmly on.

The door of the pod room burst open just as the pod slid upward into the air.

"Buckle up!" Everleigh said.

Beacon scrambled to tug on the four-point harness as the pod glided forward through a clawlike circular hatch that rotated open. Behind them, agents yelled and slammed on the glass, but the pod moved seamlessly through the opening, which spiraled shut behind them. A second clear glass hatch opened, and briny water cascaded down the pod in sheets. In moments, they were submerged.

"Whoa!" Beacon said. He'd known they were underwater, but he hadn't realized how deep. The only light was a diffuse glow some hundred feet above, casting everything into darkness and shadow. He peered through the glass at the seaweed and kelp floating in the dark water, and fish darted away from the craft like shadowy fireworks. Behind them, the UFO sat lodged in the seafloor, a solid, hulking mass of metal and lights. He stretched his neck and squinted, but he couldn't see the end of it in the murky water.

The pod jerked forward suddenly.

"Whoops," Everleigh said, just as the pod jolted to the side, then the other side, before they flipped upside down. The harness dug into Beacon's chest and blood pooled in his head. "Not a problem!" Everleigh said brightly.

She pressed more buttons, and they flipped right-side up. After a few more jumpy movements, she seemed to get the hang of it, and soon, they were cutting through the water like a shark slicing through the tide, leaving a churning white trail behind them.

"Woo-hoo!" Everleigh whooped.

Beacon joined in her celebration. But then he thought of Arthur lying curled on the ground back in that UFO, and his mirth died. How could he be celebrating when his friend was left behind? When all those other brainwashed kids were trapped?

Everleigh seemed to sense his change in mood and grew a somber expression.

"I'm sorry about your friend," she said.

Beacon nodded.

"Okay, bring me up to speed," she said after a moment.

Beacon didn't even know where to start. Everything was so screwed up.

He gave her the full update, telling her everything from his and Arthur's investigation into the vitamin injections, to their mission through the ventilation shaft of the church, to their discovery of Arthur's underwater-breathing abilities, ending with the chase through the alien craft.

"So Dad's in on it?" she asked incredulously.

Beacon nodded.

"I can't believe it."

"He admitted they gave him a shot. He acted like it was such a privilege, too." Beacon shook his head. "You should have seen him. You remember when the CDC discovered that new strain of the West Nile Virus?"

"And Dad was lit up like a Christmas tree for a month?"

"It was like that," Beacon said. "He was pitching it to me like he actually thought I'd be on board with this."

"How could he do this to us?" Everleigh asked.

"I don't know," Beacon said, "but it doesn't matter now. We just need to figure out what we're going to do."

"We need to call the cops," Everleigh said.

"You mean Sheriff Nugent? The guy who shot me?" Beacon shook his head. "We'd just end up locked up in that place again."

"Then what?" Everleigh said.

"We drive this thing to another town. The cops can't be crooked everywhere."

Or could they? Beacon remembered his dad saying he worked for the CIA. If the Central Intelligence Agency was in on it, they were doomed.

"Our best bet is going to be going far, far away from here. Back to LA, even. I'm sure Uncle Stanley and Aunt Deb would help us," Beacon said.

"With what money?" Everleigh asked.

"Don't you have anything saved?" Beacon said.

"I have twenty-five dollars."

"That's *it*?" Beacon cried.

"Why, what do *you* have?"

"Uh, like five bucks," he said sheepishly.

More like none. Money management wasn't his strong suit. He couldn't ignore the siren song of convenience store candy.

Everleigh raised a knowing eyebrow. "It doesn't matter anyway. My money is at the inn, and there's no way there aren't aliens waiting for us there in case we go back, so that's out of the question."

"Okay, it's not a big deal," Beacon said, as much to calm himself as to calm his sister. "We can hitchhike if we have to. We just need to get out of here. We'll work everything else out later. We're going to get Arthur and the rest of those kids out of there and take down those aliens."

The pod jolted. Beacon wasn't expecting it, and he banged his head against the window.

"Ow!" he cried, clutching his temple. "Be careful!"

"That wasn't me," Everleigh said. "Something hit us."

"What do you mean something hit us?"

"I mean, *something hit us.*"

He whirled around, squinting into the water, but he couldn't see anything. But something was out there, somewhere.

"Go faster!" Beacon cried.

"I'm going as fast as I can!"

The pod jolted again. Beacon pressed his face up against the glass. Nothing but blackness stared back at him. Then suddenly there was a streak of movement right outside the window. Beacon jerked back, following the wake in the water as it moved around to the front of the craft.

"Uh, Ev?"

"Yeah?"

"We have a problem."

Beacon pointed through the front window. A creature had materialized in front of the pod, its massive tentacles undulating in the water. Everleigh's eyes widened, and she wrenched the pod sharply upward just as the alien struck out with a heavy tentacle.

It was too late. It clobbered the side of their vessel. Beacon banged his head against the glass again, tasting coppery blood inside his mouth.

"What the heck? Is it trying to kill us?" As soon as Beacon said it, another thunderous boom struck the back left corner of the vessel. A crack splintered up the metal frame. Water rushed in from the gap as an alarm began blaring.

"It breached the air locks!" Everleigh said.

Frigid water gushed in, swirling up around Beacon's bare ankles.

"We've got to surface," Everleigh said. She leaned back in her chair, pulling the steering column hard toward her chest. But unlike before, when the pod jerked at every slight movement of the controls, the craft angled painfully slowly toward the surface, chugging against the current like a person trying to run through water. And they were only going to move more and more slowly as the pod took on water.

"This isn't working," Everleigh said.

Beacon cast around for something, *anything* that might save them. But it was useless. This pod would be their tomb.

"We need to jump out." Beacon unclicked his seat belt.

"What?" Everleigh screeched. "I'm not going out there with that thing! And we're in the middle of the ocean."

"We're going to be at the bottom of it if we don't get out of here."

Another jolt struck the pod, this time on the driver's side. Everleigh jumped out of the way as the window splintered like ice breaking across a lake. The crack in the body had widened from the second blow, and water moved in fast from both points; in moments, it had traveled from Beacon's kneecaps to his waist, swirling around him like an icy whirlpool. Beacon leaped up, and Everleigh frantically whipped off her harness and jumped onto the seat.

"Can you open the hatch like you did before?" Beacon asked Everleigh.

She nodded, a stunned expression on her face.

"Okay. Good," Beacon said. "When it opens, you need to swim up as hard as you can. Push off the pod to get momentum."

Everleigh swallowed.

"You'll be okay. You can breathe underwater, remember?"

"Unless being electrocuted messed with that." Everleigh said.

"Well, it doesn't really matter anyway." Beacon said. "We have no choice but to ditch this thing."

"What if it gets us?" She looked out into the black water with huge, horrified eyes.

"It won't," Beacon answered with more confidence than he felt. "It'll be too distracted attacking the pod."

Beacon almost said goodbye, but that felt too much like admitting they were probably going to die. So he just said, "See you at the top."

Everleigh pushed the button on the dash, which was just

millimeters away from being flooded. The hatch glided open. Beacon took a deep breath, just as water overtook them.

The cold was shocking, paralyzing Beacon on the spot. Through the dim electronic light of the dashboard, he saw Everleigh flailing wildly in the water. He gave a sharp tug on her shirt before diving through the hatch out into the open sea.

It was intensely dark outside the pod. He felt more than saw Everleigh slide out of the hatch after him, then launch herself off the metal body of the pod, her sneakers scraping his arm as she torpedoed up. Beacon followed suit, pushing his body hard and fast, his hands steepled toward the surface as he cut through the water.

He kicked his legs as hard as he could, but the cold made his movements frustratingly slow, as if someone had hit the slow-motion button on his life. Pressure compressed his chest. Despite the bone-chilling cold, his lungs felt as though they'd been set on fire. The urge to breathe was overwhelming. He frantically kicked through the water, but it wasn't enough. They were just too deep. Black began to creep into the edges of his vision. Any moment now, and he would be forced to breathe.

Beacon couldn't believe that this was how it was going to end. That he would die under the ocean, just like Jasper had.

But soon, light fractured off the water and hope shot through him.

They must be getting close.

He burst up, using the last of his withering strength to overtake his sister. But just as he was reaching for the surface, his fingers caught on something.

At first he thought he'd become tangled in seaweed. But that didn't make sense. They were too close to the surface. And then he saw it: the frayed edges of a rope. He realized it was a net, just as it closed around them.

15

Beacon jerked back like a fish snagged on a hook. He kicked and punched, but his arms only tangled further in the thick rope net. Before he knew what was happening, they were spit out into a room. There was a loud *whoosh* as all the water sucked out from drains in the floor. Beacon and Everleigh sat gasping and coughing in a wet heap on the metal floor of another craft.

Everleigh pushed herself up raggedly, doing languid laps around the tiny room and beating her fists on the walls and the door.

"I knew we should have stayed in the pod!" she yelled.

"Oh yeah, because we would've been way better off in a pod that was *flooding with water*," Beacon shouted back.

"At least we would have had a chance!"

"Us versus a monster squid—I'm sure it would have been a real contest. And how about a thank-you?"

"For what?"

"I just saved your life!

"Saved my life? I saved *your* life. If it weren't for me, you would still be inside that UFO. You never would have figured out how to drive that pod!"

"If it wasn't for me, you would still be a Gold Star!"

The twins glared venom at each other.

Beacon opened his mouth to argue more, but all at once, the heat went out of him. He just couldn't be mad at his sister. Not after everything they'd been through. All they had was each other.

"I'm sorry," Beacon said. He wilted to the floor. A violent shiver racked his body. He was so cold. He cradled his fist to his stomach; the cuts on his knuckles pulsed with pain.

Everleigh sighed.

"I'm sorry, too." She sat down next to him and put an arm around his shoulders. Her teeth chattered hard, her lips taking on a bluish hue.

For a while, they said nothing. But Beacon knew what they were both thinking. This was it. The last time they would be Beacon and Everleigh. Would they be turned into Gold Stars, or would the aliens just get rid of them? They certainly hadn't seemed like they wanted to keep them around ten minutes ago, when they were clobbering their pod.

The slow rush of water came into focus.

"Remember when Dad rented that RV?" Everleigh said after a while.

"And forced us to visit all the sights of small town America?" Beacon said.

Everleigh smiled dimly. "Like that giant penny, and that little village where water runs backward."

"I forgot about that place," Beacon said. "That was pretty cool."

"Jasper was so mad," Everleigh said. "He didn't talk for, like, a whole week."

He hadn't wanted to leave his friends behind for an RV trip with the family.

"Not until that amusement park in Delaware or whatever," Beacon said. "I remember riding the Twister with him, and he was trying so hard not to smile and then he just couldn't help it. We laughed so hard." Beacon felt a smile curl the edges of his trembling lips, even as a mournful feeling gathered in his chest. Those were good times. Jasper was alive. Everleigh was okay. They were all together. They hadn't realized how lucky they were then. That in a few years, everything would change. Beacon would give anything in the world to go back to that stupid little RV without air-conditioning or running water and just freeze time.

The craft slowed to a stop. Beacon's breath hitched in his chest. The twins shared wide-eyed glances.

There was a *clunk, clunk, clunk* from the other side of the door. The kids scrabbled back like crabs until their spines hit the opposite wall. The door slid up toward the ceiling. Beacon had been expecting to see the UFO's sterile white halls, or even that delivery-bay area where they kept all the pods. But when the hatch opened, they were outside. The craft floated a few feet from a rocky stretch of shore Beacon didn't recognize. Across from them, an unmarked black van was parked in waist-high yellow grass, its side door open and waiting. Their dad stood knee-deep in the murky water. A gull cawed as it circled and swooped in the dark clouds above him.

"We've got to hurry," he said, jerking his head at the van. "We don't have a lot of time."

Beacon started to climb out, but Everleigh grabbed his arm. She glared at their dad.

"Why should we trust you? You're the one who got us into this situation. You're being controlled by *them*."

"Because I just stole an alien submarine for you," he said. "And they're going to notice it's missing any minute, if they haven't already. We need to hit the road before they realize we're trying to escape. I can explain everything later."

Everleigh crossed her arms. "How about now."

He sent a pained look to the road, then heaved a sigh. "Listen, all I can tell you is that I really believed it was the right thing to move here. I wanted to keep you safe, by any means necessary, even if that meant taking away your control. But then I saw them chasing you—saw that Sov striking your pod again and again. It didn't make sense—they could have killed you! The influence of the antidote has its limits. I couldn't let any harm come to my kids." He shook his head, a stupefied look on his face. "I don't know what to believe anymore. All I know is you two are the most important things in the world to me, and if I don't have you, I don't have anything. I won't be manipulated by anyone who would try to harm you like that. Now, I can understand if you never trust me. I'll even understand if you never want to talk to me again. But if we don't get out of here, the Sov *will* catch us."

Beacon and Everleigh exchanged a glance before they climbed out of the craft, splashing after their dad and into the van. Once their dad got into the driver's seat, the vehicle jerked into motion.

The twins scrambled to latch their seat belts. It was a mark of just how scared their dad truly was that he hadn't waited to make sure they were properly belted before taking off.

The world streaked past outside the windows, a blur of green and black. Beacon's heart pounded in his ears. He swung around wildly in his seat, searching for cars, trying to see if anyone was following them.

"What about Arthur?" Beacon asked when he could finally think straight. "My friend is still back there."

The van careened around a corner, kicking up dust.

"Arthur Newell?" their dad said.

Beacon sat up straighter. "You know him?"

"I heard people talking in the cafeteria. It sounds like they're very interested in his immune abilities."

Very interested. That was one way to put it.

The van jerked to a stop. Beacon blinked at his surroundings. They were parked in the loop in front of Blackwater Lookout. The peaked roof of the bed-and-breakfast rose up into the thunderclouds, the dark vines twisted around the house like a snake choking its prey.

Beacon hadn't been paying attention to where his dad was driving, and now his stomach dropped to his knees.

"We're stopping *here*?" Everleigh squeaked, echoing Beacon's thoughts. "Won't they look for us here?"

"We need to switch cars," their dad said, unbuckling his seat belt. "Can't exactly keep you kids safe if I'm arrested for grand theft auto. Let's go. Grab whatever you can in one minute, and we'll hit the road. Hop to it, no time to waste."

Everleigh shook her head, then jumped out of the van.

"Wait!" Beacon cried. "What about Arthur? We need to help him."

"I'm afraid that won't be possible," his dad said. "His case got moved to a higher security clearance. There's no way I could even get close. Victor is *very* strict. Trust me, you don't want to mess with him. Now let's go."

"But the Sov are hurting him!" Beacon cried.

"I'm sorry, Beaks. I know he was your friend. But we have to get moving. *Now*."

Was. Past tense.

"So that's just it, then?" he said, following his dad out of the van. He practically had to run to keep up with his brisk pace. "We just leave him there? Just pretend like Arthur Newell never existed? Maybe send his grandma a sympathy card every year at Christmas?"

"I don't like it, either, Beaks, but there's nothing we can do about it. Only a four-star clearance can get close to him—I've never even been down that wing of the ship. There are armed guards at the entrance. When we get out of here, we'll make some calls. Now go up to your room and grab a few things. We need to be fast."

He banged open the front door of the inn.

Make some calls. That was it.

Beacon had never felt so helpless. It was as if a powerful current was carrying him away, and he couldn't break free, no matter how hard he tried. He didn't know whether to scream or cry.

There was a prickling sensation in Beacon's eyes; he was dangerously close to crying.

"Isn't there *anything* you can do, Dad?" Everleigh pleaded. She stood on the landing of the stairs, holding a duffel bag with clothes poking out of the zipper.

"If there was, I would do it," his dad said. "I know you want to save your friend, but we won't be able to sneak in. They have security all over the place. We wouldn't get within a hundred-foot radius of the ship before they knew about it. We might as well walk right in the front door." Their dad frowned suddenly. Beacon knew that look.

"What? What is it?" Beacon asked.

"Nothing," he said, shaking his head.

"You're lying," Beacon said. "You got an idea."

"It would never work, and it's far too dangerous. Forget I said anything. Come on, let's get going."

"You have to tell me!" Beacon cried, grabbing his arm. "What is it? Something to do with security? Walking in the front door? Come on, please!"

"I said never mind. It was a stupid idea. They'd see right through the act."

The act? What did that mean?

Suddenly all the pieces snapped into place.

"We go back through the front door," Beacon said.

His family looked at him.

"Maybe you hit your head harder than I thought in that pod crash," Everleigh said as she came down to join them.

"I'm not talking about sneaking in," Beacon said. "What Dad said gave me an idea. We walk in through the front door. So by now the Sov have noticed we're missing and have put two and two together that you helped us, right?"

"Yes . . . ," their dad said warily.

"Well, you bring us back. Drag us in there. Tell them we tried to escape and you caught us running away. We'll play the part. Kicking and screaming, and all that. You tell them we're out of control and need to be locked up until you can figure out what's wrong with us."

"That is the worst idea ever," Everleigh said.

But when their dad didn't come back with any arguments or glaring logic gaps, Beacon knew he wasn't totally off the mark. He smiled a victory smile.

"Your plan isn't going to work."

Beacon's breath stalled at the familiar voice. The whole family turned. Donna stood at the top of the stairs.

The kids scrambled away from the woman as she thumped down the stairs two at a time.

"Back away from my children," their dad ordered. He whipped a pen out of his shirt pocket and brandished it like a weapon. Donna laughed.

"Is that how you plan to fight off the Sov?" she said. "You need my help more than I thought."

Help?

"Why should we trust you?" Beacon said. "You work for the sheriff! I saw the pictures—I know you're really Donalda Pound."

"I *used* to work for the sheriff," Donna corrected. "And you'll trust me because you don't have a choice. Without me, you're going to get caught. In less than two minutes, Sheriff Nugent's going to be pulling into that driveway. I plan to tell him you left ten minutes ago, headed toward Shelburne. Unless you'd prefer to chat with him yourself, I'd suggest you move that van into the garage, where I already parked your car, and hide."

Donna and their dad eyed each other like wary cats circling. Could they trust her?

"Clock's ticking," Donna warned.

Beacon and Everleigh looked to their dad.

"Get in the garage," their dad finally said. "And stay well back. I'm pulling the van around. Go, go, go!"

The family jolted into action. Beacon and Everleigh ran outside and jerked the garage door open, while their dad backed the van up into the port next to where their Taurus was already parked. After he turned off the engine, he jumped out and pulled the garage door closed, just as a set of headlights beamed across the property. Through a crack in the door, they saw a police cruiser rumble up the driveway.

Beacon's heart raced. The sound of his family's labored breathing mixed with the quiet *tink*s coming from the cooling engine. Had the sheriff seen them? What if he noticed the fresh tire tracks leading up to the garage?

Beacon bit his lip. He felt a hand slip into his. Everleigh smiled at him grimly.

The cruiser ground to a halt in the driveway. They watched through the crack as Sheriff Nugent climbed out and stomped up the front steps. Donna emerged from the front door. She gestured animatedly and pointed east. Sheriff Nugent followed her gaze before he spoke into a radio at his belt. And then he was racing back to his cruiser. The sirens turned on as he sped back down the driveway, leaving a cloud of dust behind him.

They waited. And waited. And waited.

Finally, Donna emerged from the front door again.

"Come on out," she called over.

Five minutes later, Beacon had changed out of his Sov-issue hospital gown and into jeans and a T-shirt. He cleaned the cuts on his knuckles, and then he joined his family at the kitchen table, where they sat stiffly with mugs of hot cider.

Donna had told them that all roads leading out of Driftwood Harbor were crawling with police and Sov, and that it would be smarter to wait it out until they had all assumed that the family was long gone before finally making a break for it. Beacon wasn't sure it was the best plan, but his dad had agreed with Donna, so here they were. Sipping cider, while an alien nation and the government were after them.

Beacon eyed his mug suspiciously. He still wasn't sure he could trust Donna. Was this just her clever way of poisoning their family? Was there some type of sleeping drug in the cider, and they would all wake up inside the UFO again?

Donna rolled her eyes and swapped out her mug for Beacon's, taking a big gulp.

"See? Not dead," Donna said.

Beacon took a wary sip of his drink. If it was poison, it tasted like the best hot cider he'd ever had.

Beacon's dad cleared his throat.

"So, you used to be a deputy?" He raised his eyebrows at Donna.

"And you work for the Sov," she said. There was so much derision in her tone that the hairs on Beacon's neck stood up straight. Suddenly the burnt eggs made sense. She'd known all along that his dad worked for the Sov. And she didn't exactly like him for it.

"And yes," she said magnanimously, lifting her chin. "I was the youngest deputy the force had ever had. Not that anyone was too happy about that."

"What do you mean?" Everleigh asked.

"It was a bit of an old boys' club at the time. Not unlike how it is now, actually. No one took too kindly to the sheriff hiring a girl, never mind a nineteen-year-old girl. But that's neither here nor there."

"Tell us about the night you saw the alien craft," Beacon said.

"Why? You know all about that already." Donna sent him a knowing look, and Beacon's cheeks warmed. So she *had* seen his search history after all.

She took a sip of her cider before continuing.

"I'd been patrolling the harbor that night, following up on a tip about some kids selling drugs. Then out of nowhere, I saw a set of bright lights in the sky. The thing hovered above the water some hundred yards from the shore before finally crashing. I assumed it was a downed aircraft and called the head office for support. Sheriff Ramirez—he was in charge at the time—he had the Coast Guard there within minutes. But . . . of course you know how that turned out. They never found a trace of the craft. I knew then that there was something fishy going on. But there was a strange air about the crews that came, too. I noticed the Coast Guard whispering to each other and exchanging glances when they thought no one was looking. I was curious. Ramirez was curious, too. He kept pressuring the head office to give us more information—right until he was replaced with Nugent. Was a real uproar at the time. The head office said they needed Nugent's expertise, but it seemed like they just needed someone who wouldn't ask too many questions. But Nugent was popular with the deputies, and they got over it real fast. I wasn't so quick to warm to him. Anytime I asked Nugent about that craft, I was shut down and told to mind my own business in no uncertain terms. With Ramirez being replaced, I didn't want to take chances with my job, too, so I stopped poking around. Weeks and months went by, and I tried to forget about the craft. I did so well that Nugent took a shining to me, and I was promoted to detective. Next thing you know I'm being trusted with more and more information. Being let in on secrets no one else in the force knows about. I come to find out about the UFO in the water, and this whole government conspiracy happening right here under our noses. Not only were aliens living here, but they were helping us prepare for an upcoming threat. Or so they said."

"What do you mean?" Beacon asked.

"The Sov, they were giving these shots to the kids to help them breathe underwater. But I come to find out it also makes 'em behave. Stay in line. It all started to make sense, all the strange goings on in the town. See, ever since that craft came, there were less and less calls to the station, until it seemed like Driftwood Harbor had just . . . stopped having a crime problem. I even stopped getting called down to the pub on Saturday nights to break up fights at closing time. Now all this seemed like good news, but there were things going on in that ship that I didn't feel too comfortable about. It's one thing if someone signs up to the program willingly, and I could even make myself believe it was okay if the kids were given that shot without their knowledge, so long as their parents agreed, but they'd started bringing in adults—troublemakers in town. Once, I saw this man, Dusty, who I used to pick up at the pub as a matter of routine, lying on a stretcher. He looked dead, but the next day, I saw him in town applying for a job at the Stop 'N Save wearing a suit. After a while I noticed a pattern. Anyone who opposed the regime, anyone who asked too many questions, ended up being given this shot. It didn't make any sense. They weren't giving Dusty the shot to help him breathe underwater—they wanted to shut him up. That scared the bejesus out of me, knowing they could just make people go along with anything they wanted." She shook her head.

"Why didn't you do anything about it?" Everleigh said. "You just let all those people suffer."

"Everleigh!" their dad said.

"No, it's okay," Donna said. "Truth is, I was worried I'd lose my job if I made too many waves, after what happened to Ramirez. You don't understand what it was like back then, being a woman in law enforcement. They were chomping at the bit to find a reason to fire me. I didn't belong there, or so they told me whenever they got the chance. The boys made a sport out of harassing me, and if I stood up for myself, it just proved their point—that I was weak and not worthy of my badge. So I decided it was better to stay quiet, oppose them from the inside. I know that makes me a coward, but I'd worked hard to get where I was, and it was my passion."

Beacon just stared at her. It was too much. The Sov had been injecting children for more than forty years. That meant practically everyone in Driftwood Harbor was under their control. The kids, their parents. A whole town of complacent, docile humans under Sov control.

"If you were so loyal to the Sov, then why don't you work for them now?" Everleigh asked.

"Well, one night Nugent radioed about a participant gone Off-Program who ran away—that's what they call it when the antidote goes wonky and they can't control the kids anymore. Used to happen more, before they got the finer details ironed out. Anyway, I'd known this kid. Was a friend's son. It was raining that night—real kicker of a storm. Some of the others wanted to call off the search till morning, but I looked high and low. There wasn't a twig I didn't look underneath. But it didn't matter. He just clear went missing. No one ever saw him again."

"Is—is he alive?" Beacon asked.

All he could think about was Arthur. Once they discovered that Arthur couldn't be controlled, and even worse, that he'd been investigating them, what would happen to his friend?

"Officially, the boy was sent off to live with an aunt out of state," Donna said. "The day before, his mom had been in a panic. Then all of a sudden she didn't even want to talk about him. Every time I brought him up, she changed the subject to the weather or the projections for the upcoming fishing season. She stopped calling, stopped answering the door when I dropped by. So I asked questions, and this time I didn't give up. I went higher and higher until I finally got called into the head office. Only it wasn't Nugent there. It was some other man—Victor. Head of the Sov. Next thing I know I was discharged from the police force. I asked why I was being fired—they said 'not a good fit.' Whatever that means. But I knew the truth. Those boys could hardly stomach a woman on the force to begin with, but a strong-willed woman? A woman willing to ask the hard questions and think for herself? That was something far too dangerous to be holding a badge in this town."

"I'm so sorry," their dad said.

"Yeah, well." Donna cleared her throat.

"Why didn't they give you the injection?" Everleigh asked. "You had all that confidential information—weren't they worried you would expose them after you'd been fired?"

"This was back before everyone in town had to have a shot. After I left the force, I kept my head down and stayed out of their way. I guess they just forgot about me."

"How come you never left Driftwood Harbor?" their dad asked.

"I did," Donna said. "Or at least I tried to. I can't tell you the number of times I packed up my truck and started driving. I figured I'd just go away and let this all be someone else's problem. Maybe I'd phone in a tip from the road, once I was far out of the Sov's reach. But every time I tried to leave, I'd only get as far as the city limits before I'd turn back around again. I can't explain it. I just . . . changed my mind. I couldn't even remember why I wanted to go anymore. I think—and I know this sounds out there—but I think the Sov have some kind of power over this town. Unnatural power that has nothing to do with the shots."

Beacon had suspected this. But something about hearing it said out loud made the skin on the back of his neck prickle.

Donna cleared her throat loudly. "But enough about me. I want to help you get your friend back."

"How?" Beacon asked.

"Well, I like your plan—the one about acting as if you're escaped participants. But it won't work unless you have someone on the outside helping, too."

"What are you suggesting?" Everleigh said.

"You two kick up a real fuss while your dad hauls you back. Once you're in, you focus on finding that kid. I'll create a distraction and get you all out."

"What kind of distraction?" Beacon asked.

"Oh, I can think of a few things," she said, winking.

"But why?" Everleigh said. "You spent forty years standing by while all this happened—why are you suddenly helping us?"

Their dad opened his mouth, probably to tell Everleigh she was being rude, but then he closed it again. It seemed even he wanted to know the answer to that question.

"I just couldn't do it anymore," Donna said. "Not after I got to know the three of you. I couldn't convince myself it was okay this time. Seeing the way you changed . . ." She looked at Everleigh and shook her head. "I liked you the way you were. The way you are. It isn't right what they're doing. I've spent too long watching this town change. I'm going to be the brave woman I always wanted to be back when I was a sheriff's deputy." Her eyes watered, and she blinked fast to work the tears away.

There was a long, loaded silence.

"Come with us," Everleigh finally said. "When we get Arthur

and leave Driftwood Harbor—there's room for you in the car."

"Absolutely," their dad agreed.

Donna swallowed. "That's real kind of you. Kinder than I deserve. But I'm staying here. I need to right the wrongs of my past."

Everleigh opened her mouth to argue, but Donna was already shaking her head. "I won't go when all those kids are still in trouble. I'm one of the only adults not under their control. If I leave, what hope do they have?"

Everleigh didn't have an answer for that, but she frowned, deep and hard.

"Are we getting that kid out, or what?" Donna said, forcing a cheery tone.

"Yes!" Beacon said at the same time as his dad and sister said, "No."

Beacon gaped at his family.

"*What?!* Dad, I thought you were on board!"

"I'm all for helping Arthur if we can," his dad explained, "but what you're proposing is too flimsy. There are just too many unknown variables. One slip, and they'd be onto us. And then all of us would be trapped in there. It's too dangerous."

It was true. There were problems with the plan big enough to drive a truck through. But it was the only plan they had, and Arthur needed him.

"We can't just leave Arthur behind," Beacon said fiercely. "We're his only chance. Who knows what they'll do to him if we don't help? It's like you're always saying—do the benefits outweigh the risks? And they do. They definitely do."

Their dad looked from twin to twin. "I'm sorry, but—"

"Listen," Beacon said. "I know you don't know Arthur. I know you just want the best for us, and I know you don't want to take any chances after—after Jasper died," he said, forcing himself to say the words in one quick rush. "But I'm doing it with or without you. If I don't try and he dies because of me, because I didn't do anything to help him, then that would be on me, and I just wouldn't be okay with that. I would never forgive myself, and I would never forgive you for stopping me. I'm not asking you to help. I just need you to let me walk out that door."

There was a long, strained pause before his dad ran a hand through his thinned hair and blew out a harsh breath.

"We better get going right away then," he said. "It'll look suspicious if we've been gone for too long."

"Y-you're going to help?" Beacon asked.

"Of course I am. You don't think I'd let you do it on your own, do you?"

"Yes!" Beacon cheered, pumping a fist into the air. "Thank you, Dad."

Beacon stood up. Everleigh heaved an annoyed sigh and stood up, too.

"I get the front seat for at least a month after this," she said.

Beacon beamed. "Operation Knockdown is underway."

"Operation Knockdown?" Everleigh raised her eyebrows.

"It's this thing we do," Beacon said self-consciously. "For our club. You know, secret code names?"

"What's Knockout have to do with anything?" she said.

"Knock*down*. And I dunno." He shrugged limply. "It just sounds cool. No one said you have to be in the club if you're too cool for it."

"Are you kidding me?" Everleigh said. "Of course I'll be in your dumb club. But we're calling it Operation Sea Hammer."

16

"Ready?" the twins' dad said.

Beacon and Everleigh were sitting in the back seat of the company van. Their hands were bound behind their backs with plastic snap ties that Beacon was more than a little disturbed to discover Donna just happened to have on hand.

"Ready," Beacon said.

"I've been training for this my whole life." Everleigh cracked her neck and rolled her shoulders.

Beacon laughed, though it had a tinny quality. His heart was racing faster than their father was driving down the dusty dirt back roads of Driftwood Harbor.

"It has to look real," their dad said. "If they suspect anything, it'll all be over before it's even begun. I'm going to have to be rough with you. And mean."

They turned a corner, around an old tin house covered in rust, and the ocean came into view.

The harbor was dark and eerily tranquil. Rusted fishing boats bobbed gently against the pier, the water smooth and flat as black glass. A single seagull cawed and swooped in the charcoal sky.

"It might not look like it, but there are security cameras all over this place, and they're monitored twenty-four seven," their dad said. "The moment we get out of this car, you need to be on your A game."

He braked hard at the end of the grass embankment, sending Beacon and Everleigh lurching against their seat belts. Their headlights shone two darts of orange light across the soggy grass and the still, dark water of the ocean beyond.

"Showtime," he said.

He swung open the door and climbed out of the van without bothering to turn off the engine. Then he opened the side door. His brows were sharper than the rocks at Deadman's Wharf, and his jaw was set and rippling with fury.

"I don't want any trouble from you two, or you'll regret it," their dad said.

Beacon stiffened, because he believed him. Everything about his dad was intense, honed, and dangerous, and for a moment, Beacon could see the man who worked for a top secret intelligence agency. He'd never seen his dad like this, and he was sure he never wanted to again.

His dad leaned across the seat and shoved a rag into each of their mouths.

Beacon's eyes popped wide. That hadn't been a part of the plan.

Then he unbuckled their seat belts and grabbed Beacon and Everleigh by the collars of their shirts, hauling them upright, so that only the tips of their shoes touched the ground. Everleigh went straight into action, kicking and writhing and screaming against the rag in her mouth. Beacon had temporarily forgotten his role and jolted into action, too. As he fought, the fist holding the collar of his shirt twisted and tightened, cutting off airflow and making him gag.

"This can be easy, or this can be hard," their dad said. "Trust me, you won't like the hard way."

A frisson of fear rippled up Beacon's spine.

It's just acting, he told himself. *He warned us about this.*

A fisherman in orange chest waders emerged from a small shed on the shore—the same fisherman as the night he'd been shot by Sheriff Nugent.

Their dad gave him a small, curt nod, and the fisherman looked away quickly, scurrying off down the shore as if he were suddenly very busy.

Was he an alien, too, Beacon wondered, or just complicit in the cover-up? Just how many residents of Driftwood Harbor were in on this thing?

Beacon wasn't sure he wanted to know.

Their dad hauled the twins into the wooden shed. The moment the door closed behind them, a complicated digital panel sprang out of the rotted wood walls. He placed his hand over the handprint, and a red light scanned his palm. There was a slick *beep, beep* noise before the ground jolted and shuddered. And then it *dropped*. Beacon yelped as the shed hurtled down. Even Everleigh looked as if she were planning a full-scale retreat. Meanwhile, their dad stood with his hands clasped calmly behind his back, completely unruffled as they sped toward their death. Finally, the elevator slowed to a stop. There was an elegant *ping*, and the doors slid open soundlessly.

The twins were led by their dad out into a large warehouse-like room. Beacon had been expecting dirt and worms, but the place was so bright white that he had to blink fast against the harsh glare in his eyes. It was hard to believe they were underground.

A woman in a gray jumpsuit abruptly stopped pushing around a wet mop when she saw them. Her eyes bulged, and she scuttled away quickly, disappearing around a corner. In moments, there were thundering boots from down a distant hall, which grew louder each moment. Two, four, six armed guards ran into the room, with even more trailing in behind. They wore black helmets and black tactical vests over army-green military uniforms. Each of them carried big black guns up in front of their faces. Behind them, the janitor shrank against the wall with the mop clutched to her chest.

"Malcom McCullough," their dad said smoothly, flashing a badge from inside his jacket pocket. "Returning the AWOL participants. They're wild and need containment fast."

The words made Beacon realize that he and his sister had frozen at the sight of the guns. Now, they redoubled their acting efforts, kicking and writhing until a guard pushed a gun into Beacon's belly.

"Shut up!" the guard growled in his ear, so roughly that spittle flew onto Beacon's hot, clammy skin.

Everleigh worked out her gag, spitting it on the floor. "Leave my brother alone!" she screamed.

"I don't think the guns are quite necessary," their dad said.

"We'll decide that," the guard barked back.

"They're A-one participants," their dad said.

The guards stilled, just a bit.

"If so much as a hair is damaged on them, Victor will be furious," their dad said.

Reluctantly, the guard pulled the gun away from Beacon's belly. "Let's get moving," he ordered.

They were led out of the room, down a long white hall with no end in sight. A moving walkway, like the ones in airports, rolled slowly down the center of the tiled floor.

The guards nudged the family onto it, and before they knew it, they were speeding down the hall. Beacon had assumed they would be taking a pod to the UFO, but after a while, he realized that this must be the tunnel Everleigh mentioned that led directly to the underwater craft.

Everleigh kicked and squirmed.

"Stay still!" a guard ordered.

"Get your hands off me," Everleigh snapped back. "Dad, how can you do this?"

Tears glistened in the corners of her eyes.

"I said shut up!" the guard ordered.

"We're your kids," Everleigh continued, ignoring him. There was a thickness in her voice that didn't seem like an act. "Your own *kids*. How could you rip us away from everything we've ever known? How could you leave Jasper behind, alone in the ground, halfway across the country?"

"I'm doing this for you," their dad replied calmly. "You'll see that when you're older." He stared resolutely ahead.

Finally, they reached the end of the hall. They stumbled off the conveyor. A set of big steel doors whizzed open; a man with a dark, bushy mustache and straight black hair that fell just above his ears stood framed in the doorway. His shirtsleeves were rolled up to the elbows, revealing tanned arms covered in dark hair.

"Victor!" one of the guards said in a high-pitched tone of surprise.

A spike of fear went through Beacon.

The man didn't look particularly strong or fast, but Beacon had no trouble believing he was the fearsome leader of the Sovereign he'd heard so much about. He had a calculated air about him, the air of a man who had no doubt his orders would be carried out to a T.

"Hello, Victor," the kids' dad said smoothly, stepping forward.

A dozen safeties were removed from the guns and trained on him; he paused, but Victor made a gesture with his hand, and the guns returned to their former positions at the guards' sides. Their dad straightened his tie and advanced.

"They fell for it, just like you said they would," he said.

17

All the blood drained from Beacon's head.

"How far did they get?" Victor asked.

His dad's lips quirked into a smug smile. "Old Danbury Road."

A riot of emotions ricocheted through Beacon's body—shock, anger, hurt, confusion. He'd trusted his dad, but had he just been pretending to be on their side so he could get them to come back to the craft?

"Not bad," Victor said. "A little farther and we might have lost them. The state police are all over that county."

"I went as quickly as I could, but you know how fast and sneaky Off-Program participants can be," their dad said.

"Don't I know it. These two are particularly misbehaved," Victor said. "Nothing but problems."

Beacon glowered at his dad, resentment burning low and hot in his belly. They weren't bad kids. He got all As (and okay, a few Bs). He stuck up for kids when they were being bullied. He volunteered at the nursing home sometimes, even though the smell of the cafeteria food made him want to puke. Sure, he sometimes forgot his manners; sure, he argued with his sister. But that didn't mean he was bad.

"You tricked us!" Everleigh cried.

Beacon breathed hard and fast against the gag in his mouth. He didn't know who or what to believe anymore. Was his dad on their side or not? He willed his dad to look at him, just once—to give him a tiny sign that he hadn't betrayed them. But the man stared straight at Victor.

"All right, let's put them in Contam-A," Victor said, nodding at the guards.

"Contamination A?" their dad said. "Victor, I really think you should—"

"Don't tell him what he should do," a guard said, shoving him roughly in the chest with the butt of his gun.

The twins' dad sent Victor an affronted look, as if he were expecting him to discipline the guard, but Victor said nothing.

Beacon and Everleigh were shoved through the door. Their dad started to follow, but Victor held up a hand.

"You can return to your command post for a debriefing," Victor said meaningfully. "We want a full accounting of what happened when the kids got away."

"Oh. Of course," their dad said.

Beacon cast a glance back at his dad as he was being shepherded away, but the doors whooshed shut before he could make eye contact.

The guards led Beacon and Everleigh through hall after hall. At first they passed busy office areas buzzing with people and noises and flashing electronic equipment, and then the place thinned out and it was only a handful of curious men and women in business suits who stared at them as they passed. Then the halls emptied entirely, and it was just the kids and their captors. Their footsteps echoed through the craft. Just how big was this thing?

Abruptly, the end of the corridor loomed. They stopped in front of a set of silver doors. One of the guards scanned his badge over an electronic panel on the wall, and the doors slid open to a large white room. They stepped inside.

There were no doors. No windows. No furniture or people. Just walls so bright, he could practically see his own reflection in them. Beacon didn't get it. Where were the other prisoners? Where was the *prison*?

Where was Arthur?

Just as he had this thought, another guard punched something into another panel, and half a dozen cells shimmered into existence. Instead of bars, each cell was made up of clear glass that Beacon was certain would be shatterproof. There were three down either side of the room, with a wide corridor in between. He could see inside the cells to the plain metal bed frame and toilet in each one.

They were all empty.

One of the guards pointed his gun at the twins. Another cut the snap ties binding their arms, then ordered them to put their hands on their heads. They were searched roughly, and then Beacon was pushed into a cell. He whirled around just in time to see Everleigh shoved into a separate cell across the corridor from him. Panic overcame him. He rushed forward after the guard, but the cell door slid closed. He slammed his hands on the glass.

"Don't even *think* about trying anything funny," one guard said, stabbing his finger at him. "And, Arthur?" he added, looking farther down the row of cells. "You try that trick again and you're in for it. No going easy on you next time."

The guards stomped away and scanned their badges over the main panel. The doors swooshed open and closed again.

They were alone.

Beacon ran up to the glass and frantically searched the cells in the direction the guard had spoken. And there, in the farthest cell, tucked into the little space between the bed and the wall, was a boy. He was curled up so small and tight that Beacon hadn't seen him before. His pale white skin hadn't helped, either; he practically blended into the walls.

"Arthur!" Beacon cried.

The boy pushed his head up slowly, as if it took everything in him just to complete that one small act. The skin around his left eye was purple and swollen, and there was blood on the collar of the white jumpsuit he wore. If this was what "going easy on him" looked like, Beacon didn't want to find out what happened when you made the guards mad.

"Hey, Beacon," Arthur said weakly.

"What happened to you?" Beacon cried.

Arthur's fingers came up absently to his cheek. "Had a little disagreement with a guard's fist."

Beacon set his jaw.

"We're getting you out of here," he said.

"Shhh!" Arthur hissed, casting a frantic glance at the doors. It was the most life Beacon had seen in him. He was glad. He'd been starting to worry that whatever the Sov had done to him was permanent.

"Can you walk?" Beacon asked, quieter.

"If I had to," Arthur said.

"Can you run?"

Arthur didn't answer.

"Oh, what does it matter anyway?" Everleigh interrupted. She paced along the short walls of her cell.

"What do you mean?" Beacon said. "The plan is still the same as before." He shot a look at the door, then lowered his voice. "We're still getting out of here."

"You really think Donna's going to come through on her end?" Everleigh said, not bothering to keep quiet. "She's obviously in league with Dad and the rest of the Sov. This was all just a trick to get us to walk back into this place. And it worked, because we're fools." She kicked the bed, then sucked air through her teeth when the steel frame didn't budge.

"He said it would be like this," Beacon said, even though he'd been thinking the same thing. "He warned us."

"Yeah, well, his acting was a little too good, don't you think? They *fell for it*? What was that all about?"

"Would you guys please shut up!" Arthur cried.

"I'm sure Dad wanted to make sure it looked legit," Beacon said, lowering his voice again. "Maybe that's how he got away from the ship in the first place when we stole that pod—by saying he was coming after us."

"Wait, you stole a pod?" Arthur asked. He sat up straighter.

"I know, right?" Beacon grinned.

"Or maybe he's still brainwashed," Everleigh said. "Think about it—who came up with the plan to come back here?"

"I did," Beacon said. And then he remembered. It had actually been their dad's idea. He'd all but spelled it out for him.

A great big pit opened up in Beacon's stomach. It slapped the smile right off his face.

"Uh, what are you doing?" Arthur asked, jolting Beacon from his thoughts. He was looking at Everleigh with alarm plastered all over his face.

"Getting out of here," Everleigh said.

She reared back with all her might and kicked the glass wall. Her boot thudded hard against the clear glass, but it didn't so much as shudder.

She tried again. And again and again and again. She heaved her body against the wall like a linebacker charging an opponent. Then she jumped up onto the bed.

"Don't bother," Arthur said. "I've already tried, and there's no way out of here. You're just going to make them mad."

Everleigh ignored him and stood on her toes, stretching up her arms and feeling along the ceiling for what, Beacon didn't know.

"He'll help us," Beacon said with conviction, even though his insides were roiling. "If Dad meant for us to get caught, then why did he bring us back to the inn? Why not just drive us right back to the elevator? Why did we hide in the garage from the sheriff? It might have been his idea to come back here, but I think—I *know* he's on our side."

But Beacon's surety began to dwindle after the first hour. That didn't stop him from rattling off excuse after excuse for why no one was coming to their rescue: Dad must have been held up in that debriefing Victor mentioned. Donna was just running a little late. There must have been a snafu with her distraction plan—whatever it was. But it wouldn't be too long now! Any minute now and they'd be saved!

By the second hour, he was jumping at every imagined noise

outside the room of cells, desperate for a sign that the plan was going to start up again, even though he was pretty sure the room was soundproof. Both Arthur and Everleigh had long since drifted off to sleep, but he was wide-awake and vigilant.

By the fourth hour, he was kicking the walls, climbing onto the bed in search of a weakness in the ceiling, scouring the floors for a drain they could climb into to forge an underground escape. All he found were three holes in the concrete floor barely big enough for a beetle to scuttle inside, with a red stain he was pretty sure was blood.

By the fifth hour, he couldn't believe how stupid he'd been. He sat curled against the wall with his legs pulled up to his chest and his face buried in his knees to cover the tears that slipped down his face.

"It's okay, Beaks," his sister said quietly.

Beacon startled. He hadn't realized his sister had woken up. He swiped at his wet cheeks.

"No, it's not!" he said thickly, trying to keep his voice down so he didn't wake Arthur. That kid looked like he needed to sleep for about a century. "I never should have brought us here. You were right. It was stupid and dangerous."

"It was brave," she said. "And honorable."

He shook his head. She was just trying to make him feel better. "I'm sorry I asked you to come. I should have done this alone."

"You didn't make me do anything, the last time I checked," Everleigh said. "I wanted to help."

"Still, it was my idea. And now who knows what's going to happen to us."

"Exactly, who knows?" Everleigh said. "I bet they want to make us special ambassadors for human youth. They were just attacking our pod by accident. Victor will be down here any minute to beg for our forgiveness."

Beacon squinted at his sister through the blur of tears.

"Oh yeah," she said brightly. "This prison? Just temporary until they can get our mansion in order. It's real fancy, with pillars and a moat and everything."

A smile wobbled at the corner of his mouth. She was trying to make him smile. Trying to pave over all the bad stuff with relentless optimism, the way Beacon always did.

"I bet they'll hand-feed us grapes," Beacon said.

Everleigh smiled. "Absolutely. That's why they haven't fed us yet. They're getting a feast prepared."

"A whole table overflowing with food. Turkey, mashed potatoes, rhubarb pie," he said. "All of our favorite stuff."

His stomach rumbled. He hadn't realized just how hungry he was until he thought about how long it had been since he had any food.

"I'm sure we'll have someone to follow us around with one of those big fans just in case it gets warm, too," he said. "And someone else just to throw their jacket down over puddles like in the olden days so our shoes don't get wet."

Everleigh threw her head back and laughed. The sound echoed through the room. As it died away, she leaned against the wall. They were across the room from each other, but it felt like a hug.

They still had each other. For now, anyway.

"Listen, Beacon, I wanted to say I'm sorry," Everleigh said. "I know I haven't been very fun to be around this year." She shrugged a bit and wouldn't meet his eyes.

"It's okay," Beacon said.

"It's not, though. I was mean and cranky, and I'm sure it only made you guys feel worse when you were suffering, too. And if it wasn't for me, we wouldn't be here. Dad wouldn't have wanted to enter us into that program."

Beacon was shaking his head.

"It isn't your fault. I know you think it was—I know you blame yourself, for everything," he said meaningfully. "But you didn't know what would happen."

"I don't want to talk about this," Everleigh said, getting up and pacing around the cell.

But Beacon persisted. It had been a year. If they didn't talk about it now, when would they? The secrets and unsaid things would just eat them up inside until there was nothing of the old them left.

"We'd been swimming there a hundred times before and everything was fine. How could you know that this time there would be a current?"

Everleigh swallowed hard.

"But I get it," Beacon continued. "I blamed myself, too. For not being a better swimmer. I should have saved him."

"There's no way you'd have been able to pull him out of that current!" Everleigh said hotly, spinning around. "You can't blame yourself."

Beacon smiled a bit. They were both such hypocrites.

"I'm going to work on it," Beacon said. "Maybe you will, too?"

She nodded. "I've been thinking about it—maybe if we get out of here, I'll talk to that lady Dad wanted us to see."

"The counselor?" Beacon said.

Everleigh flushed, darting a glance at Arthur, who was still fast asleep. "I know, it's stupid."

"No, I think that's an awesome idea," Beacon said. "Maybe I'll come, too."

Everleigh gave a wan smile.

"Anyway, no one can plan how they're going to react when something like this happens," Beacon said. "I don't blame you for how you were this year. You were just trying to get through it, the same as Dad and me. Just differently is all."

"You're too nice to me," Everleigh said.

"Can you say that again a bit louder?" Beacon said, putting his hand to his ear. "I didn't quite hear you."

Everleigh grinned wider. "Love you, Beaks."

"Love you, too," Beacon said.

"This is going to sound weird," Everleigh said, "but I kind of liked this. Spending this time with you. It's the closest to normal I've felt in ages. Like old times, somehow. Even though we're fighting aliens."

"I've kind of liked it, too," Beacon said. "I missed you."

"Too bad our YAT club adventure was so short," she said.

"Our?" Arthur said, sitting up quickly. "Did you join?"

Beacon grinned. He should have known Arthur was just pretending to be asleep.

"Yeah, dude," Beacon said. "We're officially up to three members."

A broad smile split his face.

"Sweet!"

He lay back down, and they lapsed into silence.

After a while, Beacon's eyes grew heavy. He realized it had been ages since he last had a full night's sleep. He was suddenly exhausted. He wanted to stay awake. Alert. Ready at all times, in case help was on the way. But his eyelids were weighted with lead.

Before he knew it, he was inside the dream again. Only it wasn't the same dream. The coral where Jasper normally lay was empty. Fish dived over and under the reef.

Beacon heard a voice. He turned, his movements slow and languid in the water, and there was his brother. Jasper floated above him, his arms and legs spread wide like a starfish and his body backlit in the diffuse glow of the sun. He opened his mouth.

Beacon.

Beacon reached for Jasper, but no matter how hard he swam, his brother floated farther away, moving toward the light.

Jasper's lips were moving. He was trying to say something. Beacon stopped fighting and listened.

Wake up. That's what he was saying.

Wake up. Wake up. WAKE UP.

"Beacon. Beacon, WAKE UP!"

Beacon's eyes fluttered open.

He was steeped in complete darkness. For a brief, frightening moment, he didn't remember where he was. He gasped and sat up, just as a strip of neon emergency lighting flickered on along the edges of the ceiling. The pale outline of the prison came into view. Everleigh was standing with her hands pressed up against the glass. Arthur was sitting up ramrod straight.

An earsplitting alarm wailed through the ship. Beacon scrambled up, instantly awake and alert.

"What's going on?" Beacon asked.

"I don't know," Everleigh said.

Footsteps pounded the ceiling above them, and Beacon thought he could hear the muted sound of raised voices calling to one another. But otherwise, it was frustratingly silent.

Suddenly there was a deep *beep* from the door.

"A guard!" Beacon cried. The kids scrambled away from the door to the back corners of their cells. A guard stood framed in the entrance, his chest heaving in his ill-fitting uniform. It took Beacon a moment to realize that it wasn't just any guard. It was Nixon.

His green cargo pants bunched around his ankles, and his belt, notched on the tightest hole, had at least a foot of extra leather poking out. He looked like a kid playing dress-up. That didn't make him any less frightening. His wide shoulders were tensed and set, and he had his hands curled into fists. Shadows played on the sharp angles of his face.

"What are you *wearing?*" Everleigh asked.

Leave it to his sister to focus on the totally wrong thing.

"What are you doing here?" Beacon asked.

Nixon didn't answer, just stepped into the room. The door whooshed shut behind him. He closed the distance between himself and the cells in two huge, serious strides.

"Don't you dare go near my sister," Beacon yelled at the same time as Everleigh said, "Touch my brother and die." They were both pressed up to the glass.

Nixon stopped in front of Beacon. Up close, the boy towered over him. He hadn't realized just how big Nixon was.

"Our dad works here," Beacon said. "Hurt me, and he'll have you punished. Maybe even killed," he added belatedly.

"Oh yeah? That why you're locked up in Contam?" Nixon said. "Because your dad cares about you so much?"

Touché.

"I'm serious," Everleigh called out. "Hurt my brother, and I will come after you." It didn't seem to matter that it was currently impossible. There was a fiery look in her eyes that Beacon was sure glad he was not on the receiving end of. She looked like she wanted to smash through the glass walls to get to Nixon. And like she might actually be capable of it.

"Victor wants to study us," Arthur said. "If you hurt us, he'll be mad. And trust me, you don't want Victor to be mad."

"Relax," Nixon said dismissively. "I'm not here to hurt you. I'm here to get you out."

He punched something into the digital panel outside Beacon's cell, and the door opened instantly. Beacon stumbled forward. He would have run right into the Gold Star, but Nixon was already walking briskly toward Everleigh's cell. She braced her legs apart, her hands curled into fists and her chest heaving as he punched in the code. Beacon almost asked Nixon if he was sure he wanted to let her out. The girl looked feral.

He stopped at Arthur's cell last. Arthur struggled to his feet like a deer learning to walk for the first time. Nixon was already moving away before the glass had fully disappeared.

"We're going to have to move fast," Nixon said, walking toward the door. None of them followed.

"You got somewhere else to be?" Nixon said. "Because if that's the case . . ." He let his words trail off.

"Why should we trust you?" Arthur said. "You're one of them."

"Because no one else is going to get you out of here," Nixon said.

"You don't know that," Beacon said. "We have a plan."

"Does the plan involve your dad? Because yeah, that's not going to work."

Beacon's heart plummeted into his stomach.

"What did you do to him?" Everleigh said, charging forward. Beacon leaped ahead and put his arm out to stop her.

"I didn't *do* anything," Nixon said. "But Victor's not an idiot. He's got your dad tied up in interrogation and he's not going to let him go until he finds out exactly what you're up to. He's not going to be coming to break you out. Not before Victor gets here, and trust me, you don't want to be here when Victor gets here."

"But what ever happened to helping humans mutate so we can survive the floods?" Beacon asked. "I thought the Sov were supposed to be helping us."

It wasn't as if he'd ever totally believed that. But he needed answers. He felt as if he were floating in the middle of the sea with no life jacket, no help, and no idea which direction was the shore.

Nixon snorted. "Don't tell me you actually believed that." He shook his head. "There is no flood."

Beacon spluttered for words. "No storms?"

"Nothing. The side effects of that antidote? That's the real reason they're shooting us up. They want humans to be 'docile and complacent,' he said, doing air quotes. "They figured out that humans attack them in the future. Kill their people. I guess we learn space travel and decide we like their planet better than the one we've ruined. They don't want to wait around for that to happen, so they're dealing with the problem now."

"Why don't they just kill us?" Arthur said. "If they're so advanced, they could probably do it pretty easily."

Jeez, Arthur. Don't give them any ideas, Beacon thought.

"Don't think they haven't thought about it," Nixon said. "In that timeline, a different war starts up with another alien race—one that doesn't take too kindly to genocide. This way they get to make sure humans never get too smart, *and* they keep the other aliens off their back. Space politics, am I right?" He shook his head.

"Are you an alien, too?" Everleigh asked.

"Do you think I'd be telling you this if I was?" Nixon quirked an eyebrow.

"Then how do you know all this?" Beacon said. "Why would the Sov tell a kid all about their evil master plan?"

"Let's just say you're not the only ones who can figure out sneaky ways to listen in to top secret meetings." Nixon gave Beacon and Arthur a knowing look.

Beacon's cheeks warmed, remembering his grand entrance into the Gold Stars' meeting in the church basement.

"Still, how come you're telling us all this?" Everleigh said. "How come you're helping us?"

Suddenly Beacon remembered Nixon's folder in the nurse's office. The huge list of vitamin injections he'd received.

"You're Off-Program," Beacon said. "The injections—they've been wearing off. That's why you've had so many!"

"Wrong," Nixon said. "Can't be Off-Program if I was never on it to begin with."

Beacon's mouth fell open. He tried to talk, but he couldn't get the words to come out right. "What? So you were just acting this whole time?" he finally managed.

"Yeah, well, I figured out pretty quickly what happens when you don't fall in line around here. But every once in a while I slip up and they jab me again. I act for a bit longer, and the cycle continues."

"So you're immune?" Arthur asked.

"Jealous you're not the only one?" Nixon said.

"No, I mean, of course not," Arthur spluttered.

"Do you think there are more of you?" Beacon asked. "Are more people just pretending?"

"I don't know. I can't exactly ask anyone without tipping them off, can I?" Nixon said heatedly.

"Why doesn't it work on certain people?" Beacon wondered aloud.

"Not sure," Nixon said. "Should I get us some tea? Maybe a nice tray of cookies so we can theorize on this some more? Or do you maybe want to get the heck out of here?"

Nixon punched some numbers into the digital panel next to the main doors, and they slid open soundlessly.

Beacon, Everleigh, and Arthur exchanged a glance.

"Wait, what's the plan?" Everleigh asked.

"There is no plan," Nixon said without turning around.

"What?" all three kids squeaked at the same time.

"How are we going to get out of here?" Beacon said.

"Hope everyone is too distracted by the chaos to notice us leaving," Nixon said. He was halfway down the hall now.

"That's a terrible plan!" Arthur called.

"If you have a better one, by all means, use that one instead."

Beacon, Everleigh, and Arthur gaped at Nixon's retreating back.

The doors began to whoosh closed. Everleigh jumped forward, darting her hand out to grab the doors. But they weren't like elevator doors, which opened if someone walked in their path. They continued to close, nearly crunching her fingers before she got her body in between the doors and propped them open. Her muscles bunched as she struggled to keep the doors open.

"Hurry up!" she cried.

Beacon ducked under his sister's arm, and behind him, Arthur hobbled through. When they were clear, Everleigh leaped out of the way of the doors before they sealed shut.

Nixon was already at the end of the hall.

Beacon put his arm around Arthur's waist and propped him up, shouldering some of his weight, and then all three of them took off after the Gold Star.

They followed Nixon through the dark, barren halls. On their way in, it had seemed as if they'd walked forever without passing a soul, but it didn't take long for voices to come into hearing range. As soon as they did, Nixon gripped Beacon and Everleigh by the backs of their shirts, as if he were hauling off prisoners.

"You—keep up," Nixon barked at Arthur. Arthur nodded, his head ducked into his chest as he scurried along next to the others. The boy seemed to be limping more than he had before.

It wasn't much of a cover, but it worked. No one was paying much attention to them at all. The place was in utter chaos. People ran through the darkened ship, bumping into one another and calling out desperate commands. Beacon wanted to run, too—in fact, his muscles twitched with the urge to bolt—but that would have looked too suspicious.

They were passing the mouth of what looked to be the ship's headquarters when all of a sudden, the overhead lights switched on. Beacon blinked against the brightness. They were standing in the brightly lit command center of the alien ship, surrounded by Sov.

"What's going on?" Arthur whispered frantically.

The Sov didn't seem to know, either. People spoke into radios and wireless headsets and looked around with big question marks on their faces.

"My guess is they figured out I set off those alarms," Nixon said. "I thought it would buy us more time."

Beacon's stomach clenched hard.

"What now?" Everleigh asked in a squeaky voice.

Any moment now they would be recognized.

"Just keep walking," Nixon said out of the side of his mouth.

A cold sweat broke out on Beacon's skin. His chest was so tight, he could barely breathe as he went with Nixon down the corridor. They weren't invisible anymore. Several pairs of eyes landed and rested on them as they passed. A woman wearing a black skirt suit and a wireless headset squinted at Arthur before speaking in rushed tones into her headset.

"We need to hide," Nixon whispered.

He used his ID badge to swipe into a surgical suite. The four of them slipped inside. The walls were circled with windows, and they had to crouch down and flatten themselves against the wall so the people—the aliens—walking past just feet away wouldn't see them.

"We're trapped!" Arthur squeaked.

"It'll all be okay," Everleigh said. "We just need to let things calm down for a minute."

"No, I think he's right. We're totally screwed," Nixon said.

A voice came through the radio at Nixon's belt. Beacon couldn't understand the commands, but he heard the names Beacon, Everleigh, and Arthur.

They'd discovered their empty cells.

"Okay, forget about waiting," Everleigh said.

She reached for the door handle.

"Wait!" Beacon cried. "I have an idea."

The others followed his gaze to a medical cart pushed up against the wall.

"Good idea. We'll need weapons," Everleigh said.

"No," Beacon said. "We need to get *inside* the cart. They're looking for three kids. They won't look twice at a guard pushing a cart down the hall."

The cart didn't look big enough for one of them, let alone three. But they didn't have any better ideas, so the kids scurried around the perimeter of the room. Everleigh whipped open the doors of the cart, pulled out the plastic-wrapped packages contained inside, and climbed in. Arthur climbed in next, and then Beacon squeezed in the front. Or tried to, anyway. No matter how he contorted himself or how small he tried to make his body, he couldn't get the door to latch.

"Move over!" he cried.

"I'm over as far as I can go," Everleigh said.

"I can't get the door closed."

"You're not trying hard enough!"

"I think I liked you better when you were a Gold Star," Beacon muttered.

"Ha ha, so funny. I'm crying laughing," Everleigh said. "Move over. Let me try." Everleigh heaved on the door. Beacon yelped as the metal dug into his leg.

"Oh yeah, this seems like a great idea," Nixon muttered.

"We're just going to have to hold it closed," Arthur said.

"Oh, hello there!" Nixon said suddenly. It was said loudly enough that Beacon knew that it was for their benefit—they were no longer alone. Inside the cart, they fell instantly still and silent.

"On Victor's orders," Nixon said. The cart rumbled underneath them. Through the crack in the door, Beacon saw a flash of green as they passed a guard. Once they were in the hall, Nixon spun the cart around so that the doors were facing his body. Anybody who looked closely would be able to see that there was something hidden inside, but he hoped it would at least conceal them a bit better.

Beacon's leg was cramped and twisted unnaturally, and soon, a hot, prickling sensation traveled up it. Before long, he couldn't feel his leg at all. But it was working. Minutes passed, and no one stopped them.

"You! Where are you going with that cart?" The clear, commanding voice made Beacon's back go stiff.

"On Victor's orders," he heard Nixon say.

"You just wait a minute while I check with Victor."

"That's not necessary," Nixon said.

There was a strained pause before the guard said, "What do you have in that cart? Let me have a look."

It was game over.

"Run!" Nixon said.

Beacon, Everleigh, and Arthur wriggled out of the cart, numb limbs immediately forgotten.

"Stop those kids!" someone shouted.

And then they were running flat out. Even Arthur was running like he meant it. Beacon figured he just needed to get his muscles moving again. Or to be threatened with death.

It took Beacon a moment to realize where he was, but then he saw the moving walkway built into the floor. They were in the tunnel leading back to the docks. So close to escaping.

Nixon sped forward. Everleigh sprinted behind him, her ponytail flying out as she leaped onto the belt with barely a stutter in her step.

Beacon jumped onto the belt next. Unlike his sister, he landed with a wobble before he finally got his footing. Behind him, he heard a little surprised yelp before Arthur appeared at his side.

He smelled briny water and fish, and knew the elevator to the docks must be close.

For a moment, Beacon hoped there wouldn't be any guards here— that they'd all converged on the ship when they heard the alarms going off. But that hope was extinguished as the end of the corridor loomed.

A guard stood in front of the elevator, his legs braced apart and his arm raised up and trained right at them. There was something bulky and metallic strapped to his wrist. Beacon didn't have time to wonder what it was before a whirring, buzzing noise filled the corridor. Two thin cylinders whizzed up from either side of the metal device, locking into place above it with a jarring *snap-snap* sound. Blue beams of light glowed to life inside the cylinders.

"Stop right there," the guard said.

18

Nixon's footsteps stuttered. He raised his hands in surrender. Everleigh followed suit, then Beacon and Arthur. They all held their hands in the air as they glided slowly toward the guard. Beacon's heart banged in his chest. They'd been so close. So close, and one single guard was going to stop them.

Desperate ideas raged through his head, but it was useless. They might as well have been baitfish in a bucket. They were trapped.

"Don't move an inch," the guard commanded. Which seemed stupid considering they were on a moving conveyor belt. He kept the weapon trained on them while he brought a radio to his lips.

Beacon saw movement cross his vision. Before he knew what was happening, Everleigh had rolled across the ground like some kind of desert commando. The guard reacted quickly, dropping the radio and locking his arms out in front of him like he meant business as he tracked Everleigh's movements. Twin blue laser beams snapped out of the cylinders, once, twice, three times, landing just inches from Everleigh on the concrete floor. The ground sizzled where the lasers struck. His sister rolled up behind the guard, wrapped a forearm around his neck, and grabbed a baton from his belt. She fumbled with the thing for a split second before she depressed a button in its side; the baton shuddered hard, nearly rattling right out of her hand with its electric charge. When she got a good grip on it, a big smile stretched across her face.

"Neat. I wondered what that button did," Everleigh said.

The guard started to move. Everleigh pointed the baton at him, whip fast; the air still fizzed around the wand. A direct hit with that thing would probably knock a person flat for days. The guard looked at the baton as if he was thinking the same thing—and wondering if he could dodge her fast enough to escape.

"Don't even think about it," Everleigh said. She'd dropped her false, cheery tone to one so low and dangerous, it made even Beacon shake in his boots.

The guard kept still, except for his chest, which rose and fell with his quick, shallow breaths. His eyes were as round as dinner plates.

"Take off the wrist thing," Everleigh ordered. When he hesitated, she poked the baton into his belly. "Do it slow, and no funny business or I'll drop you with this thing."

She sounded like she would do it, too. Beacon shuddered.

The guard released the straps, then slid the device off his wrist.

"Drop it," Everleigh said.

Again, hesitation. She sighed and dug in the baton. The guard took a quick breath and dropped the weapon. It landed with a clatter as it hit the concrete floor, breaking into two pieces. Everleigh kicked the bulk of it down the corridor without moving her eyes from the guard. Beacon and Arthur leaped out of the way of the skidding weapon.

"Go," Everleigh ordered Beacon, Arthur, and Nixon.

Nixon started to run, then stopped when no one followed. "Come on," he said. "Before they send backup!"

"I'm not leaving without Everleigh," Beacon said, rooting himself to the spot.

"You think I'm sticking around this place?" she said. "I'll be right behind you."

"No way," Beacon said, shaking his head.

"Oh, come on!" Nixon cried, throwing his hands up. "This is our chance to escape!"

"*You* can leave anytime you want," Beacon snapped. "I'm not going anywhere without my sister."

"Me neither," Arthur said. "Well, she's not my sister, but you get the point."

Raised voices echoed from down the hall.

The guard let out a quiet grunt.

"W-what's happening?" Arthur cried.

All at once, the guard's bones shrunk; his jawline slimmed, and his entire face structure transformed; bright blond hair sprouted and curled from his head, and pink fingernails pushed through delicate, white fingers.

One minute, the guard was a thirty-year-old man. The next, a twelve-year-old girl.

Beacon and Arthur screamed, scrabbling backward. Everleigh gasped. Even Nixon's dark skin went pale. Despite all of his inside information and bravado, it was clear he'd never seen a Sov transform so quickly before. Maybe he hadn't even known they could transform this way.

"Holy cow," Arthur whispered.

Jane breathed hard and fast, her panicked blue eyes darting to the baton.

"You have to help me," she begged the boys.

"Y-you're not Jane," Beacon said. But he didn't sound so sure. She looked like Jane. How did she do that?

"What do you mean? Of course I am," the girl said.

"No. You're a Sov!" Everleigh shot back.

"Please don't hurt me," Jane begged Everleigh. "I thought we were friends."

She leveled a meek, pleading look at Everleigh. When his sister's grip on her slackened, Jane used the distraction to slip free and reach for the baton. She was lightning fast, but Everleigh jerked her hand back and retrained the weapon right at the girl. Betrayal blazed in Everleigh's eyes.

"Hands up, or I'll do it!" Everleigh ordered darkly. "Don't test me."

A slow smile curled Jane's lips.

She transformed again. In front of them stood Victor. Steely fury rippled across his face. Instead of the shirt with the sleeves casually rolled up, he now wore an intimidating black suit and matching black tie, knotted tight around his thick neck. A small part of Beacon's brain that wasn't freaking out noted how the Sov was able to shift its clothes too.

"Give me the baton," he ordered. His tone was calm, but it made a frisson of fear spike up Beacon's back. Arthur moved behind him. Based on his friend's injuries, he didn't blame the guy.

"No," Everleigh said.

"Stop her," he commanded Nixon, jutting his chin at Everleigh.

There was a small pause before Nixon stood up taller and said, "No."

His voice was thin and reedy. Nixon had told the twins that Victor wasn't someone to be messed with, and he'd meant it. Maybe he knew from firsthand experience, the same way Arthur did.

"I'll put you back on the program."

Nixon snorted. "Is that the best you can do?"

Victor's eyes narrowed dangerously.

He shifted again.

Beacon gasped, the air instantly getting sucked out of his chest.

Jasper stood a foot taller than Everleigh. If it weren't for the softness he still held in his cheeks and the awkward way he carried his body, you might have thought he was a man. Wide brown eyes met Beacon's.

"Hey, little brother," he said.

Beacon stepped forward involuntarily, but a hand grabbed his wrist. Arthur shook his head.

"It's not him," Everleigh breathed. Though her eyes didn't leave Jasper, and tears slipped down her cheeks.

"That's a mean thing to say about your favorite brother, Leigh," Jasper said.

A pained look washed over Everleigh's face. No one called her Leigh but Jasper. When he died, the nickname died, too.

Beacon fought the intense urge to reach out and touch him, just to see if he was real. But then his brother smiled at him, and all of the fight inside Beacon shook loose. The rational part of his brain knew it wasn't Jasper. His brother was in a graveyard across the country. But he wanted to believe.

"I missed you," Beacon said. "So much."

And he did. He missed his booming, infectious laugh. His bad jokes, and the way he'd always forget the punch line. He missed finding him buried underneath the car, torso out, fixing this or that. He missed him doing homework at the kitchen table, eating cereal on the couch, listening to music flopped down across his bed. He missed hearing him move around the house, seeing his car in the driveway and his shoes in the porch, always twelve feet apart and upside down because he'd launched them off his feet like missiles. He missed having Honey Nut Cheerios in the pantry, and he missed going down that aisle in the grocery store without biting his lip until it bled so that he wouldn't cry. Most of all, he missed the time when he didn't know what it was like to miss someone with your whole heart.

"Hey, don't be sad, little brother," Jasper said. "I'm right here."

"Are you real?" Beacon asked, his voice a whisper.

"Course I am." He smiled the way Jasper did, where only one side of his mouth moved and a dimple popped up in his cheek.

"You can't be real," Everleigh said. But she sounded like she was trying to convince herself.

"Put the weapon down, Leigh," Jasper said, good-naturedly.

"Don't do it," Nixon said.

Everleigh shook her head. "I'm sorry, Jasper. I can't do it."

Jasper looked at Nixon and let out a little laugh, half-disbelieving, half-dismissive. "Who's this guy? You're going to listen to him instead of me?"

Beacon had never heard his brother be even halfway rude to someone. But then again, he'd never seen his brother have an alien weapon pointed at him, either.

"If you're really Jasper, then what's my favorite car?" Everleigh challenged.

Jasper smiled. "You don't have a favorite. You love them all."

Everleigh's eyes were impossibly bright.

Boots thundered down the corridor. Nixon shot a panicked look down the tunnel. His mouth set into a grim, determined line. He turned to face the others.

"Leave Driftwood Harbor," he said. "Don't stop until you get to the next county. And listen: There's an invisible force field around this town that runs through the forest and up around the highway. It messes with your mind, discourages exit. You just have to be strong, okay? You have to want it. Push past the doubt."

"I knew it!" Arthur cried. "I knew there was something wrong with that forest."

The time slips, Beacon realized. They had happened near the perimeter of town. Could they have been side effects of the alien technology? An unexpected rush of relief washed through him. He'd been starting to think he was losing his mind.

A streak of movement jerked Beacon from his thoughts. Nixon ducked, spun, and before Everleigh could react, grabbed the guard's discarded wrist device from the floor and pointed it straight at Everleigh.

"Drop the baton," he ordered as he strapped the device to his wrist without breaking his aim.

"What is this? What are you doing?" Everleigh cried. Beacon and Arthur screamed at Nixon to put the weapon down, but he didn't budge. Didn't blink. Didn't waver for even a second.

"Drop the baton," Nixon repeated.

Everleigh's jaw tensed with fury. "That thing's broken anyway," she said.

In reply, Nixon pressed a button on the device. The two blue lasers winked to life inside the cylinders.

"Drop the baton," Nixon repeated.

Everleigh gritted her teeth. The baton landed on the concrete floor with a dull thud.

"Now take a step back," Nixon commanded.

"What?" she said.

"Just do what I say," he said. *"Please."*

Maybe it was the pleading tone, but Everleigh stepped back. The moment she moved, Nixon scooped up the baton and jumped behind Jasper, retraining the baton on him.

"What are you doing?" Beacon asked breathlessly.

"I'm making you escape," Nixon said, "because apparently none of you will do it unless I force you."

Understanding dawned on them. He was sacrificing himself.

"Come with us," Everleigh said.

"They'll kill you," Arthur added.

"They'll reprogram me," he corrected. "Now go. I mean it. I'll hurt you."

It was clear from his tone that there was no way he'd do it, but it was the permission they needed. They started for the elevator.

But it was too late.

The Sov had arrived.

The kids stepped back from the approaching army of green and black. Light glinted off the guards' myriad weapons. Not just batons and wrist lasers, but guns. Big, menacing-looking guns. Beacon's heart stuttered.

Leading the charge next to Victor—the real Victor—was the twins' dad.

For half a second, Beacon expected his dad to break away from them, or to reveal that he'd somehow convinced the others to come to their side. But the guards ground to a halt, weapons up and trained on the kids, and his dad stayed firmly behind the guards' line of protection.

He caught sight of Jasper, and his eyes went wide. The color leached from his face. "J-Jasper?" he said. He wobbled slightly, as if he were going to pass out. Beacon hated his dad right now, but he couldn't stand that look on his face. Couldn't stand knowing that his dad thought the impossible had somehow happened, and his son was back.

"It's not him," Beacon said. "It's a Sov, trying to trick us into staying."

"Aw, come on, Beaks. I thought we talked about that?" Jasper said with a wry smile.

Their dad took a steeling breath. He couldn't stop looking at Jasper.

"Deal with them," Victor commanded.

Their dad blinked hard, then shook his head, as if clearing it. He stepped forward hesitantly, one hand held out, as if he were approaching a wild animal. Beacon didn't fail to notice that he wasn't looking at Jasper anymore. Maybe he couldn't.

"Don't do anything stupid, okay?" he told the twins.

"You mean like throwing your own kids to the wolves?" Everleigh snapped.

"It's not like that," he said. "This program is to protect you."

"Oh, yeah, I feel super safe right now," Beacon said, gesturing at all the guns pointed at them. "Thanks for that, Dad. What, you didn't get enough with losing one kid?"

Their dad winced. And despite everything, Beacon winced, too.

"We just want to talk to you," their dad said.

Beacon snorted. "Talk to you. Is that a metaphor for 'stab you with a needle'?"

"Yeah, I've had a few 'conversations' with you guys," Arthur said. The bruise on his cheek looked purpler than ever.

"If you come with us, you won't get hurt. I promise you that," their dad said.

"Not happening," Everleigh said.

"This is stupid, Everleigh. Where do you think you're going

to go, huh? It's five o'clock. The sun's going down, it's going to be dark soon. You'll be all alone, with an entire army of Sov and the government chasing after you. You wouldn't make it halfway to that diner with the crinkle-cut fries before we found you. If you come with us, tomorrow will be a whole new day."

Beacon squinted. He'd never heard his dad speak so phonily before. He sounded like he was reading lines from a made-for-TV action movie.

"Just go," Nixon ordered, cutting into his thoughts.

Beacon's legs felt made of rubber. How could he leave? His dad was here. His brother—there was so much to say.

But Jasper wasn't really here, and their dad had betrayed them.

He backed up, and the others followed suit.

"Leaving so soon?" Jasper said, his head swiveling to follow him. "Come on, pal. We haven't even had a chance to catch up."

Beacon's heart clenched so hard, it hurt.

"I love you," Beacon said.

"Love me? You're leaving me." Jasper's voice had taken on an angry edge. Beacon looked away. He wanted to say goodbye—he'd never had the chance before—but his brother was long gone.

"My favorite is a seventy-three Triumph," Everleigh said on the way past. "Jasper would have known that."

Beacon, Everleigh, and Arthur got inside the elevator.

"You're making a big mistake!" their dad yelled. Victor screamed at them to stop. Guards poised their weapons.

"Don't come closer, or I'll shoot!" Nixon said. He grabbed Jasper around his neck to keep him in place, angling himself behind his body.

The elevator doors slid closed with a *ping*. Everleigh clapped a hand over her mouth. Tears slipped down Beacon's cheeks. He didn't bother to wipe them away. Arthur just stared at the floor, a shell-shocked expression on his face.

The ride up was quiet. All Beacon wanted to do was curl up in a ball. Fold into himself. Feel his dad's arms around him telling him that it would all be okay. He kept having to remind himself that his dad wasn't on their side anymore.

The elevator shuddered to a stop. As soon as the doors opened and the fresh, wet air hit his lungs, he flipped a switch. He couldn't be sad right now. He just had to be fast.

The kids ran out. Beacon desperately searched the dark harbor for Donna's truck amid all the Sov vehicles, before he remembered that she probably wasn't on their side. He felt an unexpected rush of anger. He didn't know why her betrayal hit him so hard—maybe it was just because it was finally sinking in that you could really only trust yourself.

Everleigh grabbed Beacon's hand and jerked him forward. They ran over the pebbly shore, their feet slipping and sliding on the wet rocks.

Beacon saw a beam of yellow light.

"Get down," Everleigh ordered. The three of them crouched behind a sandbar, just as a flashlight beam roved over their heads.

The shed door banged open behind them. They ducked low, close to the ground. Barely breathed. The pier crawled with guards and black vans with darkly tinted windows.

"Look!" Beacon whispered.

He pointed at the shore. Dozens of squid creatures were rising out of the water, giant tentacles moving unnaturally fast over the rocks.

"What the heck are those?" Arthur squeaked.

"You don't want to know," Everleigh whispered. "We've got to get out of here. Fast." She scoured the scene, her eyes locking on a slope of grass a few yards away. "That hill, over there," she said, nodding. "Right after these guys pass."

They kept still, their breaths held tight as a squid creature slurped past, its tentacles sending up enormous puffs of sand in its wake.

"Now," Everleigh said.

She popped up and scrambled up the hill. Beacon and Arthur skidded to a stop behind her. The three of them ducked and dived and ran, hardly breathing until they were clear of the harbor. And then they ran more. They ran until their legs shook and they couldn't do it anymore. They bent over behind the trunk of a huge pine tree, catching their breath, wheezing in harsh, short gasps. In the near distance, pale sunlight struggled through clouds, cresting over the peaked roofs of Driftwood Harbor proper.

"What do we do now?" Beacon asked.

Everleigh sank down hard and buried her face in her hands. "I don't know. We're trapped."

The words came out strangled and thick. Beacon realized that she was crying. Not a few elegant tears, but big, ugly, hiccuping gulps that came from deep inside her.

Beacon had never seen his sister cry like this. Seeing her so out of control made him feel unmoored, like a sailboat rocking hard in rough waters.

"It's okay, Ev," he said, rubbing her back. "We'll figure something out."

"How?" She looked up from between her fingers. Her eyes were puffy and bloodshot, and there was snot running from her nose into her mouth. "Dad's gone, Jasper's gone. We're all alone."

Beacon fought hard to control the frenzied beating of his heart. It couldn't be true. And yet, all of what she said held the ring of truth.

They were all alone in the world. In a world scarier and more dangerous than he'd ever thought possible. Where everything he thought he knew was wrong, where everyone he loved left him.

He thought back to his dad, his face twisted with anger. It was so unlike him that Beacon was beginning to think he'd never known him at all. How much of it was a lie? he wondered. When did it start?

When Jasper died? Or before that? Had he been pretending this whole time? Had he ever really cared?

He must have, he thought. But then he kept turning over his dad's words in that tunnel again and again. He wanted to believe him, but his words spoke for themselves. *You wouldn't make it halfway to that diner before we found you.* No, not the diner. *That diner with the crinkle-cut fries.* Beacon snorted derisively. That was a stupid thing to say. Why hadn't he just said "the Home Sweet Home diner" or "the diner we stopped at on the way here," or even just "the diner on the highway"?

He frowned suddenly. His dad was so particular. So methodical. He never said anything before he carefully thought out his words, mapped it all out in his head. Beacon went over his dad's words again. Tried to remember everything this time. *Where do you think you're going to go, huh? It's five o'clock. The sun's going down, it's going to be dark soon. You'll be all alone, with an entire army of Sov and the government chasing after you. You wouldn't make it halfway to that diner with the crinkle-cut fries before we found you. If you come with us, tomorrow will be a whole new day.*

"Everleigh. Dad didn't betray us," Beacon said.

"I know I've called you a lot of names this year, but I never thought you were this dumb," Everleigh grumbled. "How much more evidence do you need?"

"Sorry, dude, but I'm with her," Arthur said.

"Remember what he said back there?" Beacon went on. "He said we wouldn't make it to the diner with the crinkle-cut fries before they found us. He said it's five p.m., but it's only four thirty, and that was at least half an hour ago. He said tomorrow would be another day. He didn't say the name of the diner so no one else would know where we were meeting, but he said the thing about the crinkle-cut fries so we'd know!"

Everleigh lifted her head. Wet strands of hair were clinging to her flushed cheeks. Her eyes were red and glossy from crying, but there was something else there, too. Hope.

"Think about it—have you ever heard Dad talk like that before? It was definitely a clue! He wants us to meet him at that diner at five o'clock tomorrow! We'll meet up and then go to the next county over—you heard what Victor said: The state police over there are all over their butts. They'll help us blow this whole alien thing out of the water."

"That sounds great and everything," Arthur said. "Except for one small problem. How are we going to get there?"

Everleigh stood up, a grin tugging at her lips.

"We'll drive there, obviously."

19

"Hurry up," Beacon said.

Beacon was huddled in the passenger seat of the 1968 Mercury Cougar while Everleigh crouched beneath the steering wheel. She had the front panel off and was peeling back wires and twisting others together, muttering to herself. She'd been working on it for the last ten minutes, and Beacon was pretty sure it wasn't possible for his heart to race any faster.

"We're so going to get caught," Arthur said from the back seat. "I don't like this. I don't like this at all." He was rocking back and forth like he was on an amusement park ride.

Beacon looked over his shoulder. Just feet away, through the wire fence, he could see the residents of Driftwood Harbor walking up and down the cobbled path of the main square. To the casual observer, it was a peaceful scene in a beautiful small town. But Beacon knew better. He saw the mother tying her daughter's shoelaces on the bench, while casting a glance underneath it. He saw the fishermen rigging their boats, while also checking every place where three twelve-year-old kids might hide. He saw the new faces taking a stroll near the marina when new faces were ultrarare, their eyes a bit too wide and alert.

They were looking for them.

"Please hurry!" Arthur said.

"I'm going as fast as I can."

"Well, go faster!" Beacon said.

"Trust me," Everleigh replied. "When I get this thing going, no one's going to catch up to us."

Beacon bobbed his knee impatiently as she worked. Finally, there was a deep, throaty rumble as the engine roared to life, the seat vibrating underneath him.

"Yes!" Arthur cheered. "I never doubted you!"

Everleigh rolled her eyes as she popped up and adjusted her seat. Beacon tried not to worry about the fact that her feet barely reached the pedals as he buckled his seat belt.

Everleigh slid the gearshift into drive. The car jerked forward, then stopped abruptly as Everleigh slammed on the brakes. Beacon braced his hands on the dash, his eyes bulging.

"Sorry," Everleigh said. "She's touchy."

She tried again; this time, the car eased shakily forward.

"Oh God," Arthur said.

"Relax," Everleigh said. "It's going to be fine."

"Hey!" a voice called out.

The mechanic was leaning out the door of the shop, his face red and twisted with rage; a cigarette dangled from his lips. He charged toward the car.

"Lay on it!" Beacon cried.

Everleigh slammed on the gas, and Beacon flattened against the seat. They crashed through the fence.

Beacon and Arthur twisted to look behind them. The mechanic was standing in the middle of the street, glowering as a crowd of onlookers gathered around him.

"Holy smokes, did you see that?" Arthur screeched, his voice breaking. "That was the coolest thing I've ever done!"

"Save the celebrations for when we get out of this town," Everleigh said.

Without warning, the clouds broke open and it began to rain. The misty type of rain that you couldn't see falling but that drenched you in an instant. More clouds rolled in above them, the sky darkening to a dangerous slate gray. Thunder rumbled overhead.

There was a red sedan at the stop sign in front of them. It should have been moving along by the time they approached, but it didn't budge, despite there being no traffic. Everleigh honked the horn, and the driver rolled down her window and stuck out her head.

"I'm sorry! My engine doesn't seem to be working. Do you think you can call the tow truck for me? I don't have a cell phone." The woman sent them a pleading look, her bottom lip wobbling slightly.

Everleigh's eyes narrowed. She revved the engine and peeled around the car.

"Everleigh!" Beacon cried, twisting back to look at the woman. "You could have at least said something!"

"You really think her car was broken down?" Everleigh said without taking her eyes off the road. "Think about it, Beacon. She just saw a bunch of kids driving a car and she didn't say *anything* about it? She didn't even look surprised?"

Beacon felt a tingly sensation in his head. She was right.

The rain began falling in earnest. The windshield wipers whipped over the glass in a wild streak of water. Blurred red taillights shone from the next stop sign up ahead.

Lo and behold, there was a car stalled lengthwise in the middle of the road. A woman stood next to the open hood, a crying baby on her hip. Her hair and clothes were plastered against her body as she uselessly shielded herself against the onslaught. She hailed them as they passed.

A baby? They were good.

"Who knew car troubles were contagious," Arthur said.

There was a loud *thunk* as Everleigh hopped the curb, the car tilting dangerously as she drove half on, half off the sidewalk. She sped past the diversion.

The third time, there was a woman in a neon vest and hard hat holding up a giant stop sign in front of a dump truck and backhoe that blocked the entire four-way stop. Behind her, two construction workers called to each other over an open sewer drain spewing smoke. But Beacon knew better than to think this wasn't happening on purpose. The Sov had clearly planned for something like this.

Everleigh slammed on the brakes and laid on the horn with the heel of her hand. The woman frowned, and Beacon gasped.

"Mrs. Miller?" Beacon squeaked.

"Who?" Everleigh said.

"That's—that's my teacher," Beacon said.

What was she doing here? Was she even a real teacher?

A crawly feeling churned inside his gut.

There was no way around.

Beacon sent a panicked look behind them. A procession of black vans was twisting up the street toward them like ants on the scent of a discarded meal.

"We have trouble!" Arthur cried.

Everleigh scowled into the rearview mirror, then jerked the gearshift into reverse. They screeched back, careening madly toward the vans. Everleigh slammed on the brakes at the previous stop sign—the woman and her baby were gone—and then cranked the steering wheel to the left. The tires spun on the wet pavement for a frustrating moment before finally gaining purchase. They flew forward, the car's back end fishtailing.

They blew through town, passing drowning orchards and fields of soggy yellow grass. They were going so fast that there were times the tires weren't even touching the pavement. Beacon couldn't help thinking about how little experience Everleigh had driving, and what would happen to them if they crashed. He heard the earsplitting bang of metal, felt the horrifying crunch of bones breaking. A nauseous feeling roiled through him. He got the impression Arthur was feeling the same way, based on the little whimpers he was making.

He wanted to tell Everleigh to slow down, but speed was all that mattered right now.

That's what he told himself as they tore down the interstate, away from Driftwood Harbor.

The car slowed.

"What are you doing?" Beacon asked, leaning forward.

"I . . . think we should go back," Everleigh said.

"*What?*" Beacon and Arthur cried at the same time.

"This is a bad idea," she said.

"Are you nuts?" Beacon said.

"We need to get out of here before . . ." Arthur's voice trailed off. "I forget what I was going to say."

Beacon opened his mouth to tell Everleigh that they needed to go, but he suddenly couldn't remember why they needed to leave.

20

The answer floated just out of reach in Beacon's mind. The harder he tried to grasp it, the more impossible it seemed. It was as if there were a layer of dust covering everything in his head.

He frowned.

"I'm turning around," Everleigh said. The car shuddered as she pulled over onto the gravelly embankment on the side of the road.

Beacon's heart jackknifed in his chest. They couldn't stop. He didn't know how he knew. All he knew was that this was wrong. They had to drive. It was a matter of life and death.

"We need to keep going," Beacon said.

"Why?" Everleigh asked.

He wasn't sure. But he was sure that Everleigh would never accept that answer.

"Just trust me, okay?"

"I want to go home," Arthur said.

"I'm sorry, but that's not happening," Beacon told him.

Arthur leaned forward against his seat belt. "No, I mean it. I really, really need to go home. My grandma will be worried. It's been days since she's seen me."

"We have to go back, Beaks," Everleigh agreed.

"No," Beacon said firmly.

"We'll just drop him off, then." Everleigh started to turn the car around.

Beacon jerked the wheel to the right, and the car skidded back onto the road.

"What the heck!" Everleigh screeched, pushing his hand away.

"Stop the car," Arthur said, his voice getting louder, more frantic. "I want to get out."

"Don't stop the car," Beacon ordered.

"I said stop the car!" Arthur's booming voice made Beacon's shoulders hunch up around his ears.

Everleigh tapped on the brake. Beacon panicked.

He jumped into the driver's seat, landing right on his sister's lap. He slammed on the gas pedal. The car jolted forward, blasting them back against their seats. Everleigh screamed, shoving Beacon. He shoved back. The car wove dangerously across the road, a blur of green and gray outside the windows.

"You're going to kill us!" Everleigh screamed.

Beacon heard a click. He stopped. Looked into the back seat. Arthur was hanging out of the door, preparing to leap. Wind whipped at his jumpsuit, the pavement flying underneath the tires.

"Arthur!" Beacon cried. He scrambled after Arthur. His jeans got caught in the gearshift and he tripped, landing facedown on the back seat. He shot up and reached for the back of Arthur's jumpsuit at the exact same moment as Arthur let go. For a horrifying moment, Arthur was suspended in the air. But then Beacon's fingers closed around the fabric of the jumpsuit and he jerked hard. The boy folded backward like a camping chair, landing on top of Beacon and knocking the air out of him.

Suddenly Everleigh screamed. The car swerved left. The boys rolled, nearly toppling out of the open car door as it whipped around on its hinges. And then Everleigh slammed on the brakes. Tires squealed, and they went flying forward.

Beacon slammed into the back of the driver's seat.

And then: silence.

White spots danced in Beacon's vision. He tasted copper in his mouth. His brain felt like it had done a few rounds with an eggbeater.

Sound came slowly funneling back. Rain pattered gently on the roof, over the sound of their coarse breathing and the quiet ding reminding them to wear their seat belts.

Beacon groaned, rubbing his head. Next to him, Arthur patted the floor until he found his glasses. In the front seat, Everleigh stared out the windshield, a streak of blood running down her temple.

"Everleigh, you're bleeding!" Beacon said.

Everleigh touched her head, then examined her fingers with mild, fleeting interest.

"I'm fine. Just a little cut. Are you okay? Does your head hurt? Is anyone injured?" She peered into the back seat.

"Just emotionally scarred," Arthur said, sliding on his glasses.

Beacon blew out a slow breath, trying to calm the frantic pace of his heart. What had just happened?

Soon, he had his answer. He felt the fog over his brain slowly lift, like a strong wind had cleared it away. It was like waking up from a very vivid dream, where you're not sure what's real for the first few moments. But then reality shifts into place, and you can hardly remember the dream at all.

That's when he saw it. The thing they had almost hit. A sign, jutting up from the side of the road.

Wishart County.

The invisible force field. They'd just crossed it.

For a long moment, they all sat there, watching steam hiss out of the engine into the gray sky. Beacon didn't want to think about how close they'd come to just driving back into the arms of their enemies. The fact that the Sov had that kind of power over the town, over *them*, was such a monumentally frightening thought that Beacon could barely wrap his mind around it.

"Well, what do we do now?" Everleigh asked.

They were three kids, alone in the world, with an alien race and quite possibly their own government after them.

"Now, we go home," Beacon said.

21

Beacon, Everleigh, and Arthur watched the Home Sweet Home diner through the fogged-up windshield of the Mercury Cougar. Washed-out against the overcast sky, the tiny diner hunched in on itself like a delicate bird weathering a storm. A neon sign flashed the word *OPEN* from the glass of a rain-splattered door. There was a handful of cars parked outside. Beacon didn't recognize any of them, but that didn't mean anything. Any one of them could have been borrowed or rented or stolen by their dad so he could get here.

That's what Beacon told himself as he stepped out of the car and walked toward the diner.

A bell jangled as they entered. The smell of bacon and eggs wafted out at them. Beacon scanned the dimly lit diner.

An elderly couple sat side by side in a booth, studiously cutting their food. At the counter, a man watched a tiny mounted TV as he sipped amber liquid from a sweating tumbler. Otherwise, the place was empty.

"It's okay," Beacon said. "It's still early. Dad said five, and it's only ten after."

He didn't know who he was trying to convince, Everleigh or himself.

The kids sank into a booth by the window.

The waitress's ponytail swished from side to side like a happy dog's tail as she approached their booth.

The bacon-and-eggs smell hit him again, and Beacon's belly rumbled like a diesel truck. It felt wrong to be hungry right now, in the face of everything, but he couldn't remember the last time he'd had a proper meal.

"Welcome to Home Sweet Home," the waitress said, plopping down three plastic-wrapped menus onto the table. "Can I get you kids something to drink?"

"Water, please. Three of them. And we don't need these," Everleigh said, sliding the menus back. "Just bring us whatever is quickest, and a side of crinkle-cut fries."

The waitress frowned. "Anything in particular?"

"Just not seafood," Beacon said. "I never want to see lobster again in my life."

"Okay . . ." The waitress grabbed the menus and walked away, sneaking a glance back over at them.

The sound of dishes clanking and clattering came into focus. From the kitchen they heard the hiss of a deep fryer.

"So, hypothetically, if Dad doesn't show up," Everleigh said, "what then? Where do we go?"

"It's like we said before," Beacon said, "somehow we get ourselves to LA. Aunt Deb and Uncle Stanley will be able to help us out."

"What about Grams?" Arthur said. "I can't just leave her."

Beacon thought for a moment. "I'm sure she can come, too. We can pick her up on the way out."

Somehow.

But Arthur was already shaking his head. "Grams will never leave that house. It's where she grew up. It's where *I* grew up. It's where my parents lived—where they're buried."

"You can't seriously want to go back," Everleigh said. "What if the Sov come for you?"

"Driftwood Harbor is home," Arthur said. "I want to fight for it. I won't let them take it from me—from us."

Beacon understood how a place could feel like family. Like a living, breathing person. Leaving LA behind had felt like a funeral all over again. But he couldn't understand how his friend could want to go back to Driftwood Harbor after everything he'd suffered there. Knowing what—*who*—was waiting for him.

He wanted to say all of this, but he knew it wouldn't be fair. And a part of him also knew that he was just being selfish. He didn't want to lose Arthur after they'd just become friends.

There was a loaded silence.

"So I guess this is the end of YAT," Beacon said.

"Are you kidding me?" Arthur answered. "It's just starting to get interesting. And by the way—we should really call it YSAT." He grinned.

Beacon tried to smile, but he couldn't quite make his cheek muscles work.

"I vote for PSAT. You know—*People* Searching for Alien Truth. What if someone a little older wants to join?"

Beacon's heart lurched hard. He turned toward the familiar voice. His dad stood by the bathrooms, wearing his usual suit and tie. His hair was a bit mussed, and there was a clump of seaweed on his shoe, but otherwise, he looked completely fine. Perfect.

The twins jumped up from the table, screaming and laughing and crying as they embraced their dad. Even Arthur got into it.

After they were done, they sank around the table. Everleigh's face was flushed pink, and she wouldn't stop looking at their dad, as if he might disappear if she looked away for even a moment.

"How did you do it?" Everleigh asked.

"Yeah, how did you get away?" Beacon said.

"Beacon says you're like a ninja secret agent or something," Arthur said.

Their dad laughed. "Nothing so exciting as that. It's not much of a story. Basically, after you kids took off, Victor dispatched so many people after you that it left the place weak. I was able to slip away when the guards changed shifts."

"But I thought you were given the antidote?" Arthur said. "How can you be here, helping us?"

"I don't know. I can't explain that."

Arthur leaned forward across the table. "By any chance were you electrocuted recently?"

"Yes. How did you know that?"

The kids exchanged knowing looks.

"What happened?" Beacon asked.

"It was back on the ship, after I'd told you all about what was going on. I was chasing after you—trying to get you to come back. I ran around a corner and slipped in some water. I felt this hot jolt go through me, like lightning. Then I passed out. When I woke up, I was vibrating all over, and suddenly I didn't want to chase you anymore. I couldn't even remember why I'd wanted to. It was so weird."

"You were Jumpstarted," Arthur said, using the term he'd coined on the drive to the diner.

The twins' dad frowned. "I don't understand."

They explained how electrocution seemed to jolt people out of their brainwashed state. As they spoke, they could see their dad's wheels turning, going over the possibilities and implications of this at warp speed in his head.

"What about Donna?" Everleigh asked suddenly.

A grim expression came over their dad's face.

"Is she alive?" Everleigh asked.

"Was she captured?" Arthur added.

"Was she on our side?" Beacon joined in.

"I don't know," their dad said. "I haven't been able to contact her."

The kids grew somber. Beacon didn't know whether to hope that Donna had backstabbed them, or that she'd been on their side all along and had been captured, or worse. He could see the others making the same mental calculations.

Beacon opened his mouth to say something, when he caught a glimpse of the TV over the counter. Whatever he was going to say withered away.

He wouldn't have paid attention, except for the newscaster's wild-eyed look and the words *FLASH FLOODS* written on a banner at the bottom of the screen.

His heart sank like a stone dropped into the ocean. He could hear Everleigh calling him as he got up, but he didn't stop until he was standing at the counter, staring up at the TV. The newscaster's clear voice rang out over the sound of dishes clanking.

"Flash floods are expected in coastal states all across the United States, from California and Washington to Maine, New Hampshire, and New York. Scientists are baffled by this quickly moving weather system . . ."

Sound funneled away and a distant roaring filled Beacon's ears. He could feel Everleigh, Arthur, and his dad run up next to him.

Dimly, he felt a hand clasp his shoulder. Another linked fingers with him.

"The aliens were right," Arthur said, hysteria in his voice. "We're in so much trouble!"

Everleigh looked at the screen for a long moment, her brows drawn, before turning to her dad. "Is it possible the Sov are faking this?"

"What do you mean?" her dad asked.

"I mean, could these broadcasts be fake? Could they do that, if they wanted to?"

"I guess if they wanted to get something on TV, it wouldn't be all that difficult for them, what with their technology and ability to mutate into other forms. They could gain access by posing as an executive or a meteorologist, but . . . why?"

"To get us to come back!" Everleigh said. "To get us to think Nixon was lying. If we think the floods are real and we're in imminent danger, we would come running back to them for their protection— for the antidote to breathe underwater!"

"But how would they know what Nixon told us?" Beacon asked. "How would they know he's been spying on them and knows the truth about the floods?"

"Maybe these broadcasts are to trick other towns into getting the antidote?" Arthur suggested.

Their dad looked uncertainly at the TV as they slowly made their way back to the booth.

The waitress appeared at that moment. "Can I get you something, sir?"

She placed a menu on the table.

"Oh, no, I'm okay, thanks. I'll just have some of whatever they ordered." He returned his attention to the broadcast.

"Pretty scary stuff, huh?" the waitress said.

"Is it like that on every channel?" Arthur asked.

"What do the other weather reports say?" Beacon joined in.

The waitress frowned. "Same thing, I'm sure."

She reached for the menu. And that's when Beacon saw it. The bloody pinprick on her right bicep. The telltale mark of a recent shot.

Or vitamin injection, more accurately.

Beacon subtly nodded toward the waitress's arm, drawing the group's attention to the mark.

"Don't you kids concern yourselves with any of that," the waitress said. "Everything will be fine. All you have to do is behave and let the adults take care of things."

"How can you say that?" Beacon said. "Look at what they're saying!" He gestured at the TV.

"Everything will be fine," the waitress repeated. She gave them a wooden smile. Her eyes, Beacon realized—they were as vacant and glassy as a pair of marbles.

A pit formed in Beacon's stomach. They all shared a meaningful look.

It wasn't just Driftwood Harbor. The Sov had spread out, taken control of other areas, other townships, other people. Who knew how far they'd reached?

The moment the waitress was out of earshot, Beacon lowered his voice.

"We need to run," he said.

"No," their dad said. "It will look too suspicious. We don't know who's watching. We don't want to set off any alarms." He nodded toward a corridor. "There's a back door down that hall. Pretend to go to the bathroom, then slip outside. You have a car, right?"

"How'd you know about that?" Arthur asked.

"I heard the guards talking about it. Pull it around to the back. I'll meet you in a minute. She's coming back—quick, look natural."

Their dad plastered on a big, fake smile. Just then, the waitress arrived with a steaming platter of food.

"That smells great!" their dad said.

"Three Lumberjack Breakfasts, the fastest thing on the menu," she said, depositing their plates on the table. "And a side of crinkle-cut fries, of course."

"Thank you. This looks wonderful. Kids, go wash up before you eat," their dad said, giving them a meaningful look. The kids slipped out of the booth.

"Let me know if you need anything," the waitress said.

Their dad nodded and grabbed a slice of toast, bringing it to his lips. But when the waitress was out of sight, he got up and ducked quickly into the empty corridor. The kids were already gone, and the hallway was empty. Outside, he heard the rumble of an engine starting. Any minute now, Everleigh would be pulling up the car. He looked around to make sure no one was watching, then he popped open a button on his shirt. Through the gap, a wet, pink organ pushed out of his chest, wrapping around the toast. It dissolved it in a hiss of steam. Then the organ withdrew into his body with a wet slurp. He did up his button, wiped the crumbs from his shirt, and walked outside to join the kids.

22

(Fourteen Hours Earlier)

Malcolm blinked open his eyes. Harsh white light greeted him. He sat up, groaning at the pain that tore through his body. He touched his temple, and his fingers came away wet with blood. He looked around. White walls, bulletproof glass, concrete floor—he was inside the Sov's underwater prison.

He pushed himself up to his feet, feeling frantically for his cell phone in his pants pocket. But, of course, it was gone.

Beacon and Everleigh—a wave of anguish shot through him. When he last saw them, the elevator doors were closing and they were making their escape. Did they get free? Had he managed to stall the Sov long enough for them to get away? Or had they been captured, too? Or worse . . .

Were they dead?

The thought sent another wave of anguish through him. He raked his hand through his hair, pacing his cell. He screamed. He yelled. He kicked the glass walls.

Nothing happened. No one came. His kids were in danger, and there was nothing he could do.

He stopped himself short. No—he couldn't give up already. He just had to think. The Sov hadn't killed him. Back in the tunnels, after he'd failed Victor's orders to stop the kids from escaping at any cost, they could have killed him then. Instead, Victor had approached him. Victor hadn't said a word—just gestured to a Sov soldier with deadly calm, and the soldier had raised a laser gun to Malcolm's head. Before he could blink, before he could react, blue light split the air, and everything went black.

And now he was here.

Victor had spared him for a reason. Which meant he would be back. And when he came, Malcolm would have his chance.

Time passed, and he began to doubt his theory. Maybe Victor had just wanted him to suffer for his failure? For scheming to free Arthur? He shook his head. He never should have agreed to come back to this ship. What had he been thinking, agreeing to Beacon's cockamamie plan? He should have told Beacon that his friend wasn't important—that the only thing that mattered was the three of them. He should have forced them to leave this town. What did it matter if his kids hated him, if they were alive?

A long beep sounded. He whirled around just as a door in the white walls slid open. Victor stepped through.

"Good evening, Malcolm."

Malcolm rushed forward, just as two Sov guards stepped in behind Victor. They raised their guns, and Malcolm stopped in his tracks. All of his plans slipped away like sand through his fingers. What had he thought he was going to do? He was weaponless, powerless.

The door closed. Victor gestured for his guards to hang back, then stepped forward.

"Let me out of here," Malcolm demanded. Victor didn't bother to answer him. He stepped closer, squinting shrewdly at Malcolm's face, until Malcolm stepped back awkwardly, fighting the urge to cross his arms.

"What are you doing" Malcolm asked.

Victor circled him, looking at him from all angles.

Finally, he stopped in front of him and stared deeply into Malcolm's eyes. Malcolm gasped. Victor's eyes—they were moving. The dark brown irises swirled like melted chocolate in a vat. They swirled and clouded until they were a hazy light blue.

The rest happened so fast.

Bones shrunk, shifted, crunched into place. Muscle absorbed, ligaments stretched and reshaped. Skin paled and withered, hair lightened and fell away. It was all so seamless. One minute, he was Victor, and the next, he had shape-shifted into an exact replica of Malcolm. The real Malcolm gasped. It was like looking in a mirror.

"Thank you," Victor said, his voice a perfect match to Malcolm's own. "This will make everything so much easier." He turned on his heel. The Sov guards parted to allow him to pass, and the door snicked open again. Malcolm rushed forward.

"Wait! Where are you going? Come back here!"

Victor turned in the doorway.

"Sorry, Malcolm. I have dinner plans. I could really go for some crinkle-cut fries."

He winked, and then the cell doors shut behind them.